THE REE
HANGED ONE

for Janice
with love.

By
ALAN MARKLAND

Strategic Book Publishing and Rights Co.

Strategic Book Publishing and Rights Co.
12620 FM 1960, Suite A4-507
Houston TX 77065
www.sbpra.com

ISBN: 978-1-62212-553-1

Author's Notes

The Reel of the Hanged One is a work of fiction. It is dedicated to the People of Malta who will understand why it has been written.

Thomas McSweeney existed in fact and was executed by the British in 1837. His grave is tended to this day, with fresh flowers laid and candles lit. Miracles have been attributed to him and his story, in song and verse, is legendary.

I have named my character for him after exhaustive research, which has found no descendent relative of whom to ask permission. I have done this out of respect for him and for those Maltese people who still care for his memory.

All other persons, events or affirmations are entirely my invention, not to be otherwise construed.

Prologue

The stink in the underground dwelling almost chokes the boy as he awakes from a fitful sleep. The woman, huddled in skins in a corner on the ground, moans. She has moaned for days now; the boy cannot say if she is still there with him, or if she has already started her journey to the beyond. The dwelling has always stunk. The skins they wear, live in, sleep in—all stink. The smell is the smell of his home, and it is a welcome greeting when he returns from the hunt. However, now there is the stink of his mother— her foot, blackening now and swollen, oozes a foul green pus. If the priests had allowed, it could have been healing now.

He crawls from the house into the not yet light of the early morning. He goes to the pit. Squats. The bird is awake—the big bird. The boy watches as it drifts soundlessly on changing currents of air, wings broader than a man is long. Nearly still. The faint flick of a feather, least tilt of tail, keeps the bird afloat above the cliffs and the sea. The blunt head with its wicked beak continuously scours from side to side, sweeping the ground in a never-ending search for prey.

The priests are ready at the temple circle. They have counted eleven moons in preparation for today's event. The twelfth is due tonight but, before that, the sun must confirm their calculations. It must cause the Great Goddess to send her beam of living light to shine down through the massive stone structures of the temple, pierce the sacred orifice, and flood the altar.

The boy hears voices murmuring: the thin sobbing sound of a girl in terror. The mother's voice, strong, reassuring; she will walk proudly after this morning's work. The musical chanting of the priests can also be heard, and behind all this is the soft sighing of the sea on shingle.

The boy is ready; the pig's bladder bag strapped to his waist. A sharp blade of tempered olive wood at his wrist. Ready for that one chance instant he has wanted and waited for.

A small crowd has gathered outside the temple, away of course from the holy of holies. They will not see anything of the ceremony; they will only hear the sound. The sound they have waited for, and they will be glad.

Now it comes. The sun sends its first weak messenger—probing, seeking, finding at last the vital spot, and in that same instant, the chanting—

5

having arrived at a fever of imprecation—stops. The shadow of the great dark bird still circles the lightening sky. The soft sighing of the sea still sings against the shore. Then comes the scream. The sudden awful wrenching sound of a being in agony suddenly shatters the stillness of the morning air. Doves quit their brooding places in a wild flurry of wings. Bats, already homeward bound and away from the probing light of day, scurry now to find their secret sanctuaries. A dog barks. The scream rises, falters, chokes, stops.

The boy is already half way between the beach and the island—that small outcrop of rock such a short distance away. The sun sits on the horizon; its light is everywhere. The boy must dive, get beneath the waves and remain there, swimming as strongly as he can till he reaches the safety of the lea of the island, before he is seen.

Those on shore, the priests, elders, and villagers will wait now. They will drink the fermented honey. There will be dancing, feasting. The oracle will be consulted. At dusk they will gather once again at the mouth of the entrance to the holy place and when darkness falls they will wait for the promised green flash, their assurance for the coming year when the giant red ball of sun finally dips down and is extinguished in the ocean. The boy stands poised in the gathering dark. His next challenge - to get back to the mainland while the village is once again distracted.

He has lain in the sun all day, with no water, no food. His bed on the flat top of the rock was comfortable. A carpet of luxurious green foliage, soft to the touch but with sickly pale stalks—phallus shaped, topped by a rude red bud. This is the secret. This is what he has risked his life for. The whole rock, this tiny island, is sacred. The domain of a handful of the most senior elders and priests. The plant is a medicine, and its use and distribution is restricted to that same privileged few. It is said to cure almost all the ills that man could ever suffer and has been jealously guarded as such by those with the power to not only enjoy but control it. Like many other God given benefits, the plant has an evil side.

The pouch is full, comfortable on his hip as he waits for nightfall. He shivers as the wind begins to rise. Like many of the younger men in this place, he has begun to accept that theirs is not the only land. No land can be seen, that is for sure, but what of the already ancient ruts that can be found on that other side of their island where the cold comes from, those parallel tracks that disappear into the sea. Where do they rise?

He feels the cold wind on him now and it is quickening. He knows how suddenly its fury can spring. Here too is the lightning; flashing forks of fire and cracking sound. The boy knows that ashore in the village, the people will have their faces turned to the teeming sky as the rain lashes them, soaks them, and drenches the crops in their dry gasping fields. The sea is transformed into a flurry of wild confusion with so little warning. The boy is trapped. If he stays, he will surely be dashed to bits against the jagged rocks and coral. If he goes? He must go! He dives as far as he can, out into the blackness and the fury of the waves.

They find his body a day later - splayed, broken on the shingle. The pouch, split open, hangs loosely at his side, its contents gone. Among the small plots of arable land that the villagers have scratched from the bare hard rock a stranger has appeared, deathly white stems, each topped by a raw red boil about to burst. The wind, softer now, warming, gentle, fondles the interloper, eases it, coaxes it among the crops: the barley, the wheat and edible grasses. It settles - is caught here and there by a leaf, a stalk. It becomes entangled and immovable. It begins to feed.

Chapter One

The circus has come to town. Fifes and drums. Oh! The big base drum! Him in his leopard skin pinafore, bang, bang, bang, and the feller with the stick, strutting along. Silver topped stick goes flying and the pace! The marching pace on them. Left, right, left, right. Hearts of bloody oak are blocking the ports at Dublin, Cork and Derry. An iron boom across the Liffey and the same across the Shannon. We are trapped. No food. No wages. Our children are eating grass. For God's sake, do they want to kill us all?

County Cork, 1840.

They are both barefoot. She wraps her shawl closer around her shaking shoulders. It gets colder when the sun goes down and it looks like another night in a ditch somewhere if the priest will not let them in. Churches are for worship. They have tramped all day, the boy and the mother, village, hamlet—one town on top of the next to find a bed. A man sitting hopelessly by the roadside tells them how to find the Workhouse. The boy, Thomas, a man really in these times, is sixteen. An open wound gapes on the side of his otherwise handsome face.

'We must bathe that', his mother tells him, 'and God forgive Lord Hastings's man who did it'.

'I'll build you another', the boy tells his mother. 'A stone house with no grass roof to fire but slate. Hard blue slate from Valencia. Let them burn that if they can'.

Ragged lines of people, a steady stream of them, young and old, wind down the narrow path towards them. Most stare at the ground. No greeting passes between them. One, here and there, lifts a weary head to shrug.

'Nothing', a woman says. 'They're no taking in'.

And so it turns out. Town after town's poor houses have enough to do giving a roof to their own. The woman warder shakes her head. 'We've just not the room, and the new rules are… are you in work?' She looks at the boy as he shakes his head. 'In work and you're in here, that's the latest news from the English, but if you have work who would want to be in here?'

They sit on the bank by the river. Tom's mother is bathing his face; she has made ready a poultice of nettle, mustard and fennel wrapped in dock leaves.

'Me Ma would scold me for this', she says, 'It should be mad hot and make you scream'.

They eat the bit of bacon and bread that they were doled.

'I'll be shot for even that' the wardress told them.

Evening is coming on, the midges are a menace but they have known worse. The river water is clear and clean. They huddle together under a hedge. They are asleep before the dark falls.

At dawn a cock's crow awakens Tom. He snuggles in to his mother, forcing himself back to sleep. Sleep is a refuge where nothing dismays. A dog barks in a farmyard somewhere. Another dog takes up the challenge and soon it seems all the dogs in County Cork are spoiling for a fight.

'Now here's a fine young fellow!' The voice is a bellow. 'And me not into me stride even'.

Tom, startled and properly awake now, rubs his eyes. He gets to his feet. He is very hungry. A soldier stands there. Not a young man Tom thinks, a man with a moustache, one of those long pointed ones, stiff with grease. His cheeks are red, his coat is red, and a broad red stripe descends from the waist to the hem of his white duck trousers. His eyes too are red, bulging and watery.

'Take a gander of this', he says, pushing a pamphlet into Tom's hand, 'while I go and round up me band'.

"Take the King's Shilling", the broadsheet proclaims. "A life on The Main for every Fit young Man. Seven shillings and sixpence Gratuity on Signing".

Tom can hear the circus sounds, rude, brazen on the new morning air. The shrieking of the fife and the thump, thump, thump of the drum echoing up from the village green.

'All for you lad', the Sergeant says. 'All for you—and if we should let you join us—why all the world's mysteries will be at your feet. Jamaica. China. The Indies. Any fits? Syphilis? Contagion? No? of course not. Young lad, such a young, bonny lad'.

He swipes two fingers through each of his moustaches in turn, belches wetly and begins to hum

'Sign here', he says.

'Stop!' comes a shout and Margaret, Tom's mother, comes bustling up with her eyes ablaze.

'Baby snatcher!' she screams. 'Me back turned for a minute'.

'Fine boy', the Sergeant maintains, 'he's…'

'Yes, you're right. Fine boy, fine Irish boy! That paper…'

'Attestation Ma-am. A mere Attestation, a magistrate must decide, and you of course. See the sense Ma-am, the gratuity? In your hand? Three years service and a bounty? And the pressers are still about, you know? Oh, yes, still around, old Andrew's Gang and they'll take your boy for nothing. We'd be honoured to have him Ma-am, your boy, look after him, *cherish* him. Bonny boy!'

'He'd be shot' she presses her case. 'By them Whiteboys, Moonlighters, Fenians; one of them, and him fighting for the English who are starving us? My own son! But…'

'Seven and sixpence ma-am. In a jiffy, and there'll be the allotment of course, and prize money - always a chance of prize money'.

Thomas gets his uniform at Woolwich, the Marine's barracks. Cheap stuff it is, but colourful: a high black hat, red tunic, white canvas pants, black hose and boots. He is fed well, better than he has ever been. He gets on all right, survives the training. He looks forward to joining his first ship, hopes it will go abroad somewhere. He is beginning to take a pride (even though he feels alien), in performing as surely as he can, the duties of a Royal Marine Private in the service of Her Majesty The Queen.

The training is not so easy, but Tom is not afraid to get stuck in. He soon masters the musket as well as the cutlass. Life would be, could be easier but for one man - Corporal James Alum, a Liverpudlian with a hatred of Irish Catholics.

'Bog stomper', he taunts. 'Papist bastard'.

Thomas, having spent his years so far in Cork, where life, certainly in recent years, has been nothing less than tragic, is yet unused to this kind of cold hatred; he cannot understand why anyone would want to hate so badly and so much. Sure, the Irish have no love for their masters the English, that much is plain, but Tom does not have an axe to grind. He knows nothing, and cares less for politics.

Chased morning till night by this bully. Harassed, ridiculed in front of the other trainees, his life quickly becomes a misery. The others dare not support him for fear of the Corporal's wrath. Tom becomes isolated until, in despair, he takes a step in a direction he had vowed never more to go.

'Forgive me Father for I have sinned'. The usual stuff. He has no time for it, but he knows the drill and he hopes for…what?

'It'll not be you he hates', the priest is a short man but stocky. He looks strong. About fifty Tom supposes, greying but not old, although fifty *is* old where Tom comes from and his father was younger than that when he died. This man looks like a father but Tom has seen many men for whom the word might have applied. 'Dad' perhaps - a friendly word for a friendly man but he has forgotten already what it felt like, though his mother would take pains to remind him.

'He was a jewel that man'. She would say with a sigh. 'My little jewel'.

'It is Christ' the priest is telling Tom. They sit in the church, among the plaster saints and in the lovely light coming down from the great round window over the altar. The sickly smells of flowers, incense and another, older smell that seems to come from the very stones from which the church is made. *Perhaps*, Tom thinks, *perhaps it is sin*. The smell of sin. Years of sin admitted out of the mouths of the sinners, absorbed in the walls, the pillars, the high vaulted ceiling.

'They fear Him so they fear us who are fortunate enough to know Him. Do you know Him?'

'I do, I think I do', says Tom.

'And me too and that's right isn't it?' The boy is surprised but pleased to be asked, not told so much, but invited to agree.

'I think they call it belief', the priest smiles. His smile is warm. He puts out a hand. 'Call me father', he says and his grip is as warm as his smile.

And all the while the grind continues, with the Corporal inventing ever more insults and degradations.

'Hup! Hup! Hup! Keep them arms up. Keep to the outside perimeter of the parade. Is your musket heavy mister bloody Swiney? Heavy? Get your knees up! Only another four times around, and you can tell me all I want to know about your muzzle loading flintlock bloody gun and you will face the target at the one!' He strikes Tom a whipping blow to the legs with his cane. 'The kneeling position and two! The prone position and three! The orthodox-at-extended range and you will not dare to tremble Mister scum of Ireland. You will kill the bloody target or I will kill you'.

Wearily, Thomas counts the days, ticking them of in his mind the way a prisoner does on the wall of his cell, clinging to the knowledge that soon it will be over. Training done, he will be free, a soldier-sailor and with many a roving adventure to come.

It is pay parade one Friday morning. Tom's last before going to sea. He waits impatiently in the queue. His pay, after his mother's allowance is deducted and allowing for the pence he must put in the hat for the sailor's fund, will be less than ten shillings for two weeks service. He will buy a prick of tobacco leaf, a bar of hard soda soap and perhaps an item of kit out of the upkeep allowance paid for that purpose

The queue dwindles down. He holds his hat like a kettledrum before him; top uppermost to receive his money.

'McSweeney, Thomas!' the Corporal sings out and Tom steps forward smartly.

'Six nine one', he yells out his ship's book number.

And there is Alun, Lance Sergeant Alun now. Standing there looking straight into Thomas's eyes, gleefully nodding his head as in some private joke.

As Thomas steps aside to check his money, he is handed a slip of paper. A draft chit just as he had hoped. To join HMS Rambler at Woolwich Dockyard, for service in the Mediterranean. The boy is overjoyed. He leaps up and punches the air.

'Where to?' a few call out and he tells them. It's his first ship but he tells them like he was the old sailor.

'Rambler', he says, 'Second Rater - ninety guns. Mediterranean Station' and they crowd around him, his fellow trainees, patting him on the back and wishing him well and good voyage. As he turns to leave them he finds his way blocked by his hated superior, Alun, who stands there, arms folded, a look of amused mischief on his pinched little face. Tom, hesitantly at first and then with determination, steps forward, hand extended to shake that of his erstwhile foe. The corporal, arms hugged tightly to his chest, eyes Thomas with undisguised contempt and, hawking loudly from the depths of his lungs he spits on the ground at the younger man's feet.

In the church, Thomas kneels at the altar. Nothing he has heard in the now many hours of conversation, instruction really, has brought him any closer to God. Father O'Donnell agrees with him. How can you? When you consider the horror of your own father on his knees beating at the flames with his bare hands, his eyes heavenward and the helpless, hopeless plea:

'Dear merciful God, for thy son's sake Deliver us'.

Their house burned, the pig burned, the chickens burned, and when his father gripped the man's stirrup; they shot him; his brains coming out of the back of his head, frying and sizzling in the embers of his own home. Tom smelled his father's brains cooking while the village priest, his mother's confessor, mumbled in his cassock with his eyes cast down.

'God moves in a mysterious way' he told them, and 'it is not for us to know...'

The O'Donnell now, this other priest, this man has sung a different tune, a tune that Thomas has learned to appreciate and to love. It is a tale of many tales. Tales of Ireland. Of the Irish and his own connection with that land. They have sung together the old songs, and the priest has read to him, in Gaelic, the words from long past. Of the glory of Ireland, before the intruder, out of brutality and pillage, made himself the ruling resident. They have learned together, the priest and the boy, the verses of Ferguson written for The Young Irelanders. Tales of Tara and the ancient kings. Of revolution, of revenge and of the taking of the oath.

'And now' says the priest, 'them are the boys to follow. The Go Boys. The boys you should be meeting'.

Thomas says a final goodbye to his classmates. His kit has been packed two days. He walks from the barracks with a spring in his step, and in spite of the kit-bag on one shoulder and his hammock on the other, he hums a popular tune as he picks his way over the cobbles, past the railway station and the Clock House, where a passing carter gives him a lift to the jetties and the lines of waiting warships.

'I thought to welcome you'. He hears the familiar twang, that talking-down- the -nose sneering sound. Sly sound. Tom pauses in his struggle up the steep gangway. He shields his eyes against the setting sun and there he is; three broad stripes on him now. Sergeant James Alun.

'Want a hand?' He indicates with a nod Tom's kit bag, his hammock. Two or three of the lads step forward ready to greet a shipmate.

'Leave him', the sergeant tells them. 'Irish bastard'.

They sail next morning and despite all, Thomas is excited at the prospect of foreign lands. 'Gibraltar!' The old hands tell the younger, 'next stop.' He feels no shame in what he has agreed to do. A nagging voice does persist, for he is at heart an honest lad, but all it takes is the thought of the English brutality, the burning of his home, the death of his father pleading like a woman for pity. The sight of a child dead in the gutter, green grass stains about its mouth.

At Gibraltar he walks up Ragged Staff Steps, past the cemetery where many of the dead of Trafalgar lie. He sits on an old stone wall, and looks back at his ship moored in the harbour. He has been told to report on anything he sees. Anything out of the ordinary. But *everything* is out of the ordinary. This strange life of harsh discipline, wild seas, the sense of adventures yet to come. What would be extraordinary? The civilian? Perhaps. Yes, it would do no harm, and it would show his commitment at the very least.

The ship's first port of call had been Plymouth where she had been officially commissioned, and where, on the evening of their departure, a civilian gentleman had joined them. Tom had been among the party detailed to assist the man with his kit. There had been quite a lot of it, although most of the half dozen boxes were very light – empty, obviously. The Captain himself had come down to meet the new arrival, and Tom had watched and listened carefully as the man introduced himself.

'Alfred Coombes. Botanist. Your servant sir, and may I present my letters?'

The man bowed low as the Captain welcomed him warmly.

'My men will take you to your cabin Mister Coombes. Where, if I may suggest, you should rest after your journey from London. We dine in the Great Cabin at seven, by which time we shall be well clear of the Hamoaze. Perhaps it may interest you to see the new Longships Light?'

Thomas had noted the civilian gentleman's name, the date, and the empty boxes. He did not write anything down. He would remember it in the way he had been taught.

Sea days pass one into the other almost seamlessly as the ship steers always south and with just enough of eastward to keep her clear of Biscay's worst weather. There are storms here that can de-mast even the stoutest of ships and leave them stranded at the mercy of prevailing winds on the rocks of Finisterre. Tom knows his daily tasks, from the routine of Call The Hands to the final Pipe Down at the long day's end. He grows used to a life regulated by that small but persistent whistle, the Bosun's Call, as it wrenches men from their sleep.

'Away, away, away! Lash up and stow. Show a leg there! Show a leg!'

As, here and there, a hairy limb pokes from the night's slumbers and the daily grumbling and groaning begins.

'Clear lower deck!' is piped at eight o'clock; when all hands save special duty men muster and scrub decks from prow to stern. Spurnwaters are scoured with sheets of sharkskin. The binnacle, hand rails, all mahogany surfaces and furniture are buffed up with linseed so that the sun's rays bring out the beauty of the grain and the lustre of this warmest of woods. Bright work: brass fittings, copper piping, are polished brighter still, with a mixture of turpentine, naphtha and pumice.

'And don't go swigging at it', The bosun never fails to remind them, though it is rumoured that some desperate sailor boys do indeed drink it - first sieving it through a muslin cloth to remove the powders. Alcohol in any form is called a handy mate by many of these rough and hardened men; a cushion against the hardships of their daily lives.

The ship shines clean by nine o clock and all lay aft for prayers. Perhaps there will be a burial. Men die here as well as anywhere else, and not always by the battle. The Captain takes the service and afterwards a section of Ship's Articles are read: entitlements as to food, conditions, and pay. Then The Articles of War - a paragraph for every day: 'Any man found committing sodomy with man or beast shall suffer death by hanging or any other punishment which Their Lords The Commissioners For The Admiralty may from Time to Time devise'.

Much nudging and giggling is heard at this. It is by no means the only Article but it does have, in common with other, perhaps more serious crimes such as desertion, blasphemy, striking a superior: death by various means as its principle deterrent and punishment.

The sergeant of marines takes his company to a quiet corner of the poop deck where they practice cutlass drill, scrub hammocks or study and clean their side arms. It is usually here that Tom suffers most at the mouth of Sergeant Alun. What is it that makes the man so virulent? Why Tom? Why the Irish?

'Keep your head down', the man sitting cross-legged beside Tom is trying to thread a needle, squinting and probing and cursing the while. 'That's my advice'. They are sitting in the sun beneath the great sails on a "make and mend day", the nearest they ever get to a day off.

Billy Best is another Liverpudlian, signed aboard the 'Meerimac' at the saloon bar of The Baltic pub whilst drunk on cheap rum liberally supplied by the ship's husbands. 'She's a Merchantman', the kindly man told Bill and 'off for Jamaica any time'. Billy went down the tunnel to where his first ship, all singled up and tight on a back spring, had her nose in the channel, the wind at her back. He never stepped ashore for more than a year and when he did, it was to join a man-of-war.

'I'm Merchant', he told them and they said 'read your articles'. So here he was.

'Talk about a Pierhead Jump!' He is telling Thomas. 'Listen', lowering his voice to a whisper. 'Dangerous bastard he is', nodding in the sergeant's direction. 'Listen' he nudges Tom in the ribs with an elbow: 'My mam knew his mam, they went to school together. And his father, an ex-marine, kept The Talbot in Buchanan street'.

Tom likes Billy, he's about the nearest he's got to friend. He has the same nasal twang as Alun but he is matey, always a joke, the nudge in the ribs, the conspiratorial wink behind the sergeant's back.

'Charley, that's Alun's dad, shacked up with your man's mother and she's on the other foot'. He lowers his voice even further so that Tom can barely hear him. 'Catlick', he whispers, casting a glance over each shoulder: 'Devout - candles lit, plaster saints on the bloody wall, in and out of church all bloody day, and then all hell breaks loose. She's caught in the vestry with the vicar of St. Thomas's - a bloody Proddy! She gets tied to a lamppost, tarred, covered in feathers, hair cropped off, and a sign around her neck. "Apostate Whore" it says. Our Sergeant *hates* Catholics. He *is* one for Christ's sake, same as you. See?' He sighs. Punches Thomas lightly on the chin.

'Be like me', he says, 'Church o' bleedin' Turkey and bugger the lot'.

A rude disturbance interrupts:

'Away tops'l men', goes the shout. 'Reeve them shrouds'. The bosun is a tubby man, fierce but not unkind. 'Reeve I say or a shroud you will be wearing'.

Gibraltar behind them. Malta shows as a straight line to the east on the pilot's chart that was drawn only forty years earlier when Nelson chased Villeneuve, lost him, only to find and finish him in the shoals of Cape Trafalgar. Thomas has read the history - compulsory in Irish schools -of English tradition and glory. Part of him could easily succumb to the seduction, the sheer grandness of it: Drake. Nelson. Trafalgar. But what of The Boyne? What of Wolfe Tone and The United Irishmen?

'Listen to them dead-eyes knocking', Billy is saying. He licks the end of his needle again, then the thread.

'My mother used to twist it somehow,' he says, squinting at the needle with one eye tightly closed, 'little bugger, get in!' He glances up at the bulging gallants where the shrouds have been let slack: the fore, the main, the mizzen; all straining at the wooden blocks which jerk and dance and judder under the lash of the tightening ropes.

'That's a bad sign'. Billy tells Tom. 'That's Mother Death that is. Tap, tap, tapping - can you hear her on them yards? Tapping to be let in?'

Ten days out of Gibraltar and they fire off their cannon as they near the port of Malta. A fifteen-gun salute to honour the Governor. The buoy jumpers go out from the pinnace, leaping aboard the plunging platform. They take up the messenger, haul in and secure the grass rope. Six sailors man the capstan. They lean on the spars, take the strain and, at a signal from the officer of the watch, walk forward.

'Haul in handsomely', cries the bosun, and the rearing ship, protesting at the insult, is eventually tethered. Slowly now the men walk around the capstan; slowly round and round as the heavy hawser binds, sets, strains. A thin voce pipes out; a high hungry voice, plaintive, echoing and dying into the limestone walls of the old sea fortress of Malta. A man sings a line of song and the others follow him as, inch by inch, they tame the ship's anger; soothing her till she quiets, stills and rests.

In Pueblo town, there lives a girl

And her hair is a chalk cherry hue

She is tall and straight like the aspen tree

And her voice has a music sound

Await for me Pueblo Girl

I am coming back to you.

The shrill sound of the bosun's pipe brings the song to an end. Ashore on the bastions and among the steep stepped alleys, the people pause in their daily tasks; a boy milking his goat looks up. Old ladies pull back the hoods of their black faldettas to catch a glimpse of this newcomer to the fleet. A small crowd is gathered at the Upper Barraca to welcome them. Along the waterfront - The Marsa, Valletta, The Barbary Coast - the shopkeepers lay out their knick-knacks and the bars put fresh sawdust down, cutting their largest lemon so that the tang floats out onto the street.

'Inside Navy', they chant and, 'I remember you from last commission!'

The navy, the British navy, is well loved and welcome here. Napoleon came and his soldiers robbed the churches, raped the nuns. Nelson kicked the Frenchies out and made a friend of this other island race.

'Away the long boat's crew', the quartermaster goes from hatch to hatch blowing shrills on his call. 'Away special duty-men. Hands muster at the port waist'.

Billy gives Thomas a shake.

'Make a move you sleepy soldier'. They fall in line and are counted by sergeant Alun.

One by one, they make their way out along the boom, down the Jacob's ladder and into the boat. The crew, already seated at their rowlocks and with oars raised, help their shipmates into their thwarts—two at the bow and two in the stern sheets.

'Out oars'. The order is given by the coxswain, aft at his tiller and then, 'Give way together'. The boat glides out. Leaves the gently rising mother ship, and, curving his craft in an arc, the coxswain brings her back, on the other tack, to come alongside the companion way, down which the civilian gentleman carefully makes his way, holding on to the handrails until he manages the bulwarks of the boat and is helped aboard by one of the crew. Next comes the sergeant, Alun. He has a musket over one shoulder and one of the boxes over the other. More of these boxes are handed down into the boat. They are the empty boxes Tom remembers from Plymouth.

The sea is calm and the rowing makes steady progress. Even so, by the time they have left Grand Harbour, the oarsmen are glad when the order is given to rest. The two masts, main and fore, are then rigged with sail, under which the boat leaps forward as if let loose from a leash. They are soon leaving the main island behind them.

'Comino!' The sergeant informs them, pointing to an islet on the bow. 'They breed pigs there'. He looks steadily at Thomas who stares stonily ahead. 'I wonder if they sleep in the parlour like in some other places I could mention'.

They stop once in the journey, and are issued a cupful of rum and water that soon bucks them up. Before long, to the delight of their civilian passenger, they are singing lustily. Songs of battles won and women wooed. Always the ladies. And the rum. And of burial at sea with the last stitch of the shroud passed through the dead man's nose as they slide him into the deep for the fishes to nibble, the mermaids to mourn and regret.

They drop their anchor in the still, calm waters alongside a small black island that is spread out with a bright green carpet on its flat sloping top. Wading and scrambling over the wet, slippery rocks they struggle ashore where mister Coombes asks the sergeant to hold the men back in one small area while he goes ahead to reconnoitre. He soon finds what it is he is looking for and he is obviously quite excited.

'Splendid', he mutters over and over. He calls the sergeant to his side:

'Fucus Coccineus young man', he says proudly, as if he had given birth to it. 'I knew it!' He plucks at a death white stalk and immediately recoils, holding a kerchief to his nose as the foul stink assails them. He shows the men how to gather the plant, and how to wrap each individual stalk in wet moss before laying it carefully in one of the boxes. Pausing in their labours, Billy points to the slopes and gullies of the shore. The mainland is a mere few yards from where they stand and, for as far as the eye can see, the landscape is totally barren. No tree grows there. Not even a blade of grass. Nothing but bare, dry, sun-baked rock.

'Makes Toxteth Park look like paradise', Billy says and gives Tom a friendly nudge in the ribs. 'And why did we have to come all this way by boat when we could have walked it the quicker? that's what I want to know'.

Rambler sails two days later for Barcelona in Spain. Before they go, they range up a quarter of a mile off shore. Tom can easily make out the little rock where they collected the plants. He has already recorded that incident, filed it away in his memory and he looks forward to the opportunity of passing the intelligence on. He has heard that Mister Coombes will be put ashore when they reach Spain, from whence transport will take him on the long trip over the Pyrenees, through France to Calais and Dover. His precious cargo will accompany him. Thomas knows his point of rendezvous in the port of Barcelona. All he can hope is that shore leave is given there.

He ponders this question quietly, going over in his mind the various incidents - the small matters and then this latest one that he senses may be of some significance. It is not his business to make judgments about what, if any value his intelligence may contain. He is to report all and anything that appears to be in out of the normal run of naval life at sea and in port. He will do his best to do only that.

It is early evening, time to get down below to the gun deck to where he, and more than half of the total ship's company sling their hammocks. They eat there also, at long tables set up on gantries hanging from the deck-head, and in the evenings, after the supper things have been cleared away, they are allowed to prepare their hammocks for the night's rest. Of course, this cannot be done when the guns are being used either for training purposes or in real action. At the bottom of the ladder he pauses. There is the sign: "No Entry; Gunnery Practice". He is just about to begin cursing his luck when Wooosh! The Starboard cannons open fire. Woosh! Wooosh! Broadside after broadside, shaking the timbers of the ship, causing her to heel over hard to Port. A rank stink of cordite, the rotten egg smell of sulphur fills the gangways and passages.

'What the hell?' Says Billy as loose pots, pans, articles of personal gear, anything not lashed down is thrown about and rolls or slithers or rattles over the wooden deck planking, crashing into stanchions, hitting the bulkheads before fetching up somewhere at rest. A barrel, containing fresh water, rolls violently from Port to Starboard and back again in rapidly rising swings until, finally, it strikes the limber of a cannon and bursts, sending a shower of the precious fluid flying in all directions.

'Captain - playing at sailor boys again', a young marine corporal remarks, grinning at his own ancient joke. They go back up top onto the main deck.

The target turns out to be the little island from where they took the strange plant. Volley after volley is being poured into it until it is reduced to nothing more than a smouldering pile of partly submerged, smoking rubble. The helmsman brings his wheel hard over, sending the ship in a wide arc, around and around until, satisfied, the officer of the watch gives the order:

'Steer two, eight, zero'. And then, a little later:

'Wheel on - Steady as she goes'. As the top men race about the ratlines and shrouds, furling and unfurling the heavy canvas sail until the bosun turns to the cockpit and reports:

'Full Sail Ahead Sir!'

'Thank you Mister Jamison', comes the reply, and as the bell clangs out the four double peals: 'Be good enough to secure the ship for sea and then please change the watch'.

'Aye Aye sir', says the bosun.

Chapter Two

The arrival of a British man-o-war in a foreign port, signalled as it is by the pomp and ceremony, the sheer unashamed ostentation with which no other navy can be bothered, is a joyful occasion both for the crowds lining the jetties and for the sailors soon to be set free to exercise that freedom in the time honoured ways of all sailors everywhere. Many will get no further than the nearest 'boiled oil shop', where the twin requirements of wine and a woman, in that order, will be eagerly supplied by a welcoming host. Jack ashore, in his wide-brimmed going ashore hat, bell bottomed trousers and blue-jean collar, is a very welcome sight in all the world's ports and not purely for the money he will spend.

And so, masts and rigging having been manned, gun salutes fired, the ship is tied up to the mole and the pipe 'Liberty men to muster', is sounded.

Sergeant Alun inspects them. They are warned of the dangers they may encounter while ashore and reminded of the ship's sailing time. Leave expires at midnight and the ship is under sailing orders. The sergeant paces up and down before them.

'Barcelona is a papist town' he instructs them. His face up close to that of Thomas. 'Beware of them nuns all riddled with the pox and if you pass by a priest keep your bum to the wall'. Having delivered this homily he brings the small band to attention and hands them over to the midshipman who will march them to the dockyard gate for their few hours of freedom.

The sailors are normally in pairs, each having his shore going "oppo". Not necessarily a friend as such, but with enough in common to make a run ashore successful. Each will look to the others back in case of trouble. Some are loners. They are recognised as such and left alone. Tom of course would have found it hard to acquire a companion even if he had wanted one. The sergeant has made plain that any friend of the Irishman is an enemy of his. Nobody is surprised when Tom splits off as soon as they are dismissed and goes off on his own towards the town.

A general rule for going ashore is to pay no attention to the possibility of getting lost. All ports are at sea level. Most sea towns and cities are built on hills. Therefore going up to town and down to your ship is all that needs to be remembered. There is usually one main street or avenue, which, if kept to, will complete the score. In Barcelona a series of five short avenues stretches from the port to the approximate centre at the Placa del Catalunya. Collectively these streets make up The Ramblas and here a sailor on leave will find all for which he has need, and, depending on the contents of his purse, more perhaps than he bargained for.

Tom counts the Placas, the little squares. He has memorised every step from the instructions he has been given, He strides out confidently in his smart, colourful uniform and the local people, with a smile, move out of his way to let him pass. This friendly gesture, after the constraints of shipboard life, the constant nagging of his tormentor, is a pleasant experience and he revels in it.

He soon finds his goal, the Monastery, after falling in step behind a monk whose Spartan, dun brown habit reminds Tom of the Franciscans in his hometown of Mallow. He has no idea what will happen. He has only been told to have his dispatch, if any, ready to hand. He will be contacted as the nearby Cathedral clock chimes the half hour, any night or day. Instructions will be handed to him at the same time. Tom glances up at the clock. It is twenty minutes past the hour. The monk he followed earlier is seated on a bench just inside the monastery garden gate. He *looks* like a monk - well fed. Tom never saw a slender monk even when half the men and women of Cork were thin, skeleton thin, and their children with distended bellies cried out for a crust.

The monk has taken a loaf of bread from under his robe. He breaks the bread in two meaty hands and shovels a large portion into his mouth. He throws another piece onto the pathway in front of him for the waiting pigeons that swoop, settle and swagger about, pecking at the bread and at each other.

The clock strikes and abruptly the monk stands and waddles over to Tom.

'Dia duit mo mhac', he whispers, and Tom, taken aback by hearing his own tongue, can only think to thank him.

'Slainte', he says as packages are exchanged and the monk disappears back into the sanctuary. Tom, elated at having so easily performed his first real test, turns to retrace his steps.

'A squeak and your back is broke'. Strong hands grasp him from behind. The voice is an Irish voice, unmistakable in its soft inflection. A Dublin voice. 'Walk easy now and you'll be well'. Their captive is bundled into a waiting carriage for the journey back to his ship.

Back at the ship, the two men drag Tom from the carriage and fling him to the ground where he lies quietly in the dust.

'You will sign for him?' The same Irish voice, gentle, matter of fact, enquires. Less than an hour has passed since Thomas set off with such heart. His first mission gone so terribly wrong and already, dawning on him is the beginning of a fearful realisation of the extent of his dilemma. He is alone and at the mercy of forces he knows will be least likely to lend him sympathy. He is bundled up the gangway and there the final straw stands - Sergeant James Alun, grinning from ear to ear with that sinister, nodding, knowing leer. It is now at last that Tom, in his anger, fear and dismay, lashes out at the months of insult, the foul insinuations about his country, his church and his mother. Struggling from his captor's grasp, he flings himself headlong at the hated man. He takes Alun by the arms, twists him, pummels him, causing him to lose footing and fall into the ship's waist where, attempting to rise, he gasps once, and then lies still.

'You've done it now me lad', the bosun says as he signs to accept delivery of the prisoner who, resigned to his fate, allows himself to be led down below to the steering flat where he is thrust into a cell to await events which he knows already are totally outside his control.

Next morning the two men, Tom's captors, stand before the Captain in the Great Cabin. One is a tall man, the other short. They each have an air of quiet efficiency about them, a sinister calm, which, far from inducing calm in others, tends to unnerve people and put them on their guard.

'And these sir are the papers he had on him when apprehended'.

The Captain raises a hand.

'A moment if you please'. He turns and addresses his First Lieutenant. 'Instruct the bosun to place a sentry on my door and then pray return and join us here'.

The two Irishmen follow the Captain into his quarters.

'Be seated Gentlemen', the Captain invites them 'and then if you will be good enough, please to enlighten me'. He is not a little angry. He turns to his First Lieutenant.

'Do you know anything of this? Number One?'

'Not a thing sir!'

The taller of the two men clears his throat.

'I am an officer in the service of Her Majesty's Government. My name, if it pleases you sir, is here'. He produces a warrant. 'And this is my assistant', nodding towards his companion.

They all stand awkwardly. The Captain takes of his hat, a gesture they each follow.

'Well sir, I am *not* pleased but perhaps you will take some Madeira and then endeavour to please me'.

The captain pours four glasses from a wide bottomed crystal decanter.

The officer sips his wine, nods appreciatively and begins while the First Lieutenant takes notes and the Captain listen carefully.

'So', he says when the man appears to have arrived at the end of his revelations - McSweeney is a spy?' He pauses. 'What do we do with the man? Try him? Court Martial?'

'Well sir', the officer coughs discreetly. 'It is a matter of the charge you see. Oh, yes! I know, treason has been committed and we do not think a Court Martial would find otherwise but', he hesitates, 'there are in fact certain other considerations we must...er... consider. You will no doubt remember your guest of some two weeks ago, a Mr Coombes? The late Mr Coombes, I now fear...'

'What? Coombes dead?' The Captain interrupts. 'Why? How? such a pleasing gentleman!'

'Suicide', the officer tells them, 'most unfortunate. But his mission, you will recall? His task? What, I wonder, do you know of that?'

'Know?' exclaims the Captain. 'Was there something to know? I knew my orders sir and I hope I obeyed them'.

'Yes! Oh! Yes indeed! No question of that', the officer goes on, 'but the substance, the, er, flora might I say? That which was gathered and which, with your able assistance, Mister Coombes transported to England? You knew, or know, nothing of the plant? Its properties? Its potential?'

'Nothing!' replies the Captain. 'And by the sound of it I am not at all sure I would wish to know'.

'Awkward', says the man, turning to his companion who nods in agreement. 'Very awkward'.

'You see', the other man takes over. 'The plant Coombes took samples of and which you, ah... handled shall we say? Is of extreme interest to Her Majesty's Government at this time for its...mmm...propensities. I will say no more about it than that, except to stress the need for extreme secrecy about it and any matter attaching to it. This man, this Private Royal Marine, represents, at this moment, a very real threat to our national security. Fortunately, we are in possession of his report to his controllers and of theirs to him. We are confident that these two messages alone constitute the total of any recorded intelligence, and if the matter is nipped in the bud now, no embarrassment will accrue which could in any way compromise Her Majesty's Government'.

'So what?' queries the Captain 'do we do with him?' He stares about at the assembled company who gaze back at him in silence.

The tall civilian is apologetic.

'There is, sir', and he sighs, 'one other consideration'.

The Captain raises an eyebrow.

'And why would there not be?' he enquires. 'It is?'

'His Excellency The Governor of Malta has an interest, which, although not connected to our present discussion, may impinge on your deliberations'.

He hands over a letter bearing The Royal Seal. The Captain tears it open impatiently.

'From the Admiral sir?' The First Lieutenant, in his role of advisor, feels he has to say something.

The Captain looks up at him and smiles.

'Well done Number One—apparently all has been thought of'. He takes a letter from the envelope and flicking through the pages he selects one and passes it to his second in command.

'Please do read it aloud'.

The First Lieutenant moves over to catch the light from a porthole, screws a monocle into his right eye and reads:

'In the matter of the arrest and future proceedings concerning Private Thomas McSweeney and in anticipation of your request. We are pleased to Command you to Proceed Independently and to take whatever steps you will in order to obviate any threat to British National Security, which may or may not accrue out of any investigation and/or Courts Martial, which you may instigate and conclude. We need hardly tell you that your deliberations and conclusions will receive our earnest support when, it is to be wished, a timely and discreet outcome will result'.

The two naval officers eye each other as the two civilians look on silently.

'Shades of dear old Bligh of the Bounty eh?' The Captain remarks ruefully. 'Get it right and His Lordship will get his Garter. Get it wrong and I may wag for my Pennant with an early retirement'. He shakes his head, sighs and, pulling himself together, eyes his two guests evenly.

'Have you gentlemen any more shot in your locker?' he asks and this time it is the shorter of the two men who replies'

'Will you mind?' he asks the First Lieutenant. 'A moment in private?' He looks toward the Captain. 'Is their somewhere we can...?'

The Captain indicates his bedchamber.

'Will this be safe enough', he asks sardonically. And, when they are alone, the officer continues in a hushed tone.

'I can tell you sir that my department, and indeed certain highly placed gentlemen at The Admiralty, and indeed in Government, are quite cognisant of the difficulties with which you are faced. I have been asked to assure you that no small preferment may well accrue from what The Admiral's letter has just described as a successful and *discreet* conclusion?'

The Captain almost reels back from the sheer blatancy of this crass approach and he is silent for several moments.

'I await the advice of our local Advocate General,' he says. 'He has already told me that a straightforward charge of striking a superior is in itself - should the man be convicted - sufficient for the death penalty to be applied. However, and you may or may not know it, cases of this nature, with such minor complications, always succeed on appeal for Her Majesty's Clemency which would of course be his right'.

The man remains silent. The Captain goes on.

'As I understand it, we cannot try him, nor even examine him, on any charge connected with espionage as that would arouse...'

'Please - my good sir!'

'No!' The Captain, without actually shouting at the man, is firm, adamant.

'I will be heard and we are not observed. Just you and I. However, you may be right. No good can come of my spelling out what we both know to be the case.' He remains silent for a long moment and then, finally: 'Please be assured', he says. 'I know my duty and I will do it'.

They have arrived at the gangway where the First Lieutenant and the other intelligence man wait. The Captain puts an arm about the taller man's shoulder. 'I may hope that one day perhaps I will be told the full story?' He shakes the man by the hand. 'But I will not bate my breath waiting'.

Two days later Thomas McSweeney is brought before the Captain as a defaulter.

'Prisoner and Escort! By the Left, Quick March! Left right. Left right. Halt! Into line left turn. Prisoner one pace forward - March! Escort Stand at Ease'. The Master at Arms stands by the lectern, an opened book is in his hands. The Captain is positioned behind the lectern; his hands grip the sides.

'Read the charge please Master at Arms', says the Captain in a low voice.

The ship's policeman adjusts his spectacles. Clears his throat.

'Royal Marines Private, Thomas McSweeney. Ship's Book Number six nine one. Did; on the eleventh of March 1845, maliciously and purposefully strike one Sergeant James Alun of this ship with sufficient force that he fell into the waist since when, and from injuries incurred by that assault, he now lies near death...'

'Dying' cries Thomas. 'Near death? Why, it were a mere shove...'

'Silence', shouts the Master at Arms and the macabre ceremony goes on.

The Captain closes his eyes momentarily. Then he addresses the wretched figure before him.

'Thomas McSweeney,' he begins quietly; 'the charge against you of striking a superior, albeit in the face of proven and prolonged intimidation, is a very serious one. The aggravation caused by the death of your alleged victim would, if it came about, render the possible consequences so severe as to demand that your own best interests would be more justly served in a higher court than this one. I therefore stand you over to remain in custody to await a Court Martial hearing, to be held not later than one week from this date, or on the unhappy occasion of Sergeant Alun's death, whichever is the earlier and without prejudice to operational requirements. Do you understand?'

And at Thomas's nod, the Captain turns to the Master at Arms.

'Stand over and remanded in Custody'.

'Aye, Aye, sir,' says the Master at Arms. 'Stand over. Remanded. On cap. One pace backward, march! Prisoner and escort move to the left in file. Left turn! By the left quick march!'

The Master at Arms closes his book with a slam. He turns to the bosun who has been Tom's only favourable witness in providing testimony regarding the history of intimidation. The two old sailors watch the prisoner being led away.

'Poor little bugger', says the Bosun.

'Poor Captain', says the Master at Arms. 'Off he goes to wash his hands'.

Chapter Three

Monsignor Michael Spiteri, O.F.M. Cap. does not care for Dominicans. He holds a special contempt for these Ruzarjanti fellows whose grovelling poverty he finds undignified.

'What are they?' he demands to know. 'Priests? Gravediggers? What?'

'Fr. Anthony Agius of the offending brotherhood, is used to the disparagement. Princes of the Church, here in Malta or anywhere else, are not, in their elevation, generally known for getting their hands dirty or for association with common criminals. Those facing execution should not, it is felt, be part of the remit of a busy theological politician.

Father Agius presses on.

'The man is a Catholic—an Irish one at that. Is not His Grace The Archbishop an admirer of the Church in Ireland? Has he not condemned from the pulpit, England's current attitudes towards our friends in that country?'

The Monsignor is not altogether sure about any one of these statements. It is all so awkward. He will have to actually sign something, he is sure of it and that means… Damn! He swears and crosses himself. Twice.

Deep in his prison in the bowels of his ship, Thomas sits in the dark. Around him he can hear the creaking of timbers, straining as the vessel rises and falls gently and rhythmically at her moorings. From above he catches the sounds, the everyday noises of a man o' war in harbour. The sudden screech of the bosun's call tells Tom the time of day as the daily routine orders are broadcast. A burst of laughter, a sharp rebuke; echoing sounds to remind him of the normality going on around him. He reaches out in the darkness to grasp at the life from which he is so cruelly barred.

'A visitor'. The peephole on the cell door has opened without Tom knowing it; he can see the sentry's lips pushed tight against the small hole.

The door creaks open and a small form shuffles in. Tom is momentarily taken aback. The executioner already? The man - only his voice gives him away - is clothed top to bottom in a white shroud. A pointed hood completely covers his face. A white wide brimmed hat adorns his head. Two holes only are left open for the eyes to see.

The man speaks, his voice muffled by the enveloping cloak.

'Bless you my son', he intones placing a hand on top of the boy's bowed head.

Thomas falls down to his knees. He takes the other man's hand and kisses it.

'Forgive me Father for I have sinned'. He says and he is entirely sincere as his tears begin to flow.

The sentry, an off watch steers-man, sleepy and resentful for this extra duty after four long hours at the wheel, listens to the drone on the other side of the door. He likes the sound; he knows there is something like it in his own church. It is an old sound, comforting, rhythmic like a mother's lullaby as she sings to her child.

'This is my body...' and the sleepy sentry's head begins to droop.

'This is my blood...' He jerks himself awake. Found sleeping on watch and he'll be sharing Tom's cell!

He peeps though the spy hole. Thomas kneels before the hooded monk whose hand rests lightly on the penitent's head. The monk makes repeated signs of the cross.

'Gaeige a labhairt le mo teachtaireacht?'

The sound is a mumble to the sentry. Latin? It'll be the Latin that his mother always said was the Devil talking. Listen to him now, poor sod, begging forgiveness. And so would I were it me, thank God it's not! The sentry puts his eye to the hole again. The prisoner is still kneeling.

'Gratulari Deus', Tom says and yes, definitely, the sentry is reassured. He slides the spy hole cover shut. Satisfied. A priest and his lost sheep. Still - better say nothing, just in case.

There is a silence. Then, Tom speaks again. 'Planda anaitnid'. A pause. 'Rioga garraíodóir'.

The monk, again with the sign of the cross, 'In nominee Patri, Filli, et Spiritus Sancti. Amen'.

The cowled figure shuffles out onto the gangway where the Quarter Master helps him down into the gig. The bowman bangs his boathook twice on the planked deck and together he and his opposite number in the stern sheets perform the simple salutation due their passenger. First raising their hooks high into the air, a pause and then in unison, lowering them to push the gig away from the ships side as the oarsmen give way together.

All across Grand Harbour the priest mutters to himself the Gaelic parts of the conversation he has just had. He must not miss a word. Not even a letter.

The boy, poor soul, had been startled when he heard his own tongue in amongst the Sacramental Latin.

'Speak Irish my son. A message?' and Tom, recovering, answering,

'A murdering plant and a Royal gardener'.

And the days run out like water for Tom, locked in the heat and the gloom of his cell. He thinks of his mother and the last time he saw her. Like a girl she was, for all her privations. A young, vibrant girl. But there is another girl. His girl, and though he tries hard to stop her - she must not see him here - she steps lightly at night into his dreaming like a wraith, smiling at his bedside.

'No! No!' and he awakes shaking and sweating.

'Hush, Tom lad. Hush'. The sentry at the peephole speaking softly.

She persists. Sits by his cot and sighs, 'Remember me?'

And eyes wide open, in the darkness; he remembers and watches himself as he steps from the gondola at Custom House Steps, walks along the quay, past the fish market, under the Victory Gate. Alone he turns in-land, up the wide steep steps, past the open door of the church of St. Paul The Shipwreck where he is drawn by the familiar call - the ancient mystery - and refuses. He turns into Merchant Street and the smells of the souk. Spices, fruits, perfumes. The cries of the baker's boy balancing his tray on his head, twisting and turning his slender neck to direct his cry into the dark alleys, up the old worn steps, around the wounded feet of a plaster Christ Crucified high on a wall on a busy street corner where a dog pauses, sniffs and pisses urgently in the dust.

'Hobs bizette! Pastisi, Ricotta! The boy dances lightly down the worn steps.

Tom buys a small cake, bites into its hot oily flakes, savours the tang of the soft warm cheese, and brushes the crumbs with a hand at his uniform tunic. He crosses Strada Reale by the Palace, and thus enters Strait Street - The Gut to a century of sailors. This is where his sweetheart, who does not know she is his sweetheart, dances the polka for six pence a ticket or you can buy the whole book for two shillings.

'The Egyptian Queen', is run by a queen, Ramon and his very best friend Freddy, who plays the piano like Paderewski, dances The Seven Veils, and once in a while, for the sake of love, throws himself into the sea at the Manoel Bridge where the water is four inches deep. Ramon pats Tom's bottom as he strolls self-consciously through the swinging bat-wing doors.

'I should keep my hand on that if I were you soldier boy', he says with a wicked leer.

'She's over there and listen', He grabs Tom by the collar of his tunic, goes as if to kiss him and then whispers in his ear, 'She is not a whore. So be good'.

The band is a little band with just enough instruments to allow a dancing licence. The waiters, all of them men, wear long white pinafores and weave in and out of the round marble topped tables as if on skates. A leather satchel hangs from each waiter's waist for the money. Change, in as many coins as can be managed, is placed ostentatiously on the tabletops in little white saucers, to be whipped up triumphantly if you are not quick, when it is stuffed in the back pocket of the satchel for the later share-out.

Chetina sits with four of her work mates. On the table in front of each of them is the statutory 'sticky green', often also called 'a starboard light'. This peppermint concoction is dirt cheap to produce. It is non-alcoholic, for the girls have a long night ahead and many a drunken sailor, objecting to the obvious fiddle, will insist a girl has a proper drink.

'Oh! I shouldn't, but for you…' she will gush as her sticky green is whipped away to be brought back completely unaltered a few minutes later.

'It was gin dear, wasn't it? A shilling sir', and a wink for the girl.

Tom sits alone and just looks at her. He has never been so moved by anyone or anything in all his twenty-three years. He could cry just looking. She knows of course. Affects not to. But she knows and she is pleased. She also knows as the weeks have gone by that he, whoever he is, is not going to buy her a sticky green drink. Nor will he cough up the necessary for ten minutes of a waltz.

Freddy goes across to Thomas. A tenor is singing about Jeannie with the light brown hair, the dance floor is crowded with dancing couples; a fug of pipe smoke hangs like a blanket above the crowd. Freddy takes Tom by the hand, drags him across to the girl's table where a burly, bearded three-badge matelot is leering down the neckline of Chetina's dress.

'Shift', Freddy tells the man. 'This girl is taken'.

The sailor pushes back his wide, straw, 'going ashore' hat. He does not like Marines much. He looks at Freddy in his long frock, orange tinted face powder, carmined lips, and at the leather truncheon he holds menacingly in a meaty hand. He looks at Tom. He looks at the girl. He looks back at Freddy and then he hoists himself to his feet.

'Can I be best man?' He asks and wanders off.

She is, as is to be expected, a religious girl. The girls at the "Gypo", even the ones who let themselves be 'bought out', are no different to any other Maltese girl when it comes to the twin poles of heaven and hell. They know where they are going; their priest reminds them constantly. It's a matter of how long they will burn before sweet Jesus intervenes. For Chetina, Thomas is both the most beautiful thing that has ever happened, and the most terrible burden.

Their love nest, under the giant wall of the fortress, is utterly secure from prying eyes. She knows this, she is safe, and when he opens her blouse and kisses her breast she closes her eyes and sighs. She can smell the sweet perfume of the crushed carob cones on which they lie. She can feel his urgent hardness as his lips close on her nipple, sucking, biting, licking. Her legs open wide; she can smell her own woman smell, hot, liquid, mingling with the carob, rosemary and the sweat of her man. Her fingers dig in on his heaving shoulders, her nails urging him on and then the words burst into her soaring brain. The words: 'Wicked. Chetina Vella. Wicked! God watches. He sees you. Sinning! The worst sin of all sins. Sinner!' She shrivels. Dries. Her legs close firmly against the boy's urgency She pushes with her hands against his still thrusting body.

'No!' she cries, sobbing. 'No!'

They meet whenever he can get leave and when his ship goes to sea she is up on the Barracas with all the other loyal crowds, cheering. She cheers with them, hot tears stinging her eyes. She knows it is hopeless. He is a Catholic, true but he may just as well be a Martian. Her parents, her brothers, her village will not allow it. He is a foreigner, and she will be shamed if and when they are found out. Thus, darkened by the awful certainty of eventual discovery, the sweetness of their meeting continues.

The garden at the Upper Barraca will be crowded later on but now, on this particular early Sunday morning, with every one in church, they have the little park to themselves. They sit on a bench, sip sarsaparilla and watch the cats, feral and untamed, as they circle the fountain and the fish. A man walks past with a bundle across his shoulders. They watch him as he puts the bundle down, unties the leather straps and takes out a box, a wooden box, highly polished, with a large brass eye. Three sticks follow, three spindly legs, which he positions and adjusts. He looks about. Smiles at them invitingly.

'Bonju!'

He fits the box onto the legs, drapes a thick blanket over his head and speaks.

'Photo?'

'Maneesh flus'the girl tells him shaking her head, 'I have no money' and he laughs.

'Free!' He addresses Tom. 'For the soldier and his girl'.

Tom holds his girl and they smile self - consciously into the brass eye. They both jump as the magnesium flare goes off with a bang.

'Still - you must be still', the man tells them. 'Now - again and smile!'

The ships of the Mediterranean Fleet are scattered below them like so many of a small boy's toys in a bathtub. He kisses her hand and says he loves her. The sadness she saw in him that first night that drew her to him lies so heavily on him now, today.

'What time will you sail?'

'Ten', he tells her. 'In the morning at ten'.

'I'll be here'.

He forces a smile. A little boy. He looks like a little lost boy.

She takes his hand in hers.

'Come', she says and they walk out of the garden.

'Down here'.

The steps lead down to a courtyard ringed by tall multi-storeyed houses. Lines of washing hang on balcony rails. A woman beats a carpet, the dust motes rising in the slanting sun. Chickens chuckle in corners and crannies. A dog yawns. Somewhere near, a church bell tolls and down in the harbour the ships are readying for sea.

She squeezes through a narrow gap in some iron railings. He follows her. They are in a cave. Wet, green slime on the walls. She guides him into a narrow tunnel where the light gradually dies as they continue. They turn a sharp corner and there, high on a wall, lit by a sun's beam that shines through a jagged hole in the roof above them, stands a statue of Mary with the infant Jesus in her arms, a tear-drop on her pink, fresh cheek. A candle gutters feebly among a posy of dead flowers at her feet.

'Il Bambi', she tells him. 'Because of her baby face. She used to be a ship's figurehead. The ship sank on the rocks at Ricasoli. She came in here to be safe'.

Suddenly she pulls him in to her, back against the cold stone wall. She reaches down. There is a flap at the front of his trousers. His hardening flesh spills into her waiting hands as she releases the buttons. She kneels abruptly and her mouth encircles him as he begins to thrust, holding her shoulders and thrusting. He moans now and she lifts her head. Her small determined hand grips him desperately.

'Sshh!' she says. 'Wait. I want you inside me'.

She turns away from him, bending at the waist and he throws her skirts up to reveal her small naked bottom. He watches spellbound as she reaches behind with a groping hand, holds him gently and guides him into her soft demanding wetness.

"Away! Away! Away! – the scream of the pipe and the bosun's frantic cry burst rudely into Tom's dreaming. He turns restlessly on the hard boards, trying desperately to hang on to the illusion, the sweet memory, as all around him the ship is awakened and he is alone again in the darkness of his cell.

'Both watches of the hands to muster', comes another pipe and Tom can hear the rush of bare feet on wooden decks as his shipmates race to their stations at Top, Foc'sle, Quarterdeck.

The sentry opens the flap at the bottom of Tom's cell door. A tray containing a bowl of gruel and a can of water is passed through. The flap closes with a clatter.

In another part of the ship, Sergeant Alun also stirs as the ship comes alive around him. He is not a good patient. The sick bay is like a charnel house. He lies sweating in his cot, alone for most of the day. The three other beds are empty and he has no one to talk to, not that that makes a difference. He is not liked, he knows that. No friends. A bastard, a right bastard. Just like his old man, and a bastard he was to be sure. One thing though, his dad said. He said start hard and become easy. Perhaps it is time to let up a bit, especially on the bog stomper. He'd get prison, the Irish boy for striking a superior. Ninety days perhaps. Maybe the Cat, and then, well, we'll see.

That draught they gave him has made him sleepy; he can hardly keep his eyes open.

'Drink it up', the man said. 'Do you good'. So sleepy. Almonds. That's what it tastes of, smells of and he feels himself drifting, a pleasant feeling, floating, going.

The dream, is it a dream? Scares him. It is dark in the little cabin. Two figures, he cannot make out their faces, loom over him. One lifts his head, withdraws the pillow and he knows now what is coming. Scream! Scream! It is only a dream. Scream and he will wake up. He can smell the straw, the filling of the pillow, on his face, his nose. He kicks his feet out in rapid, drumming spasms. So tired. So weak. He begins to cry. He shudders and then there is nothing.

Chapter Four

The plank has been greased with goose fat so that, when the order for committal is given, the shrouded corpse slides easily from its bier and into the sea where it causes a momentary disturbance on the grey surface. It floats embarrassingly for several minutes, bobbing on the gentle eddies, causing an anxious First Lieutenant to raise an eyebrow in the direction of the sail maker, who, confident in his workmanship and in the efficacy of the bag of lead shot he has tied to the dead man's feet; smiles reassuringly as Sergeant James Alun, swaddled as a new-born babe in his own hammock, abruptly stands upright in the water before sinking slowly beneath the waves.

'Good riddance', murmurs Billy Best and just then, as the bosun goes to dismiss the assembly, the First Lieutenant steps forward with a paper in his hand.

'Sailing Orders.' He announces and then, catching the ship's navigator by the arm: 'Pilot; Captain's cabin - and in haste if you please'. He nods toward the Gunnery Officer and the Captain of Marines.

'You too,' he tells them.

The chart of the Eastern Mediterranean crackles dryly as it is unfolded and laid flat upon the dining table. The assembled officers gather around.

'It is the old, old story,' the Captain begins. 'Our erstwhile friend the Turk, enfeebled as he is in these days, is feeling more urgently than ever the hot breath of the Russian Tsar with his designs upon the Dardanelles. Our task, the navy's task that is, is to maintain the Ottoman in the Palaces of Constantinople until, of course and inevitably, he has grown so weak as to require our more proprietary attentions when a more satisfactory benefit may accrue in our own behalf.' He cocks his head to one side with a slight grin, pleased at his own eloquence.

The gunner looks perplexed.

'Keep Russia out of the Mediterranean', the Captain explains patiently and stabs a finger at a spot on the map.

The gunner is no wiser.

'The Levant?' he questions.

'Syria to be precise.' The Captain explains patiently as his eyes flick fleetingly to meet those of each in turn of his fellow officers.

He addresses the Captain of Marines.

'James, have a platoon ready to make a hostile landing at...' he studies the map again. 'D'Jabel and Mister Gunner - there will be a number of quite heavy cannon in our squadron when we may expect to bombard Sidon, Tyre and, possibly even Beirut. Do not let me be out-gunned.' The two gentlemen snap to attention.

'Aye, Aye sir,' they avow in unison, saluting the Captain who then directs his gaze at his navigating officer.

'Pilot—take me to Beirut.' And, as that gentleman turns to his charts - 'oh! And bye the bye, do get the Yeoman to hoist my new Commodores Pennant will you?' and he holds up a restraining hand as the Navigator goes to congratulate him, 'It is, I am pleased to say, a mere Second Class— leaving me my Command of course', he finishes with a chuckle.

Elements of the fleet are coming from many of the widely dispersed naval bases, some dozen ships in all including some steam and sail, as well as the more conventional man-o'-war such as the Rambler. They will rendezvous off Limasoll in Cyprus where they will be joined by yet another squadron; that of Austria, led and commanded by the young Crown Prince.

'A mere lad', the British commanders commonly agree with perhaps more than a tincture of sour grapes. 'What is he? Twenty three — and Admiral of His Fleet?'

The Commodore keeps his counsel. He looks around the table at his assembled ship's captains. Some experienced talent here; indeed more than one of them saw service with Nelson at Trafalgar. Somewhat long in the tooth now and of course that battle had been entirely sea-borne. Resentment at his elevation to Flag Rank has been quite severe among them, he knows that and can understand it. He, the younger man by far and what connections does he have? His gaze rests on Tregannon, a surly man at best, yet naturally skilled in the social arts. Well married, admirals in the family going back to Drake's day. And Marjoribanks, the old canny Scot, wedded into the Palmerston family and, with Lord Palmerston himself the architect of this Syrian adventure, surely strings will have been pulled in *his* behalf. The politics of naval high command are and always have been a quagmire and a mystery. He turns to his audience.

'We would do well to keep an eye on the Hapsburgs, I fear trouble will come from that quarter one day in the not to distant future and, in the meantime Gentlemen, Austria is our ally, the Prince is our Commander-in-

Chief and we will', he pauses, deliberates; 'as far as is *practicable*, do as we are told.'

Maps are again unfolded and the gentlemen, professional seamen all, get down to the job in hand.

'Your landing? Mister Rawlings? the Commodore addresses the Marine's Captain.

The young officer coughs and gets to his feet, always aware of the suspicions he raises among these illustrious mariners.

'A soldier? On a bloody ship?' he has heard the comments. And then there is the uniform, all that scarlet, makes of him a peacock among a bunch of dowdy sparrows.

'The D'Jabel is a fortress held by the forces of Egypt after that country's successful annexation of most of Ottoman Syria. These forces, French trained, well motivated and securely entrenched, believe that the whole of the Turkish Empire is theirs for the taking and it is very much contrary to Her Majesty's Government's present foreign policy that this should be allowed to happen. The bombardment', he turns and nods to the Gunnery officer, 'will precede the landing which must be seen to be a clear and unambiguous declaration of our allegiance to Turkey and the operation will, at its success, restore to the Ottoman Empire those territories recently annexed by Egypt'. He pauses to let his summation sink in, he has done his homework and his intention is to impress.

Naval officers, whilst traditionally inclined to obey without question, are as thankful as anybody else when the reasons why are explained to them.

'My particular honour will be' the marine officer continues, 'to first of all establish a rallying point on the highest peak atop the castle, where I will secure the Queen's Colour and then, with my company of fifty men, it is my intention to defend that rallying point to the death'.

There are murmurs of apparent approval all round and when the young man goes to regain his seat the Commodore, catching his eye, mouths the words; 'Well done!' and then, aloud; 'Any questions? No? well, one final matter to cheer you all on your way. The Lavant coast, at this time of year, is notorious for foul weather. Arrangements are in hand for large scale re-masting at Malta and it is to that safe haven, if damaged but still manoeuvrable, you should repair by whatever means at your independent disposal *post battle.*' Emphasising the last, he continues; 'I need hardly remind you to see to your various jury rigs and emergency drills at once, and now', he looks up at them, eyes every one directly.

'Thank you Gentlemen and God speed'.

Thus cautioned, perhaps mollified, his Captains return to their ships, in which, with strong and favourable winds in their canvas, they soon have the island of Cyprus on their port shoulder as they bear down silently on that most easterly shore of the Mediterranean Sea called The Levant.

Zero hour has been set for 0500, one hour before dawn and, at that exact time; the peaceful quiet of the emerging day is shattered by some twenty simultaneous salvoes from the attacking fleet. Battle flags are raised and the whole squadron, in line astern, spaced and stretched over many nautical miles and at as close a range as wrecks and reefs will allow; batter and blast the shore line from Beirut to Acre and including Sidon and Tyre. Return fire is surprisingly vigorous. Ancient cannon emplacements dot the shoreline and the opposing troops are well drilled. It is not long before hits are scored on the invading ships and, here and there, gaps begin to appear in the strict line ahead formation, as first one of the British ships drops out to tend its blazing sails or cut down a splintered mast. Then another, holed below the water line, begins to falter, halt and keel over on a hidden sand bank. On top of all this man-made mayhem, the weather, as predicted, has turned foul, in fact a full gale is blowing, visibility is down to zero and more than one ship is lost in collision with one of its own. In the ships sick bays, the stink of vomit mingles with that of brandy, which is used both as an anaesthetic and an antiseptic and the moans of a dying man sounds as descant to the screaming of another as the surgeon dips the bloody stump of an amputated limb into a vat of boiling tar.

In the Flagship, HMS Rambler, deep down below decks, a frightened Thomas McSweeney struggles to be calm, fast in his prison amid the noise, the vibrations and the obvious sounds of the battle raging above his head. His mate, Billy has volunteered to do sentry guard on him and a sympathetic bosun has agreed. It is Billy who has kept Tom informed and it is he now who, seeing the sad state of his already stressed friend, rebels in exasperation'.

'Bugger this for a game o' soldiers,' he bursts out as the bulwark alongside them is struck yet again by a scattering of grape shot. 'You hang on there me old mate - I'm getting you out of it.' And up he goes, straight to the poop deck where, at his battle station, the First Lieutenant is standing by, cutlass drawn, a group of blue-jackets at his side, ready if need be to repel boarders.

'For Christ's sake sir— your honour.' Billy stutters in his anger. 'The prisoner! It ain't bloody human. Him cooped up like that, d'yer want to drown 'im afore you hangs 'im or what? Not human, that's what it's not....' He tails off as a burly Petty Officer appears with a ropes-end in his hand.

'Now then Billy - now then! A bit of respect if you don't mind, eh?' and he slaps his bare palm with his cudgel.

'Prisoner?' the officer exclaims. 'McSweeney? The Marine? Good God man! Is he still locked up? Why......? Bosun! somebody get me the damned Bosun! and you there', he points with his sword blade to a passing able seaman; 'My respects to the Captain of Marines and ask him to join me here - at once'.

Ten minutes later, the platoon of marines gives out with a spontaneous cheer, as Tom appears, fully dressed, in uniform, blinking from the unaccustomed sunlight and carrying his musket.

The new sergeant, promoted recently after the death of Alun, is a different man altogether to the last one. He welcomes Thomas with a handshake.

'No picnic this you know? We land in ten minutes and the Turk don't take no prisoners. Still', and he clouts Tom on the back affectionately, 'beats dangling at the end of a bloody rope, eh?' And then the whistle blows, the drummer boys begin their tattoo, the fife its strident call, as down the scaling ladders the soldier-sailors scramble, into the waiting boats and off toward the shore, where they are met by a withering wall of fire. The sergeant is hit almost at once. His specific task has been to take two marines with him, scale the walls of the castle and plant the flag at the highest point and, just as he has achieved this, a musket ball strikes him in the leg. At the same time one of the two privates is shot in the head, dying instantly. This leaves, of the little band, Thomas - the remaining volunteer. Thomas McSweeney, traitor, murderer. He looks about him. He is alone on the parapet; below him the advancing marines are swarming up the hillside, their scarlet and white uniforms and their shiny black shakoes distinctive targets against the dull brown foliage. A black leather pouch sways and bounces at each man's side as they toil ever upward and on this bag is pinned a large brass badge which, catching fleetingly each dazzling sun's ray, gives the illusion that every man has been shot. Many *are* indeed shot, and already the hillside is littered with the dead and dying. They lie; some in impossible postures like so many rag dolls. Colourful, broken and discarded.

Thomas hesitates, behind him a forest of pines stretches into the distance. He could run. He should run. Into the unknown yes, but, will they pardon him, if he stays? Surely they will—won't they?

'Tom! - Tom lad! Run man!' The sergeant has raised himself up on one leg. The other appears to be missing. He leans on his musket as he shouts.

'Get away boy! Go now. While you can'.

And Tom hesitates no longer. With one last look at the lines of sheltering trees, he turns abruptly and runs down the hill to the assistance of his shipmate.

Chapter Five

The house of the Commander in Chief is not as impressive as he himself would have preferred. He had hoped for San Anton, the Palace, but the Governor General could not be shifted. So here he is. In his 'rural hovel' as he puts it. In the village of Kalkara, just outside the gates of the Bighi Hospital. He has just returned home after welcoming his fleet, or what tattered remnants remain after the pounding they suffered during the terrible storms that accompanied their most recent and otherwise successful operation. A resounding victory, which has earned him a letter of congratulation from the Queen herself. Congratulations all round in fact and he has been very pleased to inform the Commodore in charge of the operation, the Captain of HMS Rambler, that he need not bother writing the customary letter, resigning his temporary rank now that the job is done, but that instead he should write one accepting his promotion to permanent Flag Rank and the title Rear Admiral. He will be here any moment now, no doubt bearing that very letter and the C-in-C is quite looking forward to shaking his hand.

There is a knock at the door and the Admiral's personal steward announces the Commodore's arrival.

'Ah! Do come in my friend. The warrior returning eh? And Oh! What rewards too! Tell me, are you pleased, surprised, shocked or what? - I remember when I first....' but he gets no further for he can see the anger in his visitor's face.

'Rewards sir?' The other man blurts out. 'You speak to me of rewards? I care nothing for rewards sir, not when another man, whose deeds deserve better, is languishing in jail awaiting a trumped up Court Martial whose verdict is already decided. Sir! where is the justice? The lad could have fled, escaped —nothing to stop him...'

The Admirals has risen to his feet. He leans over the desk. Hackles bristling.

'How dare you speak to me, your senior officer, in that' - he searches for the word - ungrateful manner?' He stares steadily at his subordinate, his own anger, after the initial rush of indignation, somewhat tempered by an almost fatherly understanding. Of course the man is angry, he has every right to be, in fact his defensive attitude towards one of his crew is only to be applauded. He sits and motions for the other man to do likewise.

'You will take a dram?' he leans back in his chair and shouts over his shoulder. 'Steward!' and they both sit, facing each other, hushed, allowing the tension to settle, while the white jacketed Petty Officer enters on silent feet, pours their whisky, bows and departs.

'And so that is all that this outrage is about is it? This damned Irish traitor boy?'

The junior man realises he has gone far too far, no matter what the circumstances - he has no right.

'Sir, I apologise for my outburst and for my anger. Of course I am grateful for the honour you have brought me, but..'

'I know, I know, the Admiral interrupts. 'Unjust? of course it is and do you think I have not laboured over it? Well I can tell you that I have. All I can offer you is perhaps my confirmation that, something - and let me be clear, I know not what, but something is afoot in this matter. Something hidden. Something we, yes even I, in my position, are to be kept in ignorance of. The Governor ? well, all he will tell me is that it is better that I do not know. It's politics Dickie and you are going to have to learn, as I have, that politics, at the very top, is a far dirtier business than anything we are called upon to do. I have already been asked what units of the fleet may be available in order to stage a show—yes—a bloody show! in the possible event of an execution.

'Execution?' exclaims the Captain. 'Why the man has not even been tried yet and there'd be clemency, surely? there always is, an alternative; a flogging? imprisonment?

The Admiral sips his whisky. He is silent for several minutes and then:

'My congratulations again on your promotion and allow me to tell you that I, on behalf of Their Lord's The Commissioners for the Admiralty, have every confidence that you will continue to do your duty'. And with this note of obvious dismissal ringing in his ears, the Commander of HMS Rambler turns on his heel and leaves.

It is dawn in Grand Harbour one day in July. The ships lie sleeping. From the Marsa to Ricasoli and in every creek and cranny; a mighty squadron, capable when aroused of almighty destruction and cruelty, is curled up, snoring like a baby, under the guns of the fortress of Malta. On the gangway of the flagship and on every other waiting vessel, a Quartermaster stands. In his hand he holds a pocket watch and, just as the dawn is beginning to peep, he nods his head at the bosun's mate standing ready with his call to his lips.

'Wakey - wakey! Lash up and stow!' and the squadron is brought rudely awake. A Petty Officer; ropes-end ready, clenched in his hand, ducks beneath the lines of slung hammocks, giving each a thump and a shake as he goes.

'Out!' he says, straight into the bearded face of a man torn from the depths of his sleep, wrenched perhaps from a dream and the arms of a lover into the noise and bustle of another day.

In his billet by the capstan, the shipwright, grumbling automatically, climbs out from his slumbers, lashes up his hammock and, picking up his tool bag, makes his way to the Gun Room. There, the spectator's chairs are already laid out and with a row of six, more comfortable ones, facing them. A small raised enclosure is set to one side facing the front. Behind this, the carpenter takes out a round stub of cork. He mixes some glue in a pot, coats one side of the cork, and reaching up to the ceiling, presses the stub to the planks. He takes out a hammer and drives a two-inch nail through the cork and into the wooden deck head. Then he goes for his breakfast.

At 0900 the spectators have already been seated for half an hour and are beginning to stir and fidget.

An usher steps forward.

'All rise', he commands. Two Admirals, three Post Captains and a robed Judge Advocate troop solemnly in and stand before their allotted seats.

'Prisoner and Escort. Quick march!' The prisoner is lined up inside the raised box; the Master at Arms stands to attention behind him, sword aloft.

'Off Cap', comes the command and the prisoner's cap is removed. The Master at Arms, with a quick upward thrust, sticks the point of his sword up into the stub of cork in the deck head above him. The trial may be a long one and he must remain, arm extended, sword aloft, for the entire proceedings.

The trial is short lived and is more or less a re-run of the one Thomas has already been subjected too. He is not legally represented. His 'friend', appointed by the court is his divisional officer, the Marine's Major who opens his mouth once only to query the evidence of the ship's surgeon over the death of Sergeant Alun.

'Was a Coroner called in to investigate the death?' he asks.

'No', replies the surgeon.

'Why not?'

'Operational requirements forbade it'.

'So'? and it looks like the Major is on to something. 'We have only your word...'

The Judge Advocate intervenes.

'Do not bully the witness', he says sternly, and the Major sits down apologising.

The prisoner is allowed to address the court and he presents a statement of mitigation concocted for him by the Major, in which he speaks of 'this terrible accident - no malice aforethought - a mere push'. After a final plea for his life, the panel find him guilty and tell him that he shall be hanged by the neck, in his own ship, until dead.

And so it begins, the 'show' as the old Admiral called it. The local press have had several days of endless speculation. Questions have been raised: All those ships in Grand Harbour. Far more than the usual half dozen or so. Yes there is a man to be hanged but does it need most of the fleet to string a man up? The newspaper "Tal Lous," headlines the question.

'That blood sucking Itie rag!' the Admiral calls it, catering as it does for the powerful and subversive Italian element in Malta who see the coming event as aimed at themselves. It is a warning, the paper tells its readers in bold headline letters.

"British shot across our bow—a timely if crude warning?"

Keeping us in our place,' the article continues and *'Observe the Power of Her Majesty'.*

'The Gazette', in its determinedly pious and partisan way, counters with the government line:

This sad affair is an example to us all of the raging passions that may be engorged by the tensions of ship board life. For one poor soul to be so driven by anger and jealousy as to murder another—and his superior to boot—illustrates perhaps a lack of moral backbone, a legacy of the unhappy intransigence of the land of his birth.

In the streets, conversation is hushed. A boy is to be hung. A Catholic boy and no matter what his crime, if there is a crime, the people are on his side. They are already beginning to store up memories of this day, only just begun, that will still be recalled a hundred years or more from now.

High on the fortress battlements, a girl has been watching the harbour since before dawn. Most of the ships arrived during the previous few days; there are ten of them now, brought from as far away as Alexandria in the east and Gibraltar in the west, at great expense and involving considerable risk, just to watch a Private soldier hang. The ships are moored to large wooden buoys that litter the waterways that stretch from St. Elmo's Point to the Marsa, and in and out of the three creeks: Frenchman's, Dockyard and Senglea. Already, scurrying men in their white canvas uniforms are rigging and hauling the gaily coloured buntings to the fastening lines that will be hoisted sharply to the mastheads when the signal is given from the Flag Ship, prompt at 0530: 'Ships Dress Overall'.

HMS Rambler, her stern held fast at the Point of Senglea, beneath the vedette, rolls almost imperceptibly on the meagre breath of wind that rocks the small boats held fast on the swell by the standing forms of the shirt sleeved oarsmen.

A low murmuring is heard among the crowds that are beginning to muster along the battlements, at the Baraccas, by Bighi hospital and along the rocky shores at Fort Ricasoli. It is a controlled sound, seemingly without anger and yet obvious in its resentment.

A mist, low on the water, drifts on the slight breeze, rolling and eddying between the timbers of the great ships. Insidious fingers of soft grey fog that touch, caress and then turn away abruptly as if from some sudden awful discovery.

The girl, high up in a cave mouth overlooking the lines of ships, splays wide her bare legs, and gripping hard at her knees, bears down on the blanket she has spread on the ground beneath her. The sound of her cries is lost in the screaming and squealing of gulls.

The sun, massive bright red, appears as if catapulted above the dark bulk of Fort St. Angelo. The pre-dawn gloom is replaced by almost instant light. The mist melts, dew dries and warmth begins to flow again among the crowded dwellings, causing the cocks to crow. Dogs threaten each other from the sanctuary of courtyards. Church bells begin their disparate cacophonies as congregations gather to beg forgiveness for the night's transgressions, and, as is likely on this particular morning, to pray for the soul of one who is about to die.

At 0550 a bugle sounds, the buntings are raised, fluttering brightly, gaudy at the shrouds and up in the ratlines. Minutes later the first cannon is heard and sailors swarm the riggings of each of the ten assembled men-of-war, scrambling along the yards and sprits, ducking under the half moons, covering every inch of available surface, bare-headed, bare-footed and linked hand to hand in comradeship and support.

On the poop deck of Rambler, a uniformed figure stands. He is dressed ceremoniously in a full frock coat and tricorn hat. A gold epaulette at each shoulder proclaims his seniority. He wears a telescope beneath his right arm. His voice booms clearly over the water, echoing among the centuries old bastions of the ancient harbour. As he reads out the warrant, a bound hooded figure is led to the foot of the main mast. A rope is looped quickly around his neck as the priest leans forward to whisper in his ear. A second cannon shot and at exactly six o clock Thomas McSweeney is hoisted to the yards by his ship mates, two from each of the ships present who, purposefully and in defiance of strict orders, savagely jerk the falls in order to break his neck and end his terrible suffering.

'Handsomely!' The bosun protests. 'Walk back handsomely!' as the struggling prisoner, in his last desperate throes, dances in his agony to the song of the dead-eyes knocking wildly in the shrouds.

High up in the walls of the battlements, the girl bites the cord. Spits out the mingled blood of herself and her child. She ties the knot a hands breadth from the slippery body, pressing her baby to her, offering her breast. As the child's cries subside, a rhythmic pumping takes over and she feels her own short life ebbing and flowing into the small contented infant in her arms.

At half past six she watches as the shrouded shape is lowered from the mast, put into a boat and rowed away in the direction of the hospital. A collective sigh arises from the on-looking crowds as they begin to disperse. Signs of the cross are repeatedly made; an old woman beats her breast at the bottom of Crucifix Hill.

'Al Madonna!' she cries. 'Al Madonna!' Over and over in a plaintive, hopeless moan.

The girl, urgently now, ties her baby, wrapped tightly in its blanket, to the trunk of a Carob tree jutting from a crack in the rock face. She glances upward, her eyes following the worn goat path that leads to a little house with a flat-topped roof. No sign of life yet. Joe - Chetina knows him as Mister - Mister Baldachino and his wife, Jousa - will only get up when they hear their goat crying to be milked.

Chetina imagines the scene. The old man will take his wife her early morning glass of tea into which he will have poured much too much sugar.

'Blaa!' she will complain and her husband will smile as she smacks her toothless gums with pleasure.

He will pick up the wooden pail and go down the winding path and there he will find...

'Alora! The old woman will cry. 'A gift! A gift from God!'

The tolling of the Passing Bell, muffled, persistent, vibrates in the girl's ears, as she stands motionless above the wide harbour. Her gaze sweeps right, then left as she views for the last time the jutting peninsular where she was born, lived and finally loved.

She falls without sound to the rocks below.

Chapter Six

Elizabeth. Lancashire. 1880.

The corporation tram, horse drawn, glides over the cobbles with hardly a judder, cushioned on that latest import from America - pneumatic tyres. It sways as it glides, up past row upon row of newly built back-to-back houses, neatly arranged on either side of the busy main road that leads from the town to the hills and the moors beyond. The houses are an adjunct to the cotton mills and every individual dwelling with its donkey stoned front step, lace curtained windows and gas lit front room, contains, within its two up two down cramped spaces, a family of four, six, ten. A baby every year to swell the pay packet is a young wife's duty, and she will, whether she likes it or not, fulfil the expectations of her husband (and his mother), with only the ravages of age to wear her out or one of a myriad of diseases to end her toil.

The tram, continuing on its journey up the hill, stops outside number one hundred and seventeen, next door to Pilkington's Pie Shop. A young girl alights. She is about fourteen years old, slight, nimble, a trifle pinched about her pale pretty face, which already shows signs of an impending allure not altogether a boon for a girl in her position. Her blonde, almost yellow hair tumbles about her face as she skips from the tram step, delicately avoids a scattering of horse manure and approaches the row of shops. She has under her arm a bundle, which she grips tightly as she trips along.

The bell over the doorway jerks and writhes madly on its spring and produces, for all its bravado, a surprisingly weak tinkling sound.

'Hello my dear'. A bent man greets her; bowed by a hump on his back that causes him to squint upward, chin on chest. His right arm and shoulder are raised, a hand poised in the air like a claw. He is dressed warmly against the morning chill in a yellowing flannelette shirt. He wears a pair of spectacles, wire rimmed and he is in the habit of gripping them nervously between the thumb and forefinger of his good hand. With fingers splayed delicately, he lifts the glasses into focus as he addresses his clients. "Uncle Joe", they call him but he is not her uncle, nor anybody else's. The term is generic; the three brass balls above the entrance to his premises attest to his trade as pawnbroker.

Lizzie hands him the package, which he opens, spreading the contents onto the counter top. The girl watches with an embarrassed smile. She is easily embarrassed and this transaction (carried out weekly and usually on a Thursday when the week's wages have run out) never fails to bring a flush to her cheeks. There is another reason for her blush - the knowledge that today she has made up her mind; when he whispers again the awful suggestion she will acquiesce.

'Two blankets, well worn, clean. A pair of gentlemen's trousers. Waist....' He squints at the label, one hand lifting the spectacles, the other, the claw, inserting a jeweller's glass into a screwed tight eye, ...waist forty two'. He goes on cataloguing her offering.

'Two and six my little dove', he says as he issues the pledge ticket.

She takes the cash, folding the half a crown piece into her handkerchief. Then she waits. She stares fixedly at a single spot in front of her. There is a ruled yardstick, brass, polished by wear, that runs across the front edge of the mahogany counter top. She counts the inches silently, and waits.

He leans forward, he too is embarrassed, she can sense it and she is sorry for it. He places his lips close to her ear. She can smell his smell - a mixture of snuff tobacco and the camphorated oil he rubs on his chest. He wheezes into her ear. Whispers. The girl, bobbing her head in the merest of nods, reaches with one hand beneath the folds of her skirts, fumbles about in her petticoats, she lifts one leg, puts it down, then the other leg, up, down, and then; straightening, she withdraws her hand. Her fist is clenched; there is a flash of white silken cloth. She reaches out to the pile of clothing in front of her, extracts one of her father's shirts and furtively, hurriedly, she buries the contents of her fist into its folds.

Out on the street, Lizzie pauses at another doorway, a couple of shops down, where a brass plaque proclaims: "Mme Claudine Delacroix: Pianoforte, Deportement, Danse".

'Come in', says the lady of the house who in spite of her name and titles, speaks the local dialect with only an occasional descent into what may or may not be a foreign tongue. Her mouth is a vivid scarlet gash, her hair is held up at the back in what Lizzie supposes to be a *chignon;* the skin of her heavily lined face under finely drawn false eyebrows is powdered a deathly white.

'You have the money?' she enquires at once.

'Yes', says the girl, handing over a crisp five-pound note.

Later, her bones aching after the unusual activity, she walks slowly up the hill towards Belmont and the moors. She savours the ache, and as she winces at each step, she runs through in her mind's eye the movements she has just completed: *fouette, bourre, pique.* The very words are a thrill. She lifts back her head with the joy of it. A squeal of delight leaps to her throat and she allows it to escape in a cry of happiness. She is on her way.

Up high on the moors the granite wall is warm to her back. She snuggles into it, feeling the sharp edges of the age-old stones against her spine. She is alive. More alive than she has ever been. The rigours of the past weeks exercises, the demands of the dance, the stretching of every sinew and muscle, have revitalised her, cleansing her body of the poisons of the mill, where she still toils ten hours a day at the carding frames; breathing in the oil-laden air, and the flying cotton bloom.

The hot sun is in her eyes and she shades them with a hand. Below her, the town, or what can be seen of it through the fog of chimney smoke, is fringed by an arc of purple hills. A small hole, a gap in these hills, appears to the bottom right of the picture. She can just make out the crag with the man's face on it, 'The Old Man of Hoy', all the way to Wales and The Irish Sea. She knows she will go there and perhaps even further one of these days. Perhaps soon.

Chapter Seven

Lizzie's father, Samuel Reardon, is a puddler at Schofields Iron Foundry and appears at first glance to be made of the iron he handles - poured red-hot from a tilted vat, sparks flying, into a mould of sand and black plumbago. He wears braces over a collarless shirt, his moleskin trousers are drawn up at the knee by elastic bands, a flat cap sits sideways on his head and a clay pipe, short stemmed, is gripped tight between yellowing teeth. He marches smartly up the street. Past the pub on the corner, nodding 'how do' to the neighbours as he goes. The neighbours acknowledge him, 'Sam, our Sam', they say and they remember, as they watch him march, another march, a parade of flying flags and bunting. The flash of sunlight on drawn bayonets and a tub-thumping martial air from the factory band.

'Balaclava or Bust', a banner proclaimed on that happy day and less than a year later, a few stragglers returned, drawn faces over tired tread. The tap—tap—tap of a single side drum and Sam—Sergeant Samuel Reardon; eyes front, shoulders back, whiskers quivering like a porcupine's quills, bullied them, chivvied them, cheered them.

'Dig your heels in boys. Heads up. Swagger!'

And then the drinking began. The sobbing in the night. The sudden shout as he awoke, drenched in his own sweat, lashing out blindly with his fists as his wife sought to calm him.

'Hush, Sam lad, hush'.

Samuel Reardon: one of the casualties of his country's wars. His injuries deep inside himself. Hidden from sight and festering.

Lizzie lays the table for tea. On early shift, she is first home and after picking up the milk at the dairy, a loaf of bread, and a gill of ale; she has hurried home to get things ready. Poking the banked fire in the black leaded grate, she adds a lump or two of coal, carefully, each piece gripped tight in the tongs, as the grateful embers glow and burst into blue and red flame. She warms her hands and then glancing at the clock ticking on the mantle piece, she moves the soot blackened kettle into the maw of the flames, kicks off her clogs, and skips lively into the kitchen where, enjoying the cold feel of the slate flagged floor on the soles of her feet, she performs a little twirl before reaching down to unlatch the fly screened door of the meat safe.

Lizzie loves her father. His twist tobacco smell. Strong, Manly. The way his whiskers tickle her cheek. His laughter is explosive, infectious and his arms are strong as he hugs and holds her, tight against his manliness. She feels his sudden strange hardness, and she feels deep inside her a rush, a flooding, until, sharply, he pushes her away and she thinks she has angered him, but then the smile comes, lighting up the room.

'What's for tea?' he says, reaching for the pewter pot, draining the gill in one go while she watches, ever spell bound as his Adams apple bobs and dips wildly at each long gulp.

She is sorry for the secret. Two secrets. She knows that if he knew - about the dancing, about her hopes, her dreams - and the money! - if her father should ever find out, he would surely kill her. She knows his temper and she has forbidden herself to admit that his treatment of her mother, his wife, brought about her tragic death. The unexplained bruises, the worn out resignation on the poor woman's face on that last night, in the candlelight, as Lizzie, on her way to bed, caught sight of her mother, head bent in prayer at her bed side. And, next morning, the awful swinging shadow on the wall. The blood red trickle dripping from cold bare toes. Eyes bulging. Tongue lolling. The thin, cruel rope dug deeply in at the soft, white flesh of her mother's neck.

At the graveside, standing alone, Lizzie could hear the neighbours remarks furtively whispered. 'And him not turning up. His own wife. Still - there must have been something, they do say...'

The weekly visits to Uncle Joe have become more demanding. He has begun to give her instructions. Pressing into her hand a crumpled note upon which he has written his latest awful requirement. She shudders as she reads his most recent desire. How can she possibly bring herself to continue taking part in these sick games?

She tears the paper up into the smallest possible pieces, forcing them down past the iron grid, into the sewer and the darkness.

At home, in the kitchen, she stands before the mirror hanging on a nail above the kitchen sink. The mirror is cracked, an imperfection running diagonally across its face. Her father shaves in this mirror and she herself has watched herself grow in it. She looks now at her face and her face looks back at her with a lopsided grin.

She cups her hands under the flow of cold water from the single tap. She splashes her face. Buries her cheeks in the fresh folds of a clean smelling towel.

But the thoughts will not go away. She shudders in revulsion remembering the latest note. The man is sick, yes but she? What is she to pander to him? She continues to stare fixedly into the mirror. In her minds eye she sees, deep in the reflection of the glass, her mother in her nightly task of brushing her hair. Long, repeated strokes. A hundred of them and Lizzie would count. One side. Then the other. The click – click -clicking of the brush. The steady, repetitive beat and, in the background, the sound of her mother humming a popular ballad. Lizzie stares for a long time as the image in the mirror blurs and then, abruptly, changes into that of herself. The image leers silently back at her until, leaning forward and with one defiant exhalation, she clouds the glass and whispers.

'Adage. Allegro. Arabasque!'

She continues to stare into the clouded glass, as if hypnotised. She begins to sway, gently at first, side-to-side, and then with increasing tempo, as the remembered sound possesses her. The click – click - clicking of the brush. Faster and faster now and from the distance, from somewhere in the past, the sound becomes a drumming and her feet begin to dance as the sound draws nearer, louder, ever more urgent. Her hands are clenched tightly behind her back, her arms held fast by some invisible force and she watches the reflection of her feet as they drum and beat and shudder. Wilder and wilder. A crude, macabre dance, on the cold bare stones of the kitchen floor. Faster and faster. Drumming and drumming until, exhausted, she stops still and watches in the mirror as sudden hot tears flow down her cheeks. Deep sobs burst from her lips and she is wracked by such a feeling of sadness, of loss, as she has never felt before in all her life.

She stands with her hands grasping the cold edges of the sink as wave after wave of inexplicable despair engulf her. Some faint memory dances around the edges of her recollection like the remnants of a forgotten dream. It dances closer. There it is! she can touch it, hold it and then, no – it fades away, changes shape and, finally, dies.

The face in the mirror, her face, stares back at her. She wipes away her tears. Takes down her shawl from its peg on the wall.

'Adage. Allegro. Arabasque'. She breathes and, pulling the warm wool about her shoulders, she steps out into the street and, slowly at first and then with quickening step, she heads down the street to the tram stop.

Madame Delacroix has been waiting for her.

'Come in my sweetling', she coos as she takes Lizzie's hand in hers.

'Go through to the parlour', she whispers conspiratorially and there, sitting on top of the baby grand piano, is an enormous pink cake with a solitary purple candle – purple; Lizzie's favourite colour.

The Madame begins to sing, in a voice, although a little cracked, of a sweet clarity that is almost bird-like as the girl stands blushing at the unaccustomed attention.

Madame claps her hands.

'Happy birthday to you. Happy birthday to you. Happy birthday dear Elizabeth, Happy birthday to you! Blow, blow, blow out the candle, one fat candle to mean sixteen'.

They sit together in the front parlour. Their chairs are drawn up on either side of a colourfully tiled fireplace. The chair backs bear the latest fad that, it is said, the Queen herself has invented. Antimacassars; small squares of white linen to protect the Royal upholstery from a Prince's hairdressings. On the sideboard a stuffed African parrot, eyes like brilliant buttons, perches stone dead, still as the dead, in a domed glass case. It stares mutely down at them, daring them to say, 'Pretty Polly', or 'Who's a Pretty Girl?'

They eat their cakes and drink warmed Malaga wine from delicate, fluted glasses.

Lizzie is in heaven. Here is a kind of living she has always known existed. She glances around the cosy room. One wall is covered in books. Beautifully embossed leather bindings proclaim their titles and their authors. Dickens, of course. She has read copies of 'Sketches by Boz' in old issues of the *Morning Chronicle*. And here is Emile Zola - French she supposes. Anthony Trollope, yes, she has read Barchester Towers and is pleased with herself for having done so.

'You must call me Claudine', says her tutor. 'Just for tonight. We shall go now, as friends, to the theatre. There is someone I think you should meet. But first, my dear; that coat. So thin! Look!'

She stands alongside the girl, back to back, placing a hand, palm down, on top of both their heads. 'See? Same size! Now', leading the girl into the boudoir. No ordinary bedroom this but a feminine shrine of black silken sheets and flowered wallpapers.

'Try this', the older woman says, flinging across the bed a fine full-length coat with a soft high collar. 'Keep you warm, and oh so lovely! I must kiss you, lovely girl but not lips. Lips are for lovers, yes? And we? We are - friends. We *are* friends? She kisses the girl, a light touch on the side of a reddening cheek.

'And look at you! That face! So many faces I see these months, when you dance, when you sit. You are a changeling. You know what this is? A Proteus - you will read your dictionary - but tonight, you will see, you will meet another Proteus but not the Greek God - a man, only a man. You will see'.

It is raining as they leave the house to board their coach and the horses, a matching pair of bays, steam in the light from the street lamps, conjuring up giant copies of themselves on the walls of the local mill. Long trails of vapour drift from flared nostrils and the gentle snorting of harnessed beasts is punctuated by a ringing thud as an iron tipped hoof impatiently strikes the cobbles. The coachman, approaching, has a large black umbrella held before him as the older woman guides the younger one, up the step and into the cab.

At the theatre, the fire curtain is lifting as they take their seats high up in The Gods - the only way, the *real* way to see the show Madame explains lowering her voice to a whisper - 'and by far the cheapest'. She laughs softly as they take their seats.

In the pit, the orchestra has been warming up. Mouthpieces are examined and blown through, reeds wetted with probing tongues. The leading violinist scrapes his bow. A single graceful note and the rest adjust their tuning.

Lizzie has taken off her heavy coat and draped it over the soft padded rail in front of her. The band strikes up. The chorus girls come prancing on, springing from the very throat of the blaring music, sidestepping, pirouetting, bowing, kicking high. A wild exuberant dance to the tune of a fiery French frolic.

Lizzie is frozen to her seat, her eyes fixed on the bright lighting of the stage, vivid even through the fog of cheap cigar smoke and the strong reek of plug tobacco. Women – drenched in Lavender water – sniff snuff, sneezing and wheezing like nanny goats. There is a smell of pie meat, and the occasional whiff of Old Napoleon Brandy from the Gentlemen's Saloon. Painted winged cherubs strum golden harps in chubby arms. In the auditorium, the better classes; top-hatted men and their fashionable wives, perch delicately in their boxes like so many wax-work dummies, fresh from Tussauds at Blackpool. The brilliant glare of gas mantles lights up the stalls and passageways. Plush red cushions are everywhere and above the stage; plaster busts of the ancients: Sophocles, Euripides, Aristophanes, gaze serenely down on the sweating, swearing crowds as they push and shove and quarrel over who should sit where and with whom. Lizzie is entranced, breathing in the colour, the vulgarity. The sights and sounds and smells of the music hall theatre.

Backstage, after the show, a small, foreign looking man bows his head and takes Lizzie's hand in his. She does not recognise him at first, standing there, make up half on half off. He holds in one hand a sponge with which he scrubs and rubs and coaxes the clinging colours from his cheeks.

'Mister Fregoli!' she exclaims.

'Servant Ma'am',

Leopoldo Fregoli is the world's most famous Quick Change Artiste, Illusionist, and Mimic. Friend and colleague of Dan Leno, Houdini, and Marie Lloyd. He holds Lizzie's hand in his and she can feel the throb, the very presence of so many other men, even women, locked in the body of this one man who, in the blink of an eye, may release them from their chains: Disraeli, Nelson, even Florence Nightingale. A soldier for a second, a posing poet the next.

'Squeeze my hand', he commands the bewildered girl. He closes his eyes.

'Three daughters you will play—one, two, three! And I your king and father'.

Claudine claps her hands in delight.

'I knew it. Oh! I knew it'. She cries, as Lizzie, with not a single clue as to what is going on, knows all she needs to know. She is in good hands.

Madame Delacroix drops Lizzie off at the end of the lane that leads to her home; she walks carefully among the puddles of rainwater, over the polished cobbles. The lingering taste and perfume of the world she has just left, weakens, dilutes as she approaches the line of privies that back onto her terrace. She clings to her recent experience, wanting to breathe it always, but slowly at first and then with a suddenness that shocks her, the stench from the privies chases away all vestige of her dream world and brings her back with a savage jerk to the real.

Gently she turns her key in the lock, pushing the door open against the hindrance of the greatcoat placed to keep out draughts. An ember glows dimly in the grate. The only other light comes through the laced curtained window frame from the public gas lamp at the end of the row.

She takes off her coat, lays it on the back of a chair, her father's chair and it is then she smells the other smell. His smell, her father's smell and in the brief moment it takes for the information to register, she is seized from behind, thrown face down over the dining table, scattering the pots she has already laid for the morning's breakfast. A hand grips her at the back of the neck, forcing her face hard down against the tabletop. The other hand reaches under her bustle. She can smell the stink of him. He grasps her underwear, stripping, tearing. A booted foot kicks her legs apart. Hot hands spread her buttocks wide. Hot breath is on her flesh, the rasp of his face on her tenderness, his tongue licking, probing. He moans. She has made no sound. She makes no sound as his full weight falls onto her and then only the slightest gasp as she feels his hard flesh burst into her.

Seconds, only seconds and he moans again—a sound of pain? Of despair? He pulls himself out of her sharply and she lies there, exposed, thankful for the gloom. She does not hear him as he retires to his room. Is he still there? Finally she turns her head, twists her upper body to look behind her. He is gone.

Chapter Eight

Claudine Delacroix is not a sentimental woman, she did not get where she is by looking at the world through a rosy screen. A spirited woman imprisoned in a man's world she has not been content to take things lying down. Her good friend Emily, founder member of the Women's Franchise League, lives in nearby Manchester and it is to her offices in Salford that Claudine, arm in arm with her young protégé, departs from Trinity street on the nine-fifteen to Manchester, Victoria on a wet windy morning in October 1884.

Emily, her intended husband and her daughters, Sylvia and Christobel, are off to foreign climes. Political activities bring them increasing attention from the law and her husband – to – be, a barrister, has advised a short disappearance to let things cool down. That latest rally at The Exchange had nearly ended in riot, causing Emily and her daughters to ponder carefully the strident insults, rotten eggs, not all of which thrown by angry men, but by the very women whose cause they espouse.

The little group, which now includes Lizzie – Elizabeth - as the two campaigning sisters insist on, are off to emulate their gentlemen friends on what is known as The Grand Tour, courtesy of Mister Thomas Cook. The intended irony of the enterprise is apparently lost on all but a handful of those friends who, although paternally dismissive of these wilful women, cannot but admire their conviction. Lizzie travels as companion to the sisters, and until her coming event precludes it, she will dance for them in the evenings.

Mister Cohen is not at home when Miss Delacroix calls at the sign of the three brass balls. She leaves her card. The next day a message arrives to tell her that he is ready to attend her whenever she wishes it. She goes straight round and knocks quite loudly at his door.

'It is a small amount that is required', she tells the pawnbroker who fingers his beard nervously.

'A token perhaps'?

'But - my responsibility is this?'

'No of course not Mister Cohen but a young girl? A neighbour? And what of...' she lowers her voice to a whisper, 'services rendered? Certain, ah, articles supplied?' She spreads her hands dramatically, her head with its fine sculptured bones, cold white complexion, red ruby lips, is disarmingly inclined to one side.

'A hundred pounds?' She wheedles and the little bell pings on the cash register as he opens the drawer.

Lizzie has never travelled further than the moors that ring her town. She has looked out at that world, imagining what she could not see, now here she is - Folkestone and the steamer to Holland. A chain of speaking venues has been arranged throughout Europe. Always heading south, the little band is a small travelling circus and in church halls, music halls, marquees and in the open air, the two indomitable sisters preach their message: 'Votes for Women'. Lizzie absorbs this gift. The child inside her has already put a stop to the dancing, but that does not stop her learning. The venues they frequent are often pure theatre - a circus, where jugglers, wild animals, trapeze artists fill the marquee, and form a warm up for the fiery oratory. The steps of a local Town Hall. A field on the outskirts of some town. A Grand Opera House.

Lizzie watches and learns as these fiery women, in their tiers and layers of skirts, half choked by clothing designed for modesty more than fashion, control, and work their often hostile audiences. She watches also the supporting acts. The performers in their spangles and silks. The grace of a lion tamer holding the fangs of sure death inches from his heart. The accuracy and daring of the trapeze. The quick, light ease of the bareback rider as she twists and turns, leaps and bounds to the roar and stamping of the crowd. Lizzie loves the crowd. She craves the adulation, the sheer thrill of loud applause and she hopes and prays that soon, some of it will be hers.

Malta is off the beaten track as far as Europe is concerned. However, important military garrison it surely is, with its fine deep-water port, its creeks alive with the men and ships of the biggest fleet the world has ever seen. The raising and lowering of anchors, the echoes of saluting cannon. All this, and the administrative swarm that maintains it, have created a social atmosphere that is the envy of many of the more established cultural salons such as exist in Rome, Paris or London.

Maria Aloyisa greets them as they step from the bobbing gondola. The oarsman slaps his blades flat on the water to keep his boat steady.

'Call me Louisa', she speaks warmly, welcoming, and with only the merest hint of an accent other than that of a landed English Lady.

The cabriolet dips as Lizzie steps onto the footstep. The liveried footman's hand is firm yet deferential in hers. She notes the plush leather upholstery, the deep glowing polish of the bottle green coach work, the gaudy splash of colour which is the coat of arms: 'Sans Mal' the wording says.

They drive slowly through the strange streets. Out along the Mall. Under the great arches at Port de Bombes. Past The Marsa. Up the hill through Hamrun to Attard and the family home.

'You must tell me about your dance', her ladyship says, leaning closer, the better to hear Lizzie over the clip clop of the horses' hooves and the babble of noises in the streets they pass through. 'My mother wanted me to be a famous ballerina one day', she pauses and then with a twinkle, 'But I do not think that by marrying an English Lord I have much displeased her'.

She sees Lizzie to her room, dismissing the maid detailed the task. They hold hands as they mount the stairs.

'I shall call you Lizzie, will you mind? When you are famous I will tell my children I knew Lizzie Reardon the great English actress'.

They eat in the kitchen overlooking the San Anton Gardens on all occasions except when his Lordship is entertaining, or when protocol dictates that he and his wife dine formally. Otherwise, Louisa. Emily, her daughters and Lizzie enjoy pleasant days together all planned around the two sister's speaking engagements.

'The Granaries in two more days', their hostess is telling them some several weeks later. 'It will be your final challenge. It is Malta's Hyde Park Corner and you will be savaged from every angle. The Archbishop is reported to be set against you, and there have been murmurings from the pulpit. The people will do what the church tells them to do. However, there is a ground swell of support; perhaps that is more than we may expect at this stage and on this remote island'.

She turns to face an aged servant hovering at the open door.

'Yes Paul? What is it?'

'Master Phillip has arrived madam and has gone straight to his room'.

The retainer bows, retreats softly, and as the door closes behind him Lizzie is startled to catch a glimpse of a hooded figure dressed from top to toe entirely in white, gliding silently past on bare feet.

As Lizzie prepares for bed that night a note is pushed under her door asking her to meet the lady of the house in the gardens next day after breakfast.

'Thank you for coming', Louisa tells Lizzie. They sit on the low wall that surrounds a fountain among fabulous bushes, trees, shrubs and blooms imported from every continent. 'No-one will find us here and I wish to be frank'.

Lizzie is embarrassed; this woman has already done so much for her, been so kind, so many wonderful experiences, now she feels she is about to be offered even more. She steels herself. It is in her nature to reject such overt and continued kindness.

'Your child is due in less than a month', Louisa begins, 'you have told me of its origin and I admire you for the way you have borne your trials. You will have thought - I have no doubt - of the future? How you will care for your baby? Feed him, house him and yourself and raise him? No! Let me go on, please. Your career on the stage will I am sure be successful, but,' she pauses, 'the Music Hall is a demanding profession, you will *be* in demand and unless you reach the dizzy heights – a Marie Lloyd, another Gertie Gatana… well, you do see? You can have your child or you can have the stage. I have a friend…'but at this Lizzie leaps to her feet with a sob.

'I'm sorry', she cries and she runs off back the way they came, under the arches of mulberry, through the great iron studded doors, up the wide stairs to her room.

Chapter Nine

The Granaries are teaming with people. Il Fosos, they call it. This large public space, lying between the church of St. Publius and the tall, elegant buildings on Floriana Mall, is dotted at regular intervals with giant round stones that look at first glance like the bases of what must have been the massive pillars of some marvellous construction of antiquity. But they are not. They are lids, each one capping a section of a silo that runs deep under the ground. Storages for wheat, grain, built up by the Knights, against famine, drought and the ever-present threat of attempted invasion.

A platform has been set up, courtesy of Louisa's husband, whose initial disinclination towards involvement, based on centuries of family opposition to change and in particular such radical change as women's suffrage - has been modified in one night after a particularly exhilarating, if exhausting display of his wife's remarkable attention to her duty.

Christobel is the first to speak. She is the shock trooper before the more reasoned tones of her sister Sylvia. Placards placed regularly about the area all bear the familiar legend: 'Votes For Women'. Some of these have already been torn down, trampled underfoot. The speakers know the risks they are taking. They watch as a scattering of Franciscan Monks glide among the crowd. A word here, an imprecation there. Religious fervour is always simmering, ready to be tapped, and turned to political advantage. The situation looks ugly and the campaigners may have to quit, leave the stage and flee with perhaps their very lives at risk.

Suddenly there is a sound, a sound of music. Marching music. The crowd loves a band. Every parish has at least one and the restless crowd, recognising the tunes, begin to clap and sway to the well-loved airs as a small group of perhaps fifty women come toiling up Crucifix Hill. They are dressed head to toe in black, many of them are old, they all hold their Rosary Beads pressed close to their lips. They march to the beat till they reach the platform. The crowd parts to let them pass. The band: trumpeters, kettle drummers, trombonists, even the big base drum; all are played by women as they wheel, turn into line and at four loud thumps from the drum, halt. The music stops. There is silence, then, at a solitary beat from

61

the drum, each woman removes her faldetta, that sacred article of feminine subservience, that bat black all encompassing veil - and dumps it without more ceremony on the ground. The crowds are silent. They are confused. The little band of English women, Lizzie, large with child among them, join up with the new arrivals and they all set off together as the band plays a spirited march.

On the following evening Her Ladyship gives a party. A going away party. It is agreed that Lizzie will remain until recovered and then a sea passage will be arranged to take her to England. Nothing more has been said concerning Lizzie's postnatal arrangements, nor of any agreement concerning the child.

The party is a great success; the ladies competing in their finery for the attentions of the gentlemen whose own finery, especially that of the Garrison Officers in their scarlet jackets and gold braid, does not fall very far short.

Louisa takes Lizzie by the hand and leads her into the library.

'This is the friend I mentioned - Thomas Baldacino'. Louisa joins their hands and the man's grip is firm and friendly.

'Your servant Ma'am', and he bows slightly, kissing her hand.

'And may I present—my wife Hannah?'

Hannah reminds Lizzie of Madame Delacroix, though not in Claudine's looks. Nor in her ornamentation or cosmetic excess. Hannah is restrained, understated but Lizzie knows in a minute that like Claudine, she is determined.

She likes Hannah and she likes Mr Baldacino.

Lizzie, large and most uncomfortable, has sat quietly all evening, admiring the revellers, the party going on around her. She will miss it all. How, she wonders, did I ever get to this? Heavy with my own father's child, feted and coddled by near strangers, on a tiny island in the middle of the sea in the middle of the whole wide world. What twists and turns, what changes in a life yet hardly begun.

Hannah catches Lizzie's eye over her fan and takes a seat next to her on the fringes of the ballroom.

'Thomas tells me he will arrange your passage home', Hannah tells her. Lizzie is being pursued and Hannah notes her surprised look.

'Oh! Have I put my foot in it? Tom is always telling me. Oh dear' She takes Lizzie's hand.

'Never fear', Lizzie tells her. 'I did not know it was he but yes, Louisa has told me of the kind arrangement'.

Hannah smiles in the way women do when they wish to convey no threat.

'I know that Louisa has spoken to you and we do not wish to make you sad. It... look, let me be straight. We, Tom and I, are aware of your circumstances. I think perhaps you are not aware of ours - his and mine. We both want a child and I cannot bear. He needs an heir; boy or girl and we can hardly comprehend that he should not be allowed to have one, or that the law and the church can be so cruel as to prevent it. We are not allowed to adopt because we are both divorcees, even though it must be obvious that any child in our care would receive every good consideration and indeed perhaps a far better life than might otherwise be the case. Still, as I said, we have no wish to intrude and the last thing we would want is to cause you harm. You must rest and gather your strength for the event and when you are ready, Tom will make all the arrangements for your passage. Yours and the baby's if that is your wish'.

At the head of the table Louisa taps a glass with a silver spoon.

'Ladies and Gentlemen, we have an extraordinary entertainment for you tonight. A friend from Italy, who does not grace our table so often as we would like it, is nevertheless here tonight. May I now present him to you: Ladies and Gentlemen - Mr Leopoldo Fregoli'.

Lizzie is stunned and excited all at once. Is their no end to her good fortune? Mister Fregoli? Of all people! And here at her party! She looks upwards expectantly at the grand staircase where her hero is making his appearance. All around her the guests applaud. Malta is a fortress, a garrison and it is natural that many of tonight's guests are officers in either the army or the navy and when General Gordon strides briskly in they are on their feet. At first in shock - the General himself has recently been killed at Khartoum and this is still fresh in their minds - until they realise it is all an illusion. The sort that Fregoli excels in. This diminutive Italian man is one of the worlds most highly paid and respected artistes and Lizzie knows him! Or at least she has met him! Will he remember her?

The Marquis of Salisbury, Lord Randolph Churchill, all follow. Gait, demeanour, facial characteristics, all exact and when the spit of Mr Baden Powell walks in, the room is in uproar, for, sitting chatting to a lady by the piano, is the actual man in person, smiling broadly at this confrontation with himself.

'Lizzie, friend of my English friend Madame Claudine!' Leopold's large warm eyes embrace her. 'I have looked for you and - err', he notes her obvious state for the first time. 'When can we meet?' His handshake is strong although his hands shake a little after his exertions. His eyes are on fire, 'I need you for The Palace in London in two months time'.

He is gone, whisked away by the assembled company, many of whom, the men at least, try to catch his eye with a view to being caricatured in some future production, a sign these days of sure success.

Next morning Lizzie awakes early, she has begun to be a little nauseous in the mornings and her increasing bulk is an embarrassment to her. The lithe, youthful figure of a few short months ago, the agility of the trained dancer, all are hidden, smothered beneath the uncompromising signs of impending motherhood. She will be glad when it is all over and she is rid of her unwelcome intruder. She goes to the window for a breath of fresh morning air, and as she draws the curtain, a sudden awful sight makes her gasp and reel back in shock. A figure is standing there, stock-still. The same figure she caught a glimpse of earlier. A white, pointed hood with two black holes for eyes, a gaping gash for a mouth. Barefoot, the apparition stands and stares straight at her as she leans frozen against the window ledge. She lets the curtain fall and moves quickly away and out of sight.

'We will all dress nicely tonight'. Louisa claps her hands, a happy smile on her face, 'my brother Philip will join us, my handsome brother who you have not yet met. He is a bachelor you know? though you ladies will find it hard to catch him!'

Phillip is indeed handsome. Louisa has placed him at the head of the table. The Baldacino's, Thomas and Hannah, are on his left. Lizzie is on his right with her lady companions arranged along the length of the long laden table. The hostess and her husband sit grandly, side by side, opposite Phillip who, Lizzie supposes, is about thirty. His pointed beard is flecked already with grey to match his swept back sideburns and a stiff winged collar under a silk faced dinner jacket make him what he obviously is; a Gentleman. Lizzie glances at him; quick, appraising glances when he is not looking; she cannot make up her mind whether she is in awe or fear of him.

Louisa has lent Lizzie a cornflower blue dress in tulle with the new, less cumbersome bustle now in favour. With a few deft arrangements at the front and her natural ability to project, the mother to be is transformed. She has, during her recent exposure to fine living and with her natural gift for mimicry, absorbed many of the mannerisms and poses natural to the upper classes. In her speech, the flat vowels of her native home have been cleverly rounded and now, this evening, she is every inch the confident lady she has long wished to be.

'Perhaps I frightened you this morning?' Phillip asks Lizzie over the buzz of conversation. She pauses, her fork half way to her mouth. 'You?' She says. 'What…?'

'Let me explain', he goes on, placing a hand gently on her arm.

He tells her of his attachment to the religious order of the Dominican's.

'I am not a priest but a Ruzarjantia. A Member of the Confraternity of The Holy Rosary. We have certain, mainly secular, responsibilities and the strange garb I assure you does have a purpose, but it is not a sinister one'. He smiles, abruptly changing the subject.

'But tell me about you, about your dancing career'. He is charming, attentive and Lizzie is thoroughly relaxed in the warmth of his company.

Meal over, brandy sipped, cigars smoked, and noses powdered, the guests all retire to the library where Louisa sits at the piano. She strikes a chord and glances expectantly at her brother Phillip who, blushing at the attention, joins her. His voice is a subdued baritone. Not a trained voice Lizzie can tell, but sincere. His songs are English songs suited to the romanticism of the age, with an emphasis on patriotism, duty and unrequited love.

He is roundly applauded and, bowing slightly, a pleased grin on his face, he goes to re-join the others. Then Louisa, reaching to the side of the piano, produces a Spanish guitar.

'One more', she pleads. 'A Maltese song'.

Phillip's fingers caress the neck of the instrument. He taps the frets, adjusts the strings and then, in rushing bursts, dramatic pauses, tingling and teasing, the music springs wildly from his fingertips. Trills, crescendos, sobbing sighs and the voice. Phillip's voice, almost female in its pitch. A haunting sound, which reminds Lizzie of the Gypsy airs she herself has danced to, and she recognises the technique of call and response: the ancient rhythms of Africa, the Moors and of Andalusia . She is listening to a story and without knowing the words, she is captured by it and begs Phillip to teach it to her.

'Later', he tells her, smiling but pleased at her eagerness. 'When you are well', he stumbles over the words, 'after the baby'. He raises a cautionary finger. 'But I must warn you, it is not a happy tale'.

Her baby is born in a strange bed in a strangers house, that of Thomas and Hannah. It is a big house. She has every comfort. Every medical assistance.

She pushes her child, a boy, out into the world with her eyes fixed firmly high up on the wall. There are roses in the patterned wallpaper. She counts the roses, gripping tight and pulling down on the straps. Pushing, urging. She hears one sharp cry. The slight weight of her son rests briefly on the inside of her thigh. She answers his cry with her own despairing sob and abruptly, despite herself, she reaches down to gather him up. But he is gone.

The days following her confinement are a blur. Her friends, the comfort of her temporary home, the gentle pace of island life, all are the rock on which she leans and depends while the pain and anguish slowly fade.

She wanders alone down silent, sun-drenched alleyways, past ancient courtyards, returning always to the little garden beneath the palace at San Anton where she sits quietly on the warm stone balustrade that circles the little pond with its tinkling fountain. Fat carp loll on the still surface among the water lilies as they bask lazily in the warm sun. It is so gentle here, and even with her loss, she has been happy among these kind people and it is here one early morning that, reaching inside herself to caress the familiar hurt, she finds to her surprise that it has gone.

She takes a small handkerchief from her bag, dabs quickly at her eyes as she sees Phillip enter through the garden gates and walk quickly towards her.

He bows and taking her hands in his, he sits down beside her on the wall. He does not speak. She can feel the strength in him, the goodness.

'If only...' she begins, but he interrupts her, placing a hand on hers.

'It is passing now', he says firmly. 'I have watched you and I have watched it pass. All things pass', he comforts her and she nods, squeezes his hand and smiles.

'The song?' she enquires.

'The song'. He agrees and they smile together as he begins.

'Il—Ghanja ta Thomas McSweeney' is a ballad, a true story. I wrote my version as a protest really, but let me tell you the story as it was told to me by my uncle who was one of two monks who attended Thomas at his execution'.

The sun has grown too hot to sit in, and Phillip suggests they walk in the shade of the Mulberry trees that line the many pathways, among Japonica, Flambé, Bougainvillea and Oleander. His voice, with its attractive accent, rises and falls with the rhythm of the story and just as he warned her, it is not a happy tale.

'So Thomas was arrested, charged with striking a superior, a light blow apparently, but from which his protagonist conveniently died, thus allowing the authorities the opportunity to hang him. They wanted to silence him because he knew something. Something secret. In the song, a 'Royal Gardener' is mentioned and we know that a government botanist took away samples of a poisonous weed that used to grow on a rock off Gozo, our sister island. This gentleman, a Mister Coombes, committed suicide on his arrival back in England under circumstances that have never been explained. The Maltese people have never accepted the official story, which of course may be true. Their version is perhaps merely a myth that has grown with time and yes, my song may perpetuate that myth'.

They turn into the lane that leads to the gate. 'The story ends with even more sadness I'm afraid', Philip says. 'There is a girl involved, a girl called Chetina, who, after giving birth to Thomas's child, throws herself off the battlements into the sea, at almost the same spot where her lover has just been hung'.

They are almost home when Phillip stops short.

'I said just now that the story ends. What I meant was the song, my song ends. But the story goes on and now by a strange twist of fate, a coincidence? Perhaps, but you are now a part, you are in the story'.

They sit again together in the courtyard of the house in which she has been so happy. Louisa's house. Phillip's house too. How sad it will be to leave it and them. So much left behind. So much love and gladness. Her child and so much sadness.

'The child I told you about?' Philip continues, 'the child of Thomas McSweeney and Chetina? That child is Thomas Baldacino. Yes', he nods. 'Our Thomas who is now the father of your child, a child who will grow up a mixture of Irish, Maltese and English, a child of privilege who will never want and that fact at least will surely make a happier tale'.

Their feet make a crunching sound on the gravelled path as they walk slowly towards the arched main gate. The sentry, nodding sleepily in his box, hears them approach and leaping to his feet, he executes a smart salute, which, in its ferocity, nearly knocks his cap off. The couple, stifling their laughter, are suddenly sombre as they turn, hand in hand, to face one another. He looks at her, his smile turning abruptly to sadness as she waits. Their eyes lock. Moments pass. And then, turning on his heel, he walks hurriedly away without a single last glance.

The Steamer Alaunia sails at eight the next morning bound for Marseilles. Lizzie stands at the rail as the ship glides slowly past the little garden high on the fortress walls where the olive trees bend almost horizontally, looking like very old men, after centuries of high winds and storms. She sees the little watchtower on the point. The emblems etched in the weathered stone. The eye, the ear, the nose. Watch, listen, smell the wind they say and there, as the ship approaches the Palladian outline of the naval hospital at Bighi; there on the ship's Starboard side, in a cot in a nursery, in a house in the village of Kalkara, her son lies sleeping beneath the eyes and under the protection of another woman. She fingers the brooch Phillip gave her before they parted.

'A keepsake', he told her. 'Wear it and you will be protected. If you get into trouble—any trouble, go to your local Catholic church and show the priest this'.

Lizzie sits on a bed in her cabin, and as the ship grumbles, groans and gets up to full speed, she opens up a writing pad, smoothes the page and begins to write.

'THE REEL OF THE HANGED ONE'
(A solo interpretation.)
By LIZZIE REARDON.

Chapter Ten

Leopoldo Fregoli has many imitators, some he has encouraged and even, as is the case now with Lizzie, taken the trouble to teach the deeper mysteries hidden in the folds of his many, many characters. Their gestures, habits, idiosyncrasies.

'They are all me', he tells her. 'I am not an actor, I do not pretend. I *become* them - whoever they are'.

He is dressed in what he calls his workman's clothes, a simple shift of white linen that covers him from his neck to his bare feet. Lizzie sits a few rows back in the stalls of the Palace Theatre of Varieties at Hammersmith. The two months deadline Leo gave her has extended to more like two years and during this time she has not been still. Her debut at The Grand in her hometown has been followed by a whirlwind of touring. Music Halls are opening up everywhere and no act, no matter how strange, different, even bizarre (one-legged dancers are popular), the only criteria is: do the public like you? That is all that matters. And they like Lizzie, by now a skilful and accomplished dancer. And as her old friend Claudine notes with pleasure, her talent for mimicry has taken hold of her act. It is no surprise that it is Claudine who, on the now rare occasions she and Lizzie meet, has urged her to work with Fregoli.

The great man stands before her now, pristine in neutral white.

'I am nothing', he explains. 'Nobody. And then...'

A pace backwards. A pace to the right and he disappears behind a silken screen to reappear—blink, blink, blink. Lizzie's eyelids count the steps and presto! She is looking at herself. Tambourine held on high. Hand on hip. Skirts billowing. She is looking into a mirror at herself. Herself as a Gypsy Girl, one of her own most popular creations.

'You will practice with the mirrors every day. Today is Thursday and on Monday we will perform Shakespeare - Lear', he notes Lizzie's dismayed look. 'Don't know it? Neither does anybody else - a simple domestic affair of quarrels and spite and love and hate - we present only the tableaux. Three young girls you will do, two naughty ones you will act and for the other, Cordelia, be yourself'.

He goes behind the screen again emerging in a second, bearded and with a crown on his head. He speaks;

'How sharper than a serpent's tooth is to have a thankless child!' The voice of this diminutive man, turned King, rumbles round the empty theatre like the roar of a wounded lion.

The next months are a flurry of venues. Her name has spread through the pages of the theatrical newspapers where she advertises herself by the title suggested by Leopold himself: "The Female Fregoli", The popular stars of the day, ever mindful of their obligations to, and the advisability of, keeping in with those less vaunted, (today a nobody, tomorrow a star), make sure their agents are aware of Lizzie. She is soon second billing to the likes of Leno, Chaplin and Marie Lloyd and it is the latter lady, in her top hat and tails, in the cramped space between the dressing room tunnel and the wings one night, who plants a kiss on Lizzie's surprised lips and tells her; 'Get an Agent!'

James Fortune, if he had not been born with the name, would perhaps have invented it in order to attract that which he has always been convinced was his right. Somewhere out there is his fortune, and during the second curtain at The Palace one lucky night in June, he has reason to believe he has found it.

He has not been a Theatrical Agent long and tends to go for the cheaper end of the market. A specialty is in finding military units willing to provide, often at no cost, a troop of soldiers; volunteers, militia men, to form part of the padding all shows rely on. At the top of the bill there is The Star, name in big letters, an act perhaps of international fame. Lower down on the billing will be a couple of known, and often just as loved lesser names. Under these a school choir or a troop of soldiers, real soldiers, drilling to a patriotic air or re-enacting the highlights of a famous skirmish: The Siege at Rorke's Drift, The Charge of the Light Brigade, or the more recent, Death of General Gordon at Khartoum. These 'acts' cost next to nothing to produce and require only the negotiating skills of someone like Mr Fortune to stage.

James was 'born in a field in Mayo', as is his boast when describing, as he does often, his humble beginnings.

'See that?' he will demand, pointing to a perfectly ordinary chin and lower jaw.

'See the green?'

'Green?' His victim will query, seeing only pale pink with some scruffy part shaven beard. His accent is his asset, that and a tendency to believe every untruth that slides easily out of his own mouth. A card is what they call him, though some have other, more pithy epithets.

'Green!' James will insist. 'Bloody grass, that's what we had for our dinner and me Ma' boiled dog's bones for the soup'.

James is watching his lads - a platoon of Loyal North Lancashire's, turning and wheeling to the baritone strains of 'Soldiers of The Queen'. He likes The Alhambra, one of the first theatres to be purely Music Hall, and the venue being Belfast, he has no trouble with the English flavour of his shows. As a Southerner himself, he'd be strung up if he tried putting the English army on at The Abbey in Dublin say. Personally he has never had any truck with all that 'patriot game' shit.

'Patriot my arse', he tells his mates. 'Look out for number one'.

He looks up now as the master of ceremonies introduces the next act.

'Ladees and Gen'lmen!'

Bang goes the mallet in the gavel.

'Once in a very blue moon, these tired old eyes of mine are charmed by an elegance so extraordinary, a skill so sanguinary'. Here the crowd join in with mock surprise and awe.

'Ooooh!'

Bang goes the gavel.

'A vision so voluptuary'.

'Aaah!'

'Ladees and Gentlemen, I give you: The terpsichorean talents of that most delightful rising star: The Protean Artiste Extraordinaire'. He points his mallet at a fat man in the front stalls, 'Quick Change Artist to you sir! - Miss… Lizzie … Reardon!'

The crowd stamp their feet and whistle, they clap their hands and shout, smack each other on the back while the orchestra in the pit strikes up with a popular melody, and Lizzie, her small frame darting and dancing, flits behind the screen as a gypsy girl and in a flash flits back as a clown.

A range of international dances follow and with each a lightening change: A Dutch girl. An Alpine milk-maid. An Indian Squaw. A Geisha. The audience roar their approval, gasping in surprise at the speed and accuracy of the transformations and, as the act comes to a close, they object loudly, waving their programme sheets and shouting.

'More! More! As with each last curtain call, Lizzie is dragged back on stage by their incessant demand.

The stage manager catches her as she seeks refuge in the wings for the fourth or fifth time. He hugs her in his arms, turns her about, pats her bottom.

'Milk them!' he shouts. 'Milk the buggers'.

She stands at the footlights, centre stage and raises her arms for silence.

'Thank you', she says. 'Thank you. And now I would like to perform for you a dance. A montage I wrote myself. It is called 'The Reel Of The Hanged One.'

In his seat in the front stalls, James Fortune has made his mind up and when Lizzie has finally managed to get off stage, he is at the door of the dressing room she shares with most of the chorus.

'My card'.

He shouts above the din and over the heads of the scantily dressed girls who jostle and joke with each other at his presence in this all female corner of backstage. He shouts her name again. 'Lizzie', and points at the card held aloft in one hand. 'Please?' and she, flushed from the performance still, her face not entirely clean of slap, glances up at the man and at the proffered card. She has in fact already made his acquaintance - in a manner of speaking that is, about half an hour earlier when she was doing the geisha girl. She caught a glimpse of him over her fan. Saw this red headed, freckled faced boy gazing up at her adoringly - and very nearly dropped the fan. She just stared at him for what, in the split second timing of her act, seemed like an hour, but in reality can only have been a moment. After that, the rest of her performance became focused on him. It was an old stager's trick, aiming your act at one person; it seemed to have worked in more ways than one.

'No time!' she tells him, shouting above the 'ooh's' and 'aah's' of the girls, who are delighted at this spot of romance in their lives. 'My boat leaves in twenty minutes'. Dressed at last, she pushes past him and jumps into a brougham already waiting at the curb.

Aboard the night steamer, settled in a deck chair, sheltered by one of the massive draught intakes that feed air to the boiler room, Lizzie takes out her sandwiches and looks down at the stokers toiling below. She will be warm here, a favourite spot; she can snooze with only the clanging of the ship's telegraphs to disturb her.

'My card'. James says again, a big disarming smile on his handsome face. He has brought a blanket, which he drapes around her legs, tucking it in.

'You want looking after you do', he tells her in his very best brogue. And it is just about then that Lizzie, with nothing less likely on her mind, falls in love.

A month later and she is playing in her hometown at the Bolton Grand. It is just before early doors, and they are enjoying a drink and a pasty at The Golden Lion across the road.

'Mr Stoll', he enthuses over a half and half, his favourite tipple, consisting of a double scotch and a beer chaser. 'You must meet Mr Stoll. The Moss Empires, and Tony Pastor of course - and Oscar Hammerstein. My New York friends'.

She is never out of work. The man she loves is a powerhouse of energy in a whirlwind of contacts, contracts, agencies, managers, backers. He takes control of everything. Her wardrobe, her diary, the development of new acts, and he has contacts in America who will guarantee the best possible returns on the various investments they will, for the merest commission, make for her in the burgeoning markets of the New World.

The size of the lettering of her name on the billboards grows larger and larger; inching higher and higher up the lists to keep pace with the money she is making. Happier than she has been in the whole of her young life, she is content in the knowledge that, at last, she has found someone to care for her, to cherish her, and to take away the daily drudgeries of life. His drinking? Well, it is a worry, of course it is, especially since, as the workload increases, so does his intake. He is drunk most of the time now; simmering, and will often get angry if things do not go his way. She doesn't really mind, although the stink of liquor on him as he attempts to make love to her does stir an unhappy memory.

'It's my fuel', he tells her, 'my energy and look at where it has got us! Look at this', and he picks up *The Stage*, the weekly theatrical newspaper.

"Lizzie Reardon, 'The Female Fregoli". Terpsichorean and Danseuse Protean, appearing at The Palace by *Popular* Demand", he intones in a loud voice. 'And what about this?' he is getting agitated. She nods and puts a hand on his sleeve as he slams down one paper and snatches up another: 'The bloody *'Era'* no less, what more do you want? Eh? It says here:' "This graceful and accomplished dancer, transformed in a blink before our very eyes".

James opens his arms wide.

'Eh?' he demands again. 'Come on!' as the landlord collects their empty glasses.

'Everything all right sir?' he asks with an edge to his voice, as Lizzie soothes and coaxes her husband.

Back in London, Lizzie's friend Leo is in a season at the Hackney Empire and wishes she would join him as his special guest. His letters however, sent by runner, are unacknowledged. The messenger is dispatched with a flea in his ear as James Fortune, in his role of husband, manager and Lord Protector, consolidates his hold on his wife's affairs.

Chapter Eleven

RMS Campania is one of Cunard's fastest liners. With her sister ship Luciana, the company has taken the coveted Blue Riband on no less than four occasions since their launch in 1893, crossing the North Atlantic from Liverpool to New York in under six days. At seven in the morning on August 8th, 1896, Lizzie and her husband are among the milling crowd as they pass through the various check posts at the Princes Landing Stage on the River Mersey in the Port of Liverpool.

James is in a foul mood. He spent the previous night in the taproom of The Baltic pub, rolling in at their digs at Toxteth at two in the morning, roaring drunk. An altercation with their landlady had not pleased him, and hearing the row, Lizzie trembled, fearing what she knew was sure to come. He has rarely actually struck her but the fear of it and the constant uncertainty has her continually unnerved and walking on eggshells. And yet he produces. They are successful. He has talent and it comes as no surprise to her when, with typical bravado, he first announces what he calls;

'Our New World Tour'.

To Lizzie, the very idea of America was of a land so far away it might just as well be in outer space. The thought of the organisation that must go into such a trip was enough to put her off the idea altogether. However, she was well aware of the many contemporary performers, famous and otherwise, who were making the break and, attracted by big money contracts, going out to the States where theatres were opening at an alarming rate and where, with an insatiable thirst for British talent, entrepreneurs and their agents, desperate for that 'new face' were prepared to pay almost any price in the hope of discovering a 'star' and making their fortune.

Lizzie leaves everything to her manager and husband James and sure enough, due solely to his flair and energy, less than a month after he first proposed the idea, their passage is booked, their trunks packed, and they are off on the great adventure.

'Do you intend', says the customs official, 'to export any kind of subversive material from the United Kingdom into The United States? Are you in possession of any form of lewd or licentious literature or images likely to corrupt another person? Is…'

'Oh! Fuck off', James cries, turning away angrily.

'Now, now Jimmy! Now, now!' A man slips a conciliatory arm about James's shoulders. A very large man with a moustache flaring out of plump, ruddy cheeks. Check trousers in the fashionable fit, tight about his considerable bottom. At his neck, a fluttering bow tie dangles lopsidedly, and on his head, a Brown Derby hat just manages to contain a wild tumble of crow black curling locks. Mister Tony Pastor, Circus Ringmaster, Crooner, Songwriter turned Theatrical Agent, soothes the angry customs man. He has come all the way from New York to pick up these acts, and he is not about to let some lush put a goddamn spanner in the works.

'Guess you took a load on last night ugh? Jim?' He winks at the official. 'You know how it is officer? He's in my party', he gestures with an expansive arm at the little band who accompany him.

'Pastor's Summer Revue', he hands the man a card. 'Catch us on Broadway at Mister Hammerstein's Olympia… bring the missus… bring the kids. A family show. Just ask for me at the door'.

He winks again and the officer waves them through.

The brass band plays a medley of marches as the gangway is drawn up, streamers are thrown and the crowds wave fluttering handkerchiefs as the ship prepares to sail.

The massive breast lines are cast off, three men to each bollard straining at the weight and finally the remaining spring rope trails in the churning water as the ship edges away from the quay and into the muddy waters of the Mersey.

George, the Saloon barman, recognises James straight away, not that he's ever seen him before, but there is always the one. First in. Last out. The lone drinker. James orders a gill and a chaser and is well stewed by the time the ship gets to Ireland.

Lizzie looks out of her porthole at the land they are approaching. Neat rows of small cottages painted in a rainbow of colours. A line of shops, chandlers, hotels, a pub named O'Donnell's, and high on a hill towering over the town, the Cathedral in Gothic black stone. Queenstown, called Cobh by the local inhabitants resentful of the English intrusion, is the departure point for the hoards of emigrants still fleeing the effects of The Great Famine to seek their fortune in America. Lizzie watches as the Steerage port is opened up and the long lines of ragged hopefuls trudge wearily up the gangway and into the crowded dormitories below. Lizzie has been crying. How can it all have gone so terribly wrong? Here she is, on her way to her American debut, a saloon passenger aboard one of the most modern liners in the world, and the man she has loved, worshipped, suddenly turned brute. Her thoughts, though she has fought hard to prevent it, have turned to that other night in her own front parlour. The stale stink of whiskey, the pain, the bewilderment. Here it is again. Is it her fault? Does she cause this change in men? This savagery? The only two men she has ever loved and both the cause of searing pain.

A discreet tap, tap at the door brings her out of her thoughts. She dabs at her eyes with a handkerchief, pats her hair into place and opens the door.

'Mister Pastor's compliments madam, and will you join him at the Purser's office?' The steward is polite, deferential, as he waits to escort her.

James is comatose, slumped in a chair in the tiny room. Mister Pastor is settling a bill that James has apparently refused to pay at the bar. There are also some breakages. They coax James into an upright position, and with the help of the steward, they get him to their stateroom.

'You are gonna have to dump this guy' Tony Pastor tells Lizzie as she mumbles her thanks, blushing with shame as she goes to close the door. The impresario is noted for his hard-nosed business acumen, but he has a soft centre for his protégés. He reaches out and gently touches the bruise, partially hidden by make up on her cheek. He whistles low in his teeth.

'Yes siree' he murmurs. 'I got my eye on him and you tell him when he comes too that I will see him in my cabin'.

So the voyage continues. The weather is fine. James is fine. His little talk with Mister Pastor appears to have done some good.

'I'm cutting down', he tells his wife. 'We'll be alright'.

And he does cut down, makes a point of pleasing her, wooing her even, all over again. The weather is fine, the company is good, the magnificent ship nears its own record for the crossing and, in just over one week from leaving Liverpool, crowds of passengers are lining the decks for a first view of the Statue of Liberty as the great liner, with the gentle persuasion of tugs, is manoeuvred into her billet at the newly built Chelsea Piers.

Lizzie is quite used to the squalor of theatrical digs. Artistes such as herself, even with the undoubted popularity they often enjoy, are rated second, often third on the billing and are paid a pittance compared to the leading performers. Clean, comfortable accommodation rates low in a performer's expectations. Even so, it is with an increasing sense of disappointment that she views the passing scene as they toil up the hill, both horses straining and foaming at the bit as they approach the junction of Broadway and Seventh avenue.

Tony Pastor puts a hand on her arm.

'Pretty grim ugh?' He waves a hand at the mean buildings, cheap hotels, boarding houses, squalid tenements; all scarred by long flights of fire escapes that cling to the brick work, rusting and forlorn.

'Be night time soon and just you see!' Tony Pastor jollies them along.

The impresario has booked the whole fourth floor of their walk-up hotel. Lizzie and the other female members of their troupe set about their usual self-imposed task of ensuring they get as much comfort and facility as they possibly can out of the manager.

Is there hot and constant water? Is the tub communal or separate? What time is breakfast? Are chamber pots emptied as part of the service? Is there a view from the apartment window? They flutter and fuss and laugh and cajole while the men, adventurers all, go off to find a saloon and a drink. Mister Pastor takes Lizzie to one side.

'Be dark soon', he repeats himself. 'Jest take a peek from your window'.

Lizzie is alone in their room. 'Just a quick one with the boys,' James told her. 'You know how it is.' She sits on the bed, the nagging feeling in her stomach again, churning with apprehension. She sighs, kicks off her shoes and goes to run a bath.

Wallowing in hot suds, her slender form tingling with relief, Lizzie sighs again, contented despite herself. He has been good lately after all. She settles deeper in the bath and is almost asleep when she hears the door open and then close with a bang.

Startled, her heart sinking, she hesitates fearfully before she speaks.

'Jimmy? Is that you Jim?'

'Yeh! Yeh! Who'd you think? *Mister* bloody Pastor? '

Everything is spoiled again. All their hard work. This wonderful opportunity which he, yes she has to admit it; he *has* produced it. All of it ruined before it has had a chance to bloom.

She towels herself quickly.

'Jesus!' Her husband's voice is louder and she shakes with tension. 'Jays - us Kee-riste, will you come and look at this?'

He is laughing; that same old bursting pleasure of a laugh she remembers and now so seldom hears. She goes to his side at the window. Outside, the street is transformed. Gone are the mean alleys, the shady flophouses. All is lit in a blurry of flashing colour. Electricity - the new wonder of the age has arrived and with Mister Edison's Pearl Street Power Station just around the corner it does not have far to travel before literally lighting up their lives.

'Look at that', James cries again. 'And look, look, look at you!'

There are tears in his eyes as he points to her name in the flashing pinks and blues of brilliant light.

LIZZIE REARDON

DANSEUSE PROTEAN

IN HER OWN PRODUCTION OF

'THE BALLAD OF THE HANGED ONE'

Lizzie glances at his face. The joy in his eyes. Eyes she has loved and lately feared so much. Her heart is stabbed by the pity of it, the awful sadness of what she knows is now lost. He turns to her with a sob; she can smell the whiskey on him. He presses himself on her. She can feel his urgency, his need as his weight presses down on her and she opens herself to him, willingly, thankfully as he lies in her arms, crying out her name as he shudders and moans, weeping like a child on her breast and is finally still.

At the opening performance the Olympia Roof Garden is filled to capacity. The two entrepreneurs Mister Hammerstein and Mister Pastor stand together in their box in the Circle and applaud as Lizzie takes a final bow. They applaud the stage, they applaud the crowd, and smiling broadly over their cigars, they applaud each other with enthusiasm. The roar of the crowd is a great wave of warmth that thrills Lizzie as she bows and blows kisses. Left, right, to the Stalls, to the Dress Circle and higher, higher still, she lifts her head and bows again to the very heart of the theatre... the God's, where she imagines her mentor, Mme. Delacroix, cheapest ticket in hand, nodding her approval. Lizzie points to the orchestra, points to her two producers, and, hands raised in supplication, she searches in vain for the face of her husband.

The after-show party is loud with congratulations. Pffafs Oyster Lounge is used to theatrical successes. The air is thick with tobacco smoke, rich perfume, good brandy and the exaggerated greetings of actors acting the part of actors.

'Hell-O! Daaling! Cries a bright young thing in a cloche hat, while a slim, rouged gentleman of forty 'dear boys' all the dear boys he can lay his hooded eyes on.

Lizzie's is not the only hit in town. A young man by the name of Cohen is belting out his latest song sensation, "Give My Regards To Broadway", while a curly headed lad named Harry Houdini is swallowing spoons in a corner. Lizzie is ecstatic, so many fabulous people all in one place. This is show business and how lucky she is to be part of it. But where is James? He should be here, despite all, he deserves to be here and who knows? After his tears earlier....?

The crowning moment of the all night party is the early reviews. At dawn a runner is sent to Herald Square to pick up the latest news straight off the presses. Tony Pastor grabs The Herald and tips the boy a dollar note. Lizzie holds her breath as her manager flicks through the pages.

'Billy Clapp, Billy Clapp', Pastor murmurs. 'Come on Billy...ah...here, here he is'. He folds the paper to the article he has sought. 'The only damn critic in town worth a dime. Yes!' He exults, smacking the paper with a meaty paw. 'Listen up people!' He reads the piece while Lizzie, eyes closed, grips his arm tightly.

'Miss Lizzie Reardon, in her debut at The Olympia has pleased Mr Hammerstein mightily! This English Rose is a consummate dancer and a choreographer of note. Her lone interpretations and split-second timing bring a host of characters to life in a tragic tale said to be based on a real-life incident. Mr Pastor is to be blessed for bringing this kind of class from England to the rumpus rooms of Broadway'.

'Here', Pastor tells Lizzie, tucking the paper under her arm. 'Show that to the dummy you call a husband!'

Wearily, Lizzie and the few companions who have lasted the night, climb the stairs to their apartments, hushing each other and giggling as they go. She pauses at her door as the familiar apprehension grips her, the awful fear of what might or what might not happen when she enters the room.

Darkness. The room is in darkness. She crosses to the window. Draws the blind to let in the early sun. The bed has not been slept in. The open door of the closet reveals the absence of his clothes. An empty rye bottle sits on the bedside table, an empty shot glass beside it. Beneath the bottle is a note. Lizzie picks it up and begins to read.

Chapter Twelve

New York in August steams. The pavements steam, hot to the touch, they radiate their collected heat upwards in a shimmering mirage where it clings like a hot fog around the scurrying feet of the crowds passing by. The owners of these feet keep to the sidewalks. They are paved. The carriageway is not, and an inch or two of fine dry dust lies in wait until a flurry of horses hooves disturb it, whereupon it leaps up to embrace the whirring carriage wheels that fling it higher still, up and in through the ventilation slats where the passengers sit, stewing in the furnace heat, scarcely able to breathe for the scarves wound about their noses and gaping mouths. To add to the discomfort, the occasional Benz motorcar overtakes the slower brougham, belching black fumes of unburnt petrol.

James Fortune waits to cross East Houston Street. He sways unsteadily on his feet. It is noon, he is hungry, and apart from a swig every now and again from the bottle in his side pocket, nothing has passed his lips in over a day. He has begun to regret his haste in so readily walking away from the golden goose, he should at least have taken a grubstake, but no, he has to make the big gesture. He has left it all behind, perhaps hoping his shame will be lessened, but it is not, and he somehow knows it will take many, many years before that comes about. Meanwhile, here he is, hungry, broke but for a few dollars, lost in this jungle of part finished buildings, crowded thoroughfares, factories, flop-houses, foreign tongues and the scurrying feet of the world's poor. He walks miles in a day for the chance of a job.

The harsh sound of a motor horn startles James as he steps out into the busy road. He steps back sharply onto the pavement as an open topped automobile veers to a halt in front of him.

'Say feller! Can you tell me the whereabouts of…' the man pauses, lifts the heavy glass goggles from his face, squints at a paper held in his hand, 'Mister Koster and Mister Bials Emporium?'

James, angered first at the abrupt and noisy arrival of the motor and then at the ostentatious manner of the man's enquiry, is just about to demonstrate his Irish temper when two youths suddenly appear out of the milling crowds. One goes directly to the driver, who is busily divesting himself of an enormous white leather coat. The lad flips the flowing tails of this garment up and over the head and face of the by now frantically struggling driver, while the other boy, leaping like a monkey onto the back seat, proceeds to lift and carry off a large cardboard box. He jumps clear of the car and lands right in the surprised arms of James who, more out of his already aroused anger than anything else, holds on tight to the boy and screams out the first thing that comes to his lips:

'Police!' he shouts, and then, for good measure, 'Stop!' Thief!'

The boy drops the box and flees, followed by his accomplice and by a passing policeman who, obviously taking advantage of a chance at the dramatic, brandishes his nightstick and toots furiously on his whistle as he lopes along in high pursuit.

James, having been knocked to the ground in the struggle, rises and dusts himself down with the palm of his hand while the other man, having managed to rid himself of the coat at last, stands in amazement with his arms outstretched.

'Well for Chris' sake!' he bursts. 'Whadya think o' that? I been to fourteen county fairs an' many a good goat fuckin' but I ain't never seen the like o' that!' and the two men burst out laughing .

'Denver Joe Kaplinski, kineomatographer', the car driver tells James as they grip hands.

'James Fortune', the other replies. 'Theatrical Producer', he pauses, 'between engagements'.

In the deli opposite they sit at a table by the window. Joe carefully shoves the box beneath their feet as he grabs the menu.

'On me!' he proclaims. 'You hungry? You look hungry! Eat what you like. Anything. It's on expenses'. He winks at James and calls a waiter over to their booth.

'Hey! Give this guy a drink... a Martini... and me too, easy on the Italian and no goddamn glace on the cherry'.

Two hours later "Den" and "Jimmy" are bosom pals. The former has taught the latter several verses of the ruder version of "The Ballad of Dan McGrew". The barman is threatening to throw them both out if they don't can it.

'OK! OK!' says Denver. 'Keep your shirt on', as they get up and stagger to the door, 'mis'able dump anyway'.

Next morning James opens one eye. Daylight is streaming through a chink in the curtained window. He closes the eye. The express train passing by the bed, snorting and gurgling and puffing, turns out to be a snore. A loud snore. Denver is flat on his back, his mouth is wide open. His breath catches deep in his flabby throat, holds, vibrates, holds again and then escapes with a searing whistle. A loud grunt is followed by an equally loud snort, then the sequence is repeated. James digs Denver in the ribs with an elbow, and pretending it was an accident, he makes smacking sounds with his lips to indicate arousal from sleep.

'Jesus!' says his companion, making the same smacking sounds and yawning widely. 'Did we tie one on!'

Their before breakfast livener is a shared bottle of Michelob beer, after which James's host cooks bacon and beans as they begin to come around.

'So it's settled then', Denver says over coffee and James is surprised at him remembering.

'Partners'. They both say at once and they shake on it.

'Only thing', James hesitates, 'what do I know about projectors - film?'

'Easy', Denver interrupts. 'Cameras? Motion pictures? Comin' thing. I'll teach you in five minutes. You got the gab, which is all you do need'.

'In on the ground floor'. That's how James puts it years later. 'Right place at the right time,' he will say. 'Lady Luck... and a hell of a lot of damned hard work'.

Sleeping rough in sleazy flophouses, travelling in boxcars with a can of film, as fast as they laid the railroad. The haggling, the selling, as more and more of the new rage – Kineptikon - is introduced across the length and breadth of this vast country. Then the big chance: 1910 and he is a cameraman on one of the very first full-length feature films. A full seventeen minutes. Made and screened in a small, picturesque village called Hollywood. The big Directors - Selznick, Wilder, De-Mille - all competing for the best talent and among the best is Jimmy Fortune. Here, there and everywhere, he pops up with his camera and the latest techniques in lighting, angling, panning. All coming up from scratch, learning as he goes in this new and exciting industry. And here he is now at the top of his powers. The life of Riley and the fuel? What keeps him going? Why, whisky of course. Good old buddy barleycorn. Bolstering him up when the road is long, when he is lonesome, when he misses Lizzie, longing for her and nobody else will do. He stands at the wide window of his studio in downtown Beverly Hills. All around him, in the teeming streets below, the sounds and sights of the film industry are everywhere. Across the as yet unpaved road, Mack Sennet is building a set. And here he stands, Mister James Bloody Fortune. Alone with his own success. Success and money. Big money. Big time. He has it made.

There is a knock at the door and his assistant pokes her head in.

'Gen'leman to see yah'. She intones in broad Brooklyn.

The name on the card means nothing to James, seated in his swivel chair, feet up on the polished desk before him. Another small time photoshooter looking for the big dollar? Well, why not? Luck is like caviar - should be spread out, thinly yes, but spread.

'Show Mister Kanturk in', he tells his secretary.

The brogue is instantly recognisable. Even after all the years he's been in America and after only a word or two of speech, James can still pick them out.

'Sligo!' he exclaims. 'Up by them mountains there?' They shake hands across the mahogany desk.

'Connacht, yes' the man says and he has the typical softly spoken lilt of that part of Ireland.

'Born and bred', he affirms. 'And yourself?'

'Well', James pauses. 'It was a long time ago. County Mayo, my parents... you know?'

'Ah! The famine. Eighteen forty-five or six I'm guessing? And you and your da' and your ma' off to lovely Liverpool for your pains. Back Buchanan street was it, or one of them there? Four of youse to a bloody bed, and God help you if you farted?'

'Or turned over'. James laughed. 'But yes, just off the Scotty Road in fact. By the gas works and me dad played the fiddle for pennies in Tommy Clancy's place'. He smiles, remembering. He doesn't often let it happen and he is surprised to find, after all this time, that there is in fact a pleasure in the memory.

'Bastard English!' says the man out loud and James is surprised, first at the other man's vehemence, then at the sudden way in which he switches to the gentle soul again. The country boy who wouldn't say boo!

'But you are an Irishman still', the man says, smiling gently, head on one side. Catholic? Oh! I know! Who'd be a bloody Catholic? All that arsing about. But we are. Aren't we? Irish and bloody Catholic! Who'd have us, except our own mothers?'

James is beginning to fidget and the other man puts a hand up.

'Call me Tim', he demands. 'And James is it, or Jim?' He hurries on without waiting for confirmation.

'I am here on behalf of the Organisation... the Brotherhood? He pauses, noting the blank look on James's face.

'Fenian Brotherhood? We are big now. Very big here in the USA and we need your help'. He stops there. Is silent. Watching James's face. Saying nothing. Then:

'We are taking them on you see. The English'. Here his voice rises again.

James can feel the passion in the air between them. The anger. The hate.

'Out! Out! Once and for bloody all. We'll have the buggers out and not with pikes this time and them as stays will be in the hard ground.

James stares at the man. Is he pitching for a movie? A plot is it? Is he mad? What?

'Easter Time it will be, this coming Easter. In Dublin'. The man is sure. Sure of himself apparently, and of James's acquiescence. He goes on.

'Just the right man is what you are, and I expect you sing the songs? Down at the pub? Spancil Hill? God Bless Billy? Auld Ireland? All that there? Giving it stick? A patriot you'll be. Like the rest of us?'

James goes to stand and is about to call in his secretary, tell her get shut of this lunatic but the man will not be stopped.

'It's immigration you see'. He pauses, lets the word hang awhile, studies James's face. 'The authorities... bastards they are and particular too. Ten years in the state pen not unusual these days, and you'll do it breaking stones. We have the records d'you see? Who comes in. Who goes out. If you intend staying, official, it's by Ellis Island you must go, where they'll look down your throat, look up your arse, test you for blindness or pox. But you didn't do that, did you Jim?' He consults a sheet of paper:

'Arrived New York in RMS Campania 8th August, 1896. What happened Jim? Got lost did you? Many do and that's a fact, but we are not interested in the many. Only the few. The Irish few and we know them all... like we know you Jim. Born Clew Bay, Mayo. On the list you are, and that was a canny croft you were born into till the spuds went bad and the English put the rent up and burned your fields down. The fields your daddy dug and drained and planted'. He reaches out a hand, lays a palm softly on James's cheek.

'The English eh? What will we do with them?' He smiles, a crooked cynical smile, ruffles James's hair playfully. 'And who's we? I hear you say. Well, you'll remember the White Boys? Captain Midnight? The go-boys as they used to say it. Swearing the oath, up to no good with the maiming and killing - the revenge. All them we are and more now that we are organised, and with the volunteers coming in all the time. Volunteers such as yourself are what we need and indeed we have a job for you when you join us, which we know you will do. Will you not Jim?' He spreads his arms and shrugs. 'Will you not?'

He gets up abruptly, does not offer his hand.

'Today's the 16th of February. You have three weeks for an answer'. He turns and makes for the door.

'But', James begins. 'What is it you want? What do I have to do? How can I?'

Tim Kanturk stops at the door, his hand on the handle, he turns.

'We want you to make a moving picture', he says as he closes the door behind him.

Chapter Thirteen

Heavy mist has meant that the ship's whistle has sounded all night, keeping Lizzie awake and, as the ship enters the narrows, the murk thickens into a dense yellow blanket, a wall of swirling scud that clings about the funnel guys, hangs, shroud-like on the guard rails and clouds the bridge windows in a vaporous scum. The officer of the watch pulls down on the cord that opens the valve that releases the steam that vibrates the reeds that produces the deep penetrating below of the fog horn, high up on the casing of the forward funnel. Gulls, squabbling for a space on the ship's railings, take fright and soar away briefly, returning again and again to quarrel continually between the blasts.

The officer of the watch peers through the fog, searching for the appearance of the Bidston Light; which will be when, as he knows from his charts, he will need to make his change of course. Out on the bridge wings the lookouts, binoculars poised, curse the cold mist that clouds their lenses.

High in the crow's nest, the watchman, huddled in his greatcoat and keen to beat them all to it, is the first to see the faint glimmer.

'Light on Port bow sir!' he shouts through his loudhailer.

'Steer three points to starboard', orders the officer of the watch and the helmsman, repeating the command, nudges his wheel in the required direction.

Lizzie lies in her bunk, eyes open, still unable to sleep, listening to the doleful drone of the foghorn, which, in its solemnity, suits her mood and reminds her of the mourning bells of Malta. She does not cry. She has refused to cry all through the tour.

'A little trouper', Mister Pastor told her and the Summer Show had gone on. All over North America. Night after night of applause and curtain calls, mile on mile of rattling rail journeys, cramped dressing rooms in some provincial theatre in some cow town. Nights alone in a boarding room bed.

She lies now on her narrow bunk, staring into the darkness of her cabin as the ship yaws and rolls in its turning. The cabin is the same one she recently shared with her husband on the outward journey. She feels him near to her. His energy, his drive and –yes - his love.

'He is not dead'. She sits up in bed in the silence between the siren sounds and speaks the words surely in the darkness.

At the Pier Head in Liverpool a crowd is gathered to welcome home the travellers. Lizzie, in a warm coat against the morning chill, stands at the rail as the band strikes up. She watches with envy as first one and then another of the passengers catches sight of a friend, a loved one, waving wildly on the quayside.

'There she is', cries a young girl catching a sight of her mother. 'Mummy! Mummy!' and she dances up and down in her joy.

A mother. A child. And the old regret stabs hard and cruel at Lizzie's heart, as she stands at the rail alone.

And then she sees Claudine; arms full of bangles, a beaming smile lighting up her rouged cheeks as she raises a hand in greeting.

It is then that Lizzie begins to cry.

They are booked in at the Adelphi, whose opulent richness, at first overbearing to a young woman accustomed to the economy of back street digs, soothes and caresses Lizzie, reassuring her, calming her. With her friend Claudine at her side, she quickly brightens, acknowledging the fact that, to her surprise and delight, she has become a minor celebrity.

By consent of them both and without any need for discussion, Claudine, now retired from her practice, takes over the task of managing Lizzie's career.

'Common sense really', Claudine assures her. 'And', she adds with a smile, 'a few contacts'.

It turns out that, among the current clique of theatrical notables: actors, dancers, and their producers; quite a large number owe their early beginning to the tutelage of Mme Delacroix and she is not about to let them forget it.

They are sat by the big bay window in the foyer of their hotel, and, at Claudine's insistence, their seats are in the best position for them to be seen.

'The Empire Theatre' Claudine is telling her client. 'An old and respected venue and just the ticket for your triumphant return: A civilised establishment, genteel even, after the hustle and bustle of America.'

On First Night, a week later, as their carriage winds its way down by

Saint George's Hall, along the Scotland Road, on its way to the theatre, they are delayed by baying crowds and by mounted policemen holding them in check by the roadside.

'Boo!' Go the crowd. 'Shame!' shouts a top hatted gentleman, shaking his fist angrily at a small group of women as they pass in line down the middle of the road, banners held high, a small brass band preceding them.

'Votes For Women', the banners declare, 'Women's Political Union'. And at the front, who should Lizzie see but Sylvia and her sister Christobel, her old friends and benefactors, leading the procession, heads held high, striding along to the tune of the stirring march "Jerusalem".

'Stop!' cries Lizzie to the dismay of Claudine who tries to restrain her as she struggles to open the side door of the carriage, and, while the horse still plods along unheeding, Lizzie leaps to the ground, gathers up her skirts, and nipping nimbly through the ranks of marchers, throws her arms joyfully around her old friends and joins in lustily with the song:

'Jerusalem'! Jerusalem! Lift up thy voice and sing...'

Claudine, her head stuck out of a side window, one hand holding on to her hat, directs the coachman with a stabbing finger and a shout.

'Follow that march!' she yells and then, leaping down from the carriage in Lizzie's wake, she dashes, with as much decorum as she can muster, to the front of the band where, by accosting the big drummer in his leopard skin apron, she manages, between the thump, thump, thump of his drumming, to convince this gentleman that he should follow her as she leads him down Lime street to the corner of the London road where, by waving both arms imperiously in its path, she brings the whole cortège to a halt right outside the front door of the Empire Theatre.

'Genteel did you say?' Lizzie wryly quizzes Claudine.

'Well, good fun, you have to admit', the older woman nods towards Sylvia and her companions. 'And fortuitous'. She winks. 'Think of the publicity'.

With her usual panache, bare faced cheek as she herself terms it, Claudine, having charmed the theatre's front of house manager, has managed to pack not only the whole of the marchers in, but, on pain of leaving their instruments in the foyer, the brass band too. They all sit expectantly now, high up in "The Gods" waiting for the curtain to rise.

Dancing girls, acrobats, a sword swallower, a plate balancer. The compere brings them all on to the applause and occasional opprobrium of the audience.

Lizzie herself makes three separate appearances and it is on the last of these, to the shouted demand of the crowd, that she performs the dance she wrote and choreographed herself: The Reel of the Hanged One.

A white painted board is suspended over the proscenium arch on which is written, in large letters, the title of each set as it is performed. The band plays softly in the background, a medley of tunes chosen to match the mood of each presentation as, hidden from sight in the loft above the arch, a stagehand, script in hand, changes the wording on the board.

The curtain falls, its velvet folds shimmering like scarlet water as it billows and sways. Almost immediately the curtain rises again to reveal Lizzie, centre stage, lit by the limes above the orchestra pit, perfectly still, her arms rigid at her side.

At her back is a silk screen, behind which she will disappear, for no more that three seconds at any one time, to change her costume and her personae as the play progresses.

Lizzie scans the upturned faces below her, side to side. She is looking for the one person to whom she will address her performance. A friend perhaps? Claudine and her companions are all in the front row of the stalls. She smiles at them. They wave discreetly back. Then she halts her search. A woman catches her eye, a woman in some sort of uniform. A woman whose green eyes reach out to Lizzie across the brilliant beam of the burning limes. Lizzie bows her head slightly and begins to dance.

The audience gasp at the speed with which the changes are made.

A soldier in a high black shako hat, red tunic, white canvas trousers, black boots and gaiters. A girl dancing freely in a field of flowers. A fight. The soldier imprisoned. All these and more to make up the story in costume and dance while the scenery and set is altered to suit. Everything performed at lightening speed, gracefully and poignantly as Lizzie reaches the last tableau: The hanging, with the hooded priest, the soldier muffled in a sack, the rope and the final, desperate dance as Lizzie's feet rattle on the boards to the rising sound of the orchestra: flutes wailing, trumpets blaring, cymbals crashing, all combining into a shattering climax, then easing, softening, pleading, dying.

The curtain drops abruptly. There is complete silence. Then the auditorium erupts in applause.

The staff at the Adelphi Hotel are used to entertaining the well off, whose idiosyncratic behaviour is not always as restrained as the hotel's renown might suggest. Nevertheless, their diplomatic skills are a little strained by the sudden appearance at their doors of a big drummer, closely followed by a small band of women carrying banners.

Bang, bang, bang goes the drum.

'Votes For Women!' goes the shout as the drummer is persuaded to remain at the entrance while the ladies troop into the foyer.

A white-gloved attendant discreetly steers them away from the foyer, the holy of holies, where, scattered about the richly carpeted hall, beneath shimmering crystal chandeliers, a number of after-dinner guests are sipping their coffee. One of these guests, a moustachioed gentleman in a dinner jacket and tie, turns to his companion.

'Should be horse whipped', he tells her as the little group of laughing women are led discreetly to a small conference room.

Lizzie, still flushed after her performance and the unexpected reunion with her dear friends, sips delicately at her glass of champagne, wrinkling her nose at the tang of it. She has never got used to the convention of drinking alcohol, sees no point in it and can barely stand the taste but, among such friends? Surely it would be ill mannered not to join in.

Sylvia and Christobel are each in their accustomed grey and black. Bodices buttoned to the neck over ankle length skirts. Hair greying now, the weariness of their political struggle heavy in every line, every gesture. They sit laughing like schoolgirls, chattering and remembering.

Lizzie sits beside them, Claudine on her right, and her heart nearly bursts with the pride and pleasure she feels to be in such company. Her family and her friends.

She is explaining the finer points of the evening's final performance to the sisters Sylvia and Christobel, the true story behind her theatrical creation; the young lad cruelly hung, perhaps for motives other than his crime, motives possibly connected to the deaths of thousands, maybe millions in the Great Famine of Ireland; then the years of official concealment, secrecy, even to the extent of murder.

The two women listen intently. They are both aware of their friend's natural naivety, her trusting, open simplicity, and as Christobel glances at her sister's raised eyebrow, she reaches impulsively across to grasp Lizzie's hand.

'You must be careful', she tells the younger woman. 'I can think of at least a half dozen reasons for which some authority or other, even now after what…? Sixty years…? Might find cause to prevent you from reminding us of an episode we have all been too happy to forget.

'Speaking Of Ireland', says her sister Sylvia, looking up and rising to greet another woman, striding forward to meet them.

'And of the devil' adds Christobel quietly, smiling a welcome, as they stand to welcome an old friend.

Lizzie is accustomed to the demeanour of her companions: Claudine, the two sisters, and their mother Emily. Aristocratic in their speech and in their mannerisms, they yet have the common touch, combining a masculine vigour in their political protestations with an extreme of feminine guile. They are not ordinary women, and while Lizzie is entirely comfortable in their company, she is still in awe of them.

'The Countess Kramerivitz' announces Sylvia as she presents the newcomer to Claudine and Lizzie, both of whom stand awkwardly not knowing whether to curtsey, bow or what.

'Constance, please!' the lady demands, embracing them both at once in a hug that would shame a bear.

Lizzie, recognising her as the lady for whom she has just performed, runs an eye over her, an expert eye from one well versed in the art of theatrical presentation. Constance, Lizzie decides at once, is an actress. Whatever else she may also be. She exudes theatre in every gesture. And the clothes! A plumed bonnet sits jauntily on one side of a mass of auburn curls, her jacket—more a tunic—fits neatly over her womanly curves. Tight trousers are tucked into calf-length boots. Under one arm she grips a swagger stick, and, green eyed to match the colour of her uniform, she is every inch a soldier as she notes Lizzie's appraisal.

'Captain, second battalion, Irish Citizen Army', she announces, gripping Lizzie's hand in hers.

A new bottle of champagne is opened, then another and Lizzie is glad when, at some time just after dawn, a member of the hotel staff is seen discreetly hovering at the door, coughing into a white-gloved hand. The party breaks up and Lizzie escorts her guests to their waiting carriages. Constance grips her hand again.

'I have friends', she says, 'a new theatre, an Irish theatre, in Dublin. You will have heard of Mister O'Casey? Yeats? Come and see us when next you are in Ireland'.

And, as they rattle in their carriage through the deserted streets in the first streaks of morning light they pass a lone newsboy selling his wares.

'Read all about it,' he shouts and by his side is a poster on which he has written, in large black letters:

"ARCHDUKE ASSASSINATED IN SARAJEVO".

Chapter Fourteen

Lizzie is not getting any younger. She sits in front of her mirror, carefully massaging cold cream into the few lines that are beginning to appear on her still handsome face. Engagements are getting fewer. The war has spawned a host of new acts. Patriotic balladeers with their anthems of recruitment. Troops of marching girls in mock military uniform. James, she muses wryly, would be in his element.

Her Suffragette friends have, for the duration of the war, suspended their acts of civil disobedience. They have gone to work making munitions or learning the arts of nursing for those few poor and wasted youths already returning in cattle trucks from the carnage of France. Lizzie herself is attending part time classes in the treatment of bullet wounds, gas poisoning and the effects of shell shock. The sights, sounds and smells of all this horror have appalled her and she has quickly become, to the disappointment of all her women friends, including Claudine, vehemently opposed to the fighting.

'Coming from you, your popularity', Sylvia tells her. 'A refusal to support your country could easily deter many a potential warrior from joining the cause'.

Lizzie's answer is to create a new dance in which of course she performs all the parts alone except for one other, a younger girl, a newcomer to the stage, who sings in the background, to Lizzie's rapid enactments, her own version of a popular recruitment song:

'I don't want to lose you and I think you should not go!...........'

The girl's plaintive plea, her sweet poignant voice, at first convince the audience of the song's jingoistic authenticity, but when first a few, and then the many, catch on to the scathing satire, a loud booing begins, programmes are waved, feet stamped.

'Get her off!' cries one angry patron from his expensive box in the wings.

'The Stage Magazine' for that week, headlines the story: 'Quick Change Artist Changes Her Tune'. It goes on to print the song's anti-war words in full.

In London, Lizzie feels the lack of her friends more keenly. Claudine gone back into retirement. The Parkhurst's making their displeasure known. She feels deserted and bewildered, unable to properly comprehend their hearty and full support of the war. Patriots yes! She understands that and would describe herself as one. But, the killing! The slaughter! An army lost at Mons. Young men, legless, begging in the streets or gibbering and trembling in shop doorways. Train loads of replacements, barely trained, leaving every train station bound for Dover, Calais and The Front. Her only recourse and comfort is her act, the applause of an audience and her determination to protest.

Arriving for rehearsal next day at The Palace Theatre of Varieties, where over recent months she has become almost a resident act, the first thing she sees as she steps from her cab, is a broad, newly painted slash through her name on the bill boards.

"Cancelled".

As she turns to retrace her steps, a small crowd gathers around her. One holds aloft a banner: "Traitor!" it proclaims in blood red painted letters. In silence, a woman steps forward and pins a white feather to the front of Lizzie's coat.

Her digs are in a little back street off Saint Martin's Lane. She climbs the worn stairs, struggles for a moment with the door key. The smell of frying fish from the jellied eel stall across the alley hits her as she closes the door behind her. She sits at the tiny dressing table and stares into the mirror. She pours, a little unsteadily, a tumbler of sherry. She continues to stare. She stares at her face in the mirror. At the bottle standing half empty. At the front page of *The Stage Magazine* on her dressing table and then, this time with a steadier hand, she pours another tumbler. Tomorrow she will begin the rounds of the agencies.

'No such a thing as bad publicity'. Aaron Fisk declares expansively. He is a short man. Fat and with little piggy eyes that dart and roam continually. He sits at his desk and looks at the pictures on the wall. Signed pictures of past clients. He looks at the ceiling as he twiddles his thumbs, he looks through a grimy window, swivelling on his chair, he looks at the wall of the building opposite.

Finally he turns to her, his eyes refusing to meet hers.

'But... your age... ahem! Forty something is it? A little bit more? Not the end of the world of course. No'. He leans forward, as far as his bulk will let him, in his chair.

'People will come to see you, I can guarantee it, they may be a trifle…
umm… difficult but you'll handle that, eh? Old trouper?' Look, he spreads
his hands wide, 'strike while the iron's hot, that's the ticket. Publicity, good
or bad, does not last long. I can get you a full month of engagements, the
length of the country, one end to the other, one night stands… you'll move
fast and who knows with the public eh? Love you one minute, the next …
let's be honest, it's make or break and after all, as I say - forty something?'

He lets the words hang as Lizzie, only now realising the extent of the
damage, accepts gratefully the glass he hands to her across the desk. He
raises his own in salute.

'Fifty per cent?' he says and they clink glasses.

Chapter Fifteen

The pavements are still wet after the sudden squall of the early afternoon as Lizzie walks from Piccadilly Circus, down the crowded Haymarket. She is remembering the last time she appeared at Her Majesty's Theatre, her name in large letters at the top of the bill. She pauses now at the box office doors and scans the posters.

"Supporting Cast". One says and in small black letters, "Miss Lizzie Reardon".

At the stage door, the autograph hunters, the simply curious, and the star struck hopefuls look past her and through her as she slips via a small side door into the stone stairwell that leads to the dressing rooms. A warm smell reaches her as she slowly climbs the stairs. The old, mingled smells, of sawdust and grease paint and cheap perfume, of stale cigar smoke and of people. The smell is still the same as it always was, as it has always been and it welcomes her as she reaches the top of the stairs and steps out into the dusty, dimly lit corridor that leads to the wings and the curtained stage.

A man is lighting the powder trays at the front of the stage and above the orchestra pit. A slight, bluish smoke wafts gently upwards to where it hangs momentarily on the quiet, perfumed air, then, as the man fans with his hands at the glowing embers, the misty smoke leaps suddenly skyward, disappearing into the loft where it is lost among long forgotten sets, back-drop scenery, ropes, wires - all the para-phernalia of the illusion of the stage. A bright, white glow starts up in the trays and the limelight illuminates the emptiness. This is theatre. Her theatre. Her home. Surely it will not be taken from her?

She has stopped reading the reviews, closing her eyes and her ears to the anger she is engendering. She travels from town to town, venue to venue. Lost by day in the anonymity of a railway carriage, sleeping fitfully at night in the cheapest digs. She earns her pay and will be glad when it is all over and she can forget Mister Fisk. One last performance and after that she will rent a small house. Put up a plaque:

"Madam Elizabeth Reardon". it will say. "Dance and Deportment; Terms by Arrangement."

In rehearsal she is met with polite disdain. The old friendly banter is gone. She is tolerated but only barely and, when the curtain rings down at Her Majesty's, she is not sorry to quit London, the scene of so many successes, and head for the boat train and Ireland.

The night steamer from Holyhead ploughs sluggishly through the misery of an Atlantic gale. Lizzie is cold even here in her old favourite spot between the funnels. She pulls the blanket around her shoulders, remembering. The cold seeps deeper into her bones. She shivers as, in her memory, a voice, a soft Irish voice, speaks to her in the dark:

'You need looking after you do'.

There is no one to meet her at the Belfast terminal. The rain is a thin, misty fog, clinging to Lizzie's cloak as she rides from the quay to the theatre. It is already nearly noon and she has a matinee performance at two. No time to find digs, no time for anything. The same old rush that she used to enjoy, has thrived on for all these years, is now but a memory.

She wipes the isinglass window with a sleeve and peers out at the passing traffic. Down Queen Street and over the bridge the coach lurches and sways. Past the ornate gates of the shipyards where lines of shuffling men queue for work. In the giant dock they are caulking the seams of yet another warship. The roar of steel on steel, the rapid rattle of the rivet gun, echoes and reverberates all over the town like waves of applause. This is the new theatre, the new rage. One of the many supporting acts in the drama of war.

The coach turns sharply into a cobbled side street and comes to a halt, the horses steaming, snorting, glad of the short respite from their labours.

'Alhambra!' the conductor shouts as Lizzie alights and looks up at the old familiar building.

"Royal Alhambra. Theatre of Varieties". The sign says and Lizzie quickly scans the billboards until she sees her own name: "Miss Lizzie Reardon. International Artiste Protean. Direct From Her American Success".

Well, Lizzie notes wryly. Fifteen years direct! Her agent has been here already, obviously. But still - she runs an eye over the famous façade and, despite herself, the old familiar thrill envelops her, embraces her like an old persistent suitor determined to hold her affections.

Second billing too, she notes, and as she enters, the Stage Door Keeper, head on one side, squints up at her from his cubby-hole.

'Marnin' Miss Reardon!' he greets her and his remembering brings tears to her eyes.

'You'll do The Reel of course'. Aaron Fisk is adamant. 'That should stir them up here in English Ireland'. He laughs heartily, a podgy arm about Lizzie's shoulders. 'Blood is what they are after, what they have come for. You are the solitary sacrifice in an arena of sand, waiting for the lions to eat you up. Give them just that bit of gore and by the time we get to 'Derry they'll be fighting each other to get in'.

Lizzie's is the opening act. First on after the chorus girls. On they troop in their spangles and stars: side-step, high-kick, pirouette, twirl. Warming up the audience, they smile and simper, caress and coax until, in a final salute and a rude blare of trombones, they present their frilly-knickered bottoms to the crowd.

The music dies. The curtain rises. Lizzie, centre stage, motionless, looks out at the audience, seeking out a friendly face. They know her here and have always greeted her warmly. A few scattered handclaps start up, tentative, hesitant and then die, as the patrons look about them, unsure. No one likes to be shown up and in that split second of uncertainty, Lizzie, no stranger to hostile or indifferent audiences, knows she will have to win them. The music starts, she begins the dance, and slowly, the magic of her performance seduces them, beguiles them till they begin to warm to her and applaud each lightning transformation: Girl, Soldier, Judge, Priest. The story unfolds until, shrouded, bound, the rope at her neck, Lizzie dances the final reel and rat-a-tat go her struggling feet to the rattle of a kettledrum and the doleful tolling of the passing bell.

Lizzie is at the footlights taking her bows, the curtain falling and rising repeatedly at the demand of the crowd. She opens her arms to the auditorium, humbly acknowledging the appreciation. These are her family. How can she leave them? She bows one last time and then, waving till the end, she disappears into the wings and runs straight into the arms of a policeman.

Chapter Sixteen

'Routine enquiries' the constable tells her, and will she mind accompanying him to the station. She looks around for her agent, Mister Fisk. He is nowhere to be seen. The kindly bobby, jovial, helpful and apologetic the while, keeps a firm steady grip on her arm as he escorts her, through the evening crowds, to the police station, where she is told to sit on one of the hard benches and wait. She sits. She waits. A clock ticks. There is a strong smell of urine, not quite staunched by the competing tang of Lysol disinfectant and Lizzie is reminded of the waiting room at the Infirmary that day as a child when she broke her ankle. The same hard wooden benches, well worn. The same colour paint on the cold stone walls. Dark green below, a sickly yellow above and a stern black line separating the two. Where have all the years gone? Claudine - the Parkhurst's, and Jim her husband? All gone now, all her kin, all her friends and she is alone in this awful place.

'This way miss'. The sergeant is elderly, kindly, efficient. He holds in one hand a sheaf of foolscap papers and in the other a bunch of keys.

Standing beside the sergeant is another man. He is very young. His wig is new and he is hesitant, unsure of himself as he addresses his client.

'I am your Brief', he tells Lizzie, as the sergeant, with a quick, sympathetic glance in her direction, turns and leaves them. 'Well... actually', the young man glances at his papers, 'your guardian ad litem'.

Lizzie lifts an eyebrow.

'A legal phrase, er, definition that is'. He clears his throat and Lizzie is sorry for him. She forces a smile.

'Thank you for coming', she says, first extending a hand to shake his and then, as a sudden fit of nervousness grips her, quickly withdrawing the hand to place it behind her back where she holds it fast against the trembling.

'The solicitor is reading from his notes. She hears the words; 'injunction' …… 'diminished responsibility'…….. 'and so therefore…'. He rambles on but Lizzie has lost the thread. She has begun to shake ever more violently. The lawyer looks up from his papers and is alarmed, shocked at the sudden deterioration in his client. He goes to the door and calls out.

'I say!' he cries and Lizzie hears the rattle of keys as the warder approaches.

Locked up once again in her cell, Lizzie tosses and turns. Sleeping fitfully through the rest of the day and into the long night, she awakes with a jerk and cries out:

'Help me! Somebody! Help me!'

And the sound of her voice echoes and returns, hollow and distorted in the stillness of her prison.

The warder observes her through the bars. He has a cup in his hand.

'Miss Reardon?' His voice is soft, respectful. She staggers to the cell door, grips the bars as the man reaches out an arm. He holds her head steady and firmly as he places the cup to her lips.

'Brandy', he whispers, 'cheap stuff but sup it up there's a good lass'.

Lizzie, retching as the sting of the liquor runs through her, gulps, sips again, drains the cup and sits on the side of her bunk. The warder looks on in pity. Lizzie is not the first he has seen in this state. It shouldn't be allowed. Should be a law.

'Don't worry miss', he whispers. 'I'll see you right but you must try to sleep. They'll be coming for you at nine.'

She does not sleep and the hours drag by. She is fed at what she presumes is breakfast time – a mug of tea, a slice of bread and then silence, until she hears again the sound of approaching feet and she is led, flanked by a policeman on either side, preceded by her brief, to an ante room where, seated on what looks like some kind of a throne, is a be-wigged gentleman in scarlet robes. He sits unsmiling in a raised chair over which is emblazoned the Royal Coat of Arms. He coughs; leaning forward to look down at Lizzie and when he speaks his voice is surprisingly gentle.

'This is a hearing'. He assures Lizzie. 'You are not on trial and we are met here today, in Chambers, to consider an Injunction Plea brought by His Majesty's Government, under the Defence of The Realm Act 1915, against you Elizabeth Reardon, Actress, of no fixed abode'.

Lizzie looks about her. Oak panelling on the walls, a picture of The King, bearded, stern, in army uniform, red tabs on his collar; looking down at her from his perch on the back of a horse. Her legal representative is on her left, the judge in his high backed chair, and in the corner of the room, silent in the gloom, sits a figure dressed entirely in black; arms outstretched, clenched fists resting on his knees.

Lizzie turns her gaze to look up at the judge. Violet, she decides, her professional eye running over the man. Not scarlet. His robe is violet and it is faced in taffeta. Lilac taffeta. A black - sash is it? She considers the broad strip of silk looped about the judge's ample middle, a scarf perhaps? And the wig, full bottomed, falling in a drape over the hunched shoulders, is yellow with age and looks prickly to the touch.

Lizzie is brought out of her musing by a discreet cough from her Brief. The judge continues. 'Specifically, it is alleged that One, in certain parts of your act, you deploy or utter...' Here the judge, spectacles perched precariously, reads from a document in his hand.... 'statements prejudicial to the war effort in that they may seriously and adversely affect the patriotic fervour presently enjoyed by the country's recruitment drive'. There is a pause. 'Two; in another part of said act, you have consistently and for several years sought to portray, in song and in dance a misrepresentation of an event that took place, er...' The judge grips his spectacles, adjusts them on his nose... 'some years ago apparently'. He pauses, bites his lip, considers the document closely and then goes on, 'and which is still subject to a Restricted Publication Order'.

He puts the paper down on the tabletop and peers at Lizzie over his glasses.

'Now my dear', he begins, 'I have it in my power under The Defence of the Realm Act', he stops, adjusts his spectacles again, coughs and squints at the young man sitting silently beside Lizzie, who, nodding wisely every now and again, has been doing his best to appear au fait with the proceedings so far. The judge shifts his gaze to stare directly at the lawyer.

'You will, I am certain, have already acquainted your client with the ramifications, as far as they affect her, of the Act I refer to, and of course, and in particular', he rivets the young man with eyes that are at once solicitous and demanding. 'And in particular', he repeats slowly, 'the recent changes to said Act with regard to freedom of speech?'

The question hangs silently in the air, a heavy cloud impending rain. The solicitor opens his mouth. Closes it.

'Never mind'. Says the judge dryly as he turns again to Lizzie and smiles. 'The law my dear, has within its scope, recently defined articles specifically directed at the Theatre and of course your good self'. He leans forward, his smile widening and for a moment Lizzie is sure he intends to take her hand in his and kiss it. 'Censorship, in time of war, is indeed a weapon of war and we must all abide by these, um, inconveniences, for the, um, time being - d'you see?'

Lizzie nods.

The judge looks relieved. ' Now', he goes on, 'it is within my gift to bind you over to keep the peace and abide by said law with regard to your act. You must remove the offensive material referred to, specifically....' He snaps his fingers at the Brief who, rummaging frantically in his valise, is relieved to find the required document. He hands it to the judge who thanks him.

'Well done'. He tells the younger man, stifling, but only barely, a wry sigh.

'Ah! Here we are' he reads - 'all and any act or theatrical performance deemed prejudicial to the war effort, and which may in particular give comfort and aid to the enemy. And Two - with reference to that part of your performance known as The Reel of The Hanged One ...' He glances enquiringly down at Lizzie who again can only nod.

'This too, is to be deleted from your repertoire, effective immediately, as, it is alleged', and here he pauses again, goes over the wording silently, a finger following the words on the paper, 'um - alleged - that it may infringe an open and standing statute of limitation regarding publication'. He sits back in his chair and regards Lizzie more sternly now but still with some concern.

'I can accept, if you will give it, your word that the changes will be made and that you will henceforth refrain from using the said material in your act ...' He glances at the solitary figure in the darkened corner who has sat quietly throughout the whole proceedings. 'And from uttering or causing to be uttered any such material in the future'.

Lizzie does not hesitate; she puts a hand out to prevent the intervention of her brief who has risen to his feet.

'No' she says, in a small but determined voice. 'I will not give my word. I am opposed to the war and I will say so'.

The judge sits silently for a moment and then, rising stiffly from his chair.

'I am sorry', he tells her. 'I am very sorry'.

The door shuts gently behind him as the man in the corner, the man dressed in black, also rises, goes to the door and opens it.

'Come in', he commands and two people enter. A man and a woman. The man carries a small black leather bag, which he places on the tabletop in front of Lizzie. He is a small man, wisps of gingery hair over a fiery complexion. He stands there, stiffly. Coughs. He eyes Lizzie briefly and then, arms folded, looks steadily upward at the ceiling.

The woman is big, and she holds in her arms what looks like a garment. Canvas. The woman's face is set in stone, expressionless, as she slowly unfolds the article to reveal dangling tapes, buckled straps.

Lizzie is bewildered. This is one of her own stage props surely. The shroud! Thomas's death shroud! She looks up into the face of the small man looming over her, the hairs in his nostrils are like bristles, she can feel his hot breath on her cheek. He grips her hand and she feels a sharp prick in the ball of her thumb.

'Now then! Now then!' the woman's voice is harsh, commanding, as the straps are tightened and Lizzie feels herself sinking. She tries to scream, but no sound comes. She is held, hugged fast by the buckled belts. A hard canvas ball is forced into her mouth as her panic mounts. She cannot move. She is drowning in her own fear as strong hands lift her, dragging her towards the open door. She is helpless. Only her feet are free! They have removed her shoes and she can feel the rough boards as she is drawn along. They stand her upright and in that instant the drumming begins. A rapid knock, knock, knocking sound. Louder and louder. Faster and faster. A frantic, desperate sound that forces Lizzie to look downward for its source. She is surprised to find it is her own two feet.

Chapter Seventeen

There are twenty-six beds. Lizzie has counted them, thirteen on each side of the ward. Her bed is at the far end, furthest away from the locked door, by the side of which, in an enclosed glass box, sits the night nurse. The box is known as "the office". An orange coloured light offers a dim glow that illuminates the bars through which Lizzie can see the nurse - stiffly starched, blue uniformed, immobile. Her head droops every now and again and is brought back with a sudden jerk to the upright as the woman forces herself out of a weary slumber. The clock ticks loudly, hollow in the still of the night. Lizzie lies prone, the edge of the blanket, rough and sour to the taste, is pressed firmly to her mouth by both of her hands. She is rigid, tight, held together by her stillness. If she relaxes she will scream. She looks at the clock hung high on the wall. Five hours to go. The long night, punctuated by the screams and moans of those in torment around her, drags and ticks through the endless hours. Finally, dawn inches up; its meagre light scarcely penetrating the grime of the metal barred windowpanes.

At ten to ten she is ready, dressed, sitting on the edge of her bed, calmer after early morning medication. And this has been the pattern of her days and nights. Every last one of them and she has counted. Every new day she has pulled out a hair from her head. She has laid it side by side, pressed in the leaves of the bible, her only allowed reading. When she has collected forty-nine hairs, she has tied the fiftieth about them to make a little stook, just like the bigger ones, which rank in long lines in the farmer's fields beyond the high wall.

She has seen them and smelt them, these sheaves of fresh mown hay at the harvest. She has stood on a chair, gripped the bars on the window, high on the wall of her cell. She has peered out in the late summer time and she has watched the young labourers as they have tossed each golden bundle into the mouth of the thresher. And in winter the fields have lain bare until spring when the plough has turned the furrows again and she has heard the cuckoo and the bleating of newborn lambs.

She counts the little loops. Passing each from one hand to the other. One at a time. There are ten of them. Five hundred days in this madhouse.

There is a rattling of keys, the door swings open and two nurses approach her. They are in a hurry. Nurses are always in a hurry. Quick, purposeful tread in polished sensible shoes. Swish, go their skirts on coarse, black woollen stockings.

They have come to collect her and she is ready.

The board consists of two doctors, both of them are men. Lizzie recognises one, a member of Staff. The other is a stranger. They are both pink. Pink faces, pink hands, well scrubbed. Their pinstriped trousers match their pinstriped jackets and each wears a carnation in his buttonhole. One red. One white. There is one other person in the room, a woman who smiles as Lizzie takes her seat, a slight, slim woman, not young but feminine in the latest Paris mode, delicate and poised. Lizzie can smell her perfume. Expensive.

'You know the Countess of course?' The staff doctor addresses Lizzie and it is only then it dawns on her. This tiny, beautiful lady is the same soldierly, mannish woman she last met at The Adelphi Hotel in Liverpool.

'Have I changed that much?' the voice is soft, seductive and then:

'For advantages I hope', the Countess winks at Lizzie with a glance either side at the two gentlemen.

'Conduct?' Red carnation enquires of white.

'Oh! Excellent! Very good!' enthuses the latter gentleman, smiling indulgently at Lizzie. 'Five consecutive quarters... yes, fifteen months I see, of, ah...' He scans her report sheet, 'very good progress'.

Constance and Lizzie sit silently while the two doctors confer. The eyes of the two women meet briefly as each medical point, each legal requirement is debated, and as the men's voices drone on, Lizzie is comforted, reassured by the strength and certainty of the other woman's presence.

Finally the men reach agreement. Papers are signed.

'You will remain ward of court', red carnation tells Lizzie, stern but not unkindly, 'for a trial period of twenty eight days, under the stewardship of m'lady present'. He nods at the Countess deferentially. 'And now you may go'.

Central station is alive with men in khaki. Line after line of them. Laughing, joshing, posing for photographs. Raised thumbs and wide grins for the cameras. Bang goes the magnesium flare as, boys and young men, volunteers all, go off to their great adventure.

In the first class buffet, away from the noise, Constance and Lizzie sip their tea as they await the Dublin train.

'And now', the Countess begins. 'To work'. She takes out a small tin from the depths of her reticule, extracts a cheroot, and taps it gently on a thumbnail.

'The theatre, I am afraid, must wait'. She strikes a sulphur match, lights the cigar, leans back and exhales a long blue stream of smoke that fills the little restaurant with its aroma and shocks an elderly gentleman sitting nearby. She gazes out through the open door at the soldiers passing.

'Ulster boys', she observes, 'off to do England's dirty work for the price of a gill and a pair of boots'. She sucks in the tobacco smoke angrily.

'Well, 'tis not the only war going on and there may yet be a few that will remain to fight for their own'.

Lizzie is still somewhat bewildered by the day's events. To be released, to be free after the long months of despair has left her drained, unsure, fearful of the future. The train rumbles on through a moonless night as, staring out into the blackness, she sees only her own face, reflected in the dusty window, staring back at her. The faint glimmer of a turf fire in the grate of some lonely croft briefly punctuates the gloom as they rattle and sway towards Dublin.

Click, go the wheels on the iron rails. Click, click. Rising, falling, quickening. Her feet pick up the urgency as, nearing sleep, she dances down the years of her life.

At Connolly station they are met by a posse of men. More soldiers, Lizzie notes but different in their uniform: Slouch hats, green cloth instead of khaki. Their commander steps smartly forward, behind him a bearer flourishes a flag - seven white stars on a blue ground. The Countess returns his salute and the two ladies are escorted to their carriage for the drive to the Countess's home.

'Sit', the Lady invites, or is it a command? She herself remains standing, pacing the floor behind a massive mahogany desk, a cloud of aromatic blue cigar smoke enshrouding her shoulders like a cloak.

They are in the library of a small Georgian town house in the grounds of the Cathedral.

'My mother's old house', Constance tells Lizzie absently, obviously deep in thought.

'In the next few hours', she begins carefully. 'My country will be at war with yours. We will not win this war, not in the conventional sense, we are too small and we have not the equipment. When it is over, I, along with many others of the leadership will be tied to a post in a prison yard and shot'.

The sound of bees, busy at work in the Wisteria, can be heard through the open French windows. In the distance, fields away, a dog barks.

'A friend... William... a supporter, is writing about it.' The Countess goes on. 'A kind of beauty— a *terrible* beauty he calls it, will be born in these coming few days that will, in the long off days to come, give us the truer victory'.

Lizzie takes the hand of Constance in hers.

'How can I help?' She asks.

'Thank you', the Countess replies and, tightening her grip, 'come, I will show you'.

The sharp clip of hooves on cobbles precludes all conversation as their carriage rattles over the bridge, past Trinity College, along crowded Grafton Street to the gates of a park, where the coach-man checks his horses with a commanding 'Whoa!'

Lizzie, in the comfort of expensive leather, recalls another cobbled street and the horse-drawn tram that took her up the hill to Uncle Joe and his Pawn Shop, Madame Delacroix, the first faltering ballet steps and the years now past.

'Stephens' Green', The Countess explains, embracing the park with a sweep of her arm. Lizzie nods politely, her eyes following her friend's gesture, taking in the bandstand with its slate-tiled roof, the neat rows of fine trees, the Corporation's flower beds in their regulated patterns, and the criss-crossing paths trod by both barefoot children of the ragged, and by the perambulated babies of the better off.

The Countess points towards the arc of buildings opposite and to the bow fronted windows of a smart hotel.

'The Shelbourne', she says with a half smile. 'Which, it is to be hoped, will provide some fine sport on a day not far off. And that', she nods in the direction of the bandstand, 'will be your infirmary'.

Chapter Eighteen

The stink from the river is a miasma. It hovers on the water, almost visible, a vague fog compounded of human waste, dead dogs, rotted fish, and all the effluence of industry. A rusting barge lies alongside the wall. Its mooring ropes hang slack, waiting on the changing tide when, at high water, any detritus ensnared by the ropes will be washed away, to be replaced at the ebb by more, equally forlorn human flotsam. One of the industries, the biggest, is the brewery, which not only discharges its waste into the river but sucks its lifeblood from it in the first place. No wonder, some say, a pint of it sports such a fine creamy head.

A boy sits silently on the wall beside the river. He has tied his handkerchief about his lower face and nose against the smell. A whiff of it gets through every now and again, but he doesn't mind it so much. In fact it is welcome, there are ingredients in the river stench that help to keep his stomach from crying out in hunger, and twice in the twenty four hour cycle, when they open up the mash tubs, you could get drunk on the sweet sour smells of brewing stout. He glances up at the clock high on the wall of the barracks opposite. Nearly noon and he has not yet caught his breakfast. He lifts his pole, examines the bait, casts out again with a flick of his wrist and as he does so, his eye catches a movement out to sea. A ship is turning into the mouth of the river. A grey ship, low in the water with a long, raking stern. She is approaching fast, her ensign stretched proudly behind her above the threshing wake. The boy notes the broad red cross on a white background. 'British!' he exclaims as the first puff of yellow smoke is followed a split second later by the sharp bang of a gun that startles the gulls preening on the quay walls, rocks echoing among the wharfs and the warehouses lining the river, rolls like thunder in and out of the brewery yards, up over the wooded hill, past Saint James's church and the jail, and is finally lost in the green open spaces of Phoenix Park.

Bang! She goes again and the ship heels over under the recoil as the gunner finds his range on the old stone walls of Liberty Hall.

Bang! A direct hit sets ablaze the linen placard with its hand painted legend proclaiming: 'Neither King nor Kaiser'.

The banging goes on, joined by enfilading fire from the British batteries at Trinity College. The boy, looking on, takes off his cap and waving it wildly, shouts out loud into the wind and the roaring cannon.

'Go on! Go on! Blast away! And it's welcome you are while we show you the door!'

At last the events the boy has witnessed over the past few days have begun to come together in his mind. He winds in his line, wraps his tackle in the old tarpaulin, hiding it in the bushes to be returned to later when this is all over. He arranges the foliage carefully, making sure his precious rod cannot be seen and, as he straightens up, he hears the first crack of small arms fire; rifle by the sound of it, and behind it the occasional rapid stutter of a machine gun. He cocks an ear and, standing on tiptoe, he swivels side to side till his ears pick up the direction.

'O'Connell Street', he murmurs. 'I knew it!' He starts to run down the quays in the direction of the sounds of battle, remembering as he goes, the events of the last few days that are only now making sense. His father, big Mick, they call him, Michael Flaherty same as himself, winding on the puttees, polishing and re-polishing his already shining boots, carefully angling the slouch hat over his raven curls. Mick, young Mick, is no stranger to manoeuvres and it has been like any other Sunday up to now. Mass at Saint James's, him and his Ma, walking home together, her hand in his. Souls white as snow after the devotions. And then the trap arriving and his dad giving him the pony's head to hold while his mother and his sisters, still in their Sunday best, stepped daintily into the carriage, and, waving bravely, were borne away.

'To the races', his father said. 'To Sandy Mount Strand for the Easter'.

Then the meeting, downstairs in the front parlour. Famous men looking ordinary in their celluloid collars and outside, on the street, the tramping of feet, hushed commands and lines of militia, some with rifles, some with pikes, some in uniform, some in bowler hats. No drill this; the old wheeling and turning, "Slope arms, Order arms, Fix and unfix bayonets". Drilling and practicing, every Sunday and for what? For this, that's what.

The boy has arrived at the bridge, breathless, he leans on the wall. While he watches, lines of green clad men cross the other bridge, The Ha'penny, and turn into the broad sweep of O'Connell Street. Tramp, tramp, tramp, goes the sound of their feet on the hard flint cobblestones.

'Squa-aad! Halt!' bellows the Sergeant Major and they come to a stop, more or less all together, panting from their exertions.

'Stand—at—Ease! Cries their leader, his voice hollow in the empty street, while the twin stone statues of Daniel O'Connell and Lord Nelson, blackened by time, splashed white by intemperate pigeons, gaze down at them, perhaps in pity.

An old man shuffles up and he too leans on the wall, catching his breath. He nods good morning at Mick, glancing contemptuously at the troops steaming and sweating in the early sunshine. He spits wetly into the swirling waters of the river below.

'Same old story', he murmurs. 'And on Easter Monday too. Have they no respect?'

In North Earl Street, opposite the Post Office, a small group of men are assembling their instruments. Big men, well fed by the looks of things. They are all dressed alike; plus-fours or knickers as the Americans call them - large flat caps and two-tone shoes. A folding canvas chair has been placed among the booms and gantries, the cameras and the magnesium lighting screens.

On the back of the chair, stencilled letters proclaim the name:

"James Fortune – Director". And, as Mick watches, the man in the chair sits forward, an arm raised.

'Steady!' he speaks quietly as if to avoid breaking the silence. The crew around him stand poised, immobile. Eyes fixed on the large wooden doors of the General Post Office across the deserted street. Then, with a sudden crash of sound, the silence is rudely broken.

'Roll 'em!' Comes the command as the whole first floor of the building erupts in a shower of tinkling glass. Windowpanes are shattered by the butts of rifles and a flag; the Tricolour – bands of green, white and orange, is poked tentatively out from among the smashed splinters.

The door of the Post Office bursts open and a man comes out with a paper in his hand.

He adjusts his glasses nervously, but when he speaks his voice is clear and confident.

'In the name of an Irish Republic…' he begins as, down O'Connell Street, comes the rattle of harnessed horses, the rumble of wheeled gun carriages and the regular tramp of many more feet, different feet, disciplined, orderly, sure. A fusillade of rifle fire cracks out and, behind all this, the many churches of the town ring out a joyful, if premature, pealing of bells.

James pans his camera down the street, straight into the maw of approaching British cavalry advancing at the trot in scarlet jackets, with drawn swords and polished boots, the rowels of their spurs caressing the tender flanks of their mounts.

'Spacing!' calls the Company Corporal. 'Pick up your dressing!'

Disciplined, drilled, determined; a mounted brigade in full trot. Veterans of Loos and Mons with a shaming defeat to avenge.

Inside the post office the rebel leaders confer among the chaos as shells from surrounding emplacements pound the sturdy walls. Strange, heavily armoured vehicles rake the gaping windows with the staccato rattle of machine guns.

Michael Flaherty, like any other boy in any other town, knows his way around. At an age when the stature of adulthood has barely stained his childish innocence, a natural urge to grow, to be rid of physical weaknesses, to be a man, burns in him like a searing flame. He is born into a family of rebels where his own mother's lullabies sang of death and martyrdom. Wolf Tone, Robert Emmet and her own younger brother 'a lad of fourteen summers', hung from a tree while the prophesies of poets promised freedom. Michael has become a patriot like his father, his father's father, and all the fathers back to the Hill of Tara and the ancient Kings of Ireland. Like all patriots everywhere, moved by love, he can be driven to acts that those untouched by such ardour will know only as madness.

Crouched in a shop doorway, he watches helplessly as the English bombardment gets into its stride. A field gun is rushed onto the scene by a crew in naval uniform; the limber is swung about, the barrel pointed at the post office door

'A Nation from a Province', the banner, proudly placed only hours ago, hangs limply now, proclaiming one minute an Irish victory and then whoosh! it disappears in a sheet of vivid flame. And now, as Michael can plainly see, hope is ended, the Rising has failed, the plans are in tatters like the tri-colour flag, which, wrenched from the window by a well-aimed English shell, now lies shamefully on the cold, hard pavement among the shards of shattered glass and the ruins of a dream.

As the boy watches he sees the big wooden post office door swing slowly open and a man, a man familiar to the boy, stooped low to avoid a sniper's bullet, emerges tentatively. He carefully scans the length of O'Connell Street. Left. Right. And then, in one short dash, he flings himself to the ground on top of the flag. Michael watches in awe as, struggling to rise, the man is hit. Once, twice - the bullets gouge a hole in the fabric of his tunic, another in his trouser leg. Three times and more, the whole body of the man jerks and twitches with each impact. He rears up, tries to sit, the flag is caught, bunched tight in a defiant fist and as he cries out in pain, his eyes come to rest on the sight of his son running full pelt towards him.

'Daddy!' Michael cries as the cameras roll and James Fortune, his blood, his Irish blood now, boiling in anger. Without further thought he abandons his instruments and heads straight for the boy and, as he runs, he screams instructions to his camera crew to keep on filming.

'Get it! Can it! Shoot the fucking lot!'

The column of mounted cavalry have come to a halt, the horses toss their heads as they clench their teeth and froth at their bits, their riders reach out an assuring hand and caress the steaming beasts.

'Hush!' They tell the frightened horses. 'Whoa there! Steady!' as with a quick flurry of feet, a line of infantry is marched to the forefront where they halt, wheel and face the Post Office.

They kneel abruptly at a single command, aiming their rifles at the open door and at the boy.

Michael has taken the flag from his father's body, draping it like a shroud around his shoulders. He stands and, while the bullets ping and thud, he walks steadily towards the soldiers.

Chapter Nineteen

At Saint Stephen's Green, the Countess is preparing, under pressure, to withdraw her troops. A delegation, with a white flag of truce, has been sent to reason with her.

'It is the Dressing Station you see ma-am', the Major is solicitous, gentlemanly in that typically English manner which only angers the Countess more.

'My orders are explicit... I must return your fire and engage you by midnight and surely you will not be so unkind as to make me do so while you shelter behind your hospital? And in any case you must know your cause is lost? We occupy the Four Courts. The Castle is secure. The General Post Office is on the point of surrender. Retire ma-am, lay down your arms and I will personally escort you to safety'.

The Countess, defiant to the last, fighting hard to maintain her manners in the face of such arrogant assumption, eyes the man coolly and with disdain.

'The day is yet young sir, and I have no need of either your patronage or your protection. My hospital facilities, such as they are, will be removed to the Four Courts by midnight when I will, with the greatest of pleasure and from where I now stand, continue my resistance to your rude attentions'.

The Major is silent for a moment, then, with practiced indolence, he raises his swagger stick, taps the peak of his cap in salute.

'My compliments then ma-am... and my regrets'.

He and his escort march smartly away and back across the road to the comfort of their redoubt in the Shelbourne Hotel.

'Two Pink Gins, sir?' The waiter places little saucers on the polished mahogany tabletop. Bending low and balancing his tray expertly in white-gloved hands, he adds a frosted glass to each carefully set place. Into each glass he adds the merest splash of Angostura Bitters. He rolls each glass delicately, upside down between warming palms, spreading the blood red herb evenly. He adds the liquor, a squirt of sparkling tonic water and, with a final flourish, attaches a small wedge of lemon to the lip of each glass.

'Cheers!' The Major salutes the Adjutant.

'Cheers!' replies the latter as they clink glasses.

They are seated in the bay window of the saloon bar of the hotel, smoking a cigar after a satisfactory dinner. Their vantage point overlooks the lush grass and carefully regimented flower beds of The Green where, on any normal day, babies in prams attended by clucking nannies will navigate the pleasant paths and lawns, stopping to admire each others charges, sharing perhaps a discreet morsel of gossip. Older children, free of adult controls, will run wild amid the mock-fright screaming of the girls and the playful taunting of the boys. The park keeper will stroll in his peaked capped uniform, nodding a dutiful *sláinte* to passers-by. Keeping order.

But not today. Not on this Holy Easter Monday, while the rifles crack and the dead lie stiffening by the roadside, on makeshift barricades and on the steps of the sanctity of churches.

The Major lets out a plume of cigar smoke and turns toward his companion.

'In a day or two', he sighs, 'when we have tidied this...' he searches for the correct word... 'inconvenience, and we have shot the likes of milady the Countess, it will not be of traitors the poets will sing but heroes'.

In a tent in the park, among the mingling smells of cordite, iodine and death, a woman kneels by a bed. Her once pristine uniform is splashed with new blood the colour of the cross on her cap, from which escapes a strand of greying hair.

A young man, a soldier, is bleeding from a wound in his stomach and the woman has stuffed a pillow into the gaping hole where the boy's intestines, raw red and blue, struggle and writhe to escape.

'Margaret!' the soldier cries, holding out a hand.

'Yes love', the nurse grips his hand. 'It is me. I am here'.

Her voice is cracked, weary, she is not a young woman and the strain and horror of recent days has drained her. She has lost count of the numbers of dying men and the days and nights have been long, but when she stands she still moves skilfully and silently among the crowded cots, she is full of grace and accustomed poise. She remains a dancer in this pit of hell.

She bends to kiss the boys cheek and with a gentle caress, closes the staring eyes. Blue eyes. Soft warm blue and tight black curls on a freckled brow. She remains stooped over the dead soldier, her eyes fixed, vacant, staring into the distance and seemingly removed from this awful place, lost in her pain and the memory of another boy, long ago and gone now. Him with his eyes and his curls and his charm. She stares and remembers. Bites down on the hurt.

A commotion outside jerks her wearily to her feet. Voices are raised, cursing. The tent flap is swept angrily aside as a man struggles to manoeuvre his burden through the small space. In his arms he holds a child, a boy even younger than the one she is nursing. The boy is wrapped in a flag and the woman can see at a glance he is dead.

The man lays the body gently down on the floor of the tent.

'Save him', he pleads.

She kneels; automatically her fingers feel for a pulse at the neck. Seconds pass. She raises her eyes.

'Dead', she tells the man. 'He is dead'.

She is cold, matter of fact. As a nurse she must manage her own injuries, mask them under a cloak of efficiency.

'Are you the father? She asks the man, her voice already softening.

She sees before her the typical parent in the immediate shock of grief. Disbelieving, angry, pitifully vulnerable.

She reaches out a hand and their eyes meet. Hold. They stare at each other in disbelief.

'Liz?' He says. 'Lizzie?

Chapter Twenty

London. 2010.

Rob awakes slowly, carefully, opens one eye. He knows where he is. Cups rattling, murmuring voices, the stink of disinfectants. Has it gone? Is it over? The *music* has gone... strange music. Russian? Melancholic. Persistent. Coming from the walls, the radiators and the screen... the picture screen, look at the screen flickering. An old silent movie. Flickering, night and day and the films, are they films? Horror films?

Men in trenches either side of a long dirt road, red dirt, red dust billowing up around the approaching Jeeps as they roar and tilt and bump and leap, and their passengers, stiff to attention, salute the men below them in the ditches. The men, the soldiers, naked from the waist up, pause in their labours to watch their superiors pass. Braces dangle at their thighs. Their faces and lower arms are burnt brown by the fierce sun. They smoke cigarettes and spit and curse and laugh as the Generals salute them, and then they bend again to their task. Bayoneting the pregnant women, opening their swollen bellies as with one quick, twist of a wrist, out pops a baby, which is clubbed by a rifle butt.

On a small hill away from the stink of death and the wailing mothers with their screaming babies, a piper pipes a lively reel. Left foot tap, tap, tapping. He punches his bag with a vicious elbow, fingers dancing on the chanter pipe, his swollen cheeks near bursting through the skirling and the drone.

Rob jerks fully awake, Sweat pouring, heart pounding, a lump like a football in his bone dry throat. Looking upwards and to either side of his cot he sees two inverted plastic bottles hanging from their gantries, each is half filled with a colourless liquid. He knows these bottles and their contents: Hemineverine on one side to reduce the delirium, and on the other side, a saline drip. Thin plastic tubes are connected from the bottles to his wrists where bright coloured plastic valves have been inserted - pink on the left, blue on the right. They *could* give him more of the Emineverin, blessed Emineverin. If they would. But they won't. Even when he begs.

'Are you seeing anything now?' The consultant, doing his rounds, is surrounded by white-coated acolytes, peering, prodding, pronouncing.

They laugh dutifully at the great man's jokes.

Ron tells him about the soldiers and the scissors that came in the night. Two pairs of bright steel scissors, walking like stiff legged men on their outstretched blades. Snip, Snip, Snip they went as they nibbled the softness of the dangling capillary tubes, his lifelines. Snip, Snip, Snip and Rob yells out, back arched, skin prickling in fear. He can smell his own fear.

'Nurse! Nurse! Please! My tubes!'

'Ssshh! She sighs. Hush now. We've a man dying over here. Have some respect'.

He lays back in his own sweat, gasping, shallow breathing, shaking uncontrollably, wrenched every few minutes by a vicious spasm, his whole upper body jack-knifed in pain and retching.

An arm slips around him, around his shoulders. A slender arm. A woman's arm. He can smell her perfume. She doesn't speak. He can *feel* her. He can hear her heart beating. Her lips brush his cheek and she whispers softly in his ear:

'We can help you', she says and she presses a slip of paper into his trembling hand.

And the days and nights pass, as they always do. The routine of drying out is predictable. The shakes take some time but the images; the awful, unreal reality of them – they will be gone in a day or two. He knows that but knowing does not help when slimy snakes creep up his legs. Sliding, slithering. Prickling his skin with hot fear. He watches the man in the bed opposite. An old man. He is strapped to the bed-head with towels to stop him falling out of his cot. The nurse, as she hurries by, sticks the old man's catheter back on.

'Tommy!', she says. 'Keep the bugger on or you'll pee all over.'

The old man laughs, a toothless cackle.

'Dementia', the nurse tells Rob. 'Alcohol. He's forty-one years old and he is you - quicker than you think'.

And a few more days later Rob is discharged. Gets his watch back, his signet ring.

'See you next time.' The nurse says. And as soon as he gets home he gets on the phone.

'Green door', she says. He holds the phone unsteady in his hand and he recognises her voice at once.

'There'll be a little card hanging from the doorknob. And take it easy with the stairs.'

And he stops now, half way up, leaning against the banister rail, catching his breath. He looks upwards to where the stairs continue, winding until they reach a landing on the top floor, and over this a single beam from a skylight pierces the gloom. Rob sits down on the cold stone step. He watches as dust motes jig and flutter in the light. Look for the logo she told him. Can't miss it. He hoists himself up and continues the climb.

The little card is there, hanging on its piece of string. Two large letters of the alphabet in stark black, the same letter written twice and he is reminded at once of the famous motoring insurance company. The card is lopsided. He straightens it. He can hear the hum of voices, the clink of a teacup in a saucer, the harsh scraping of a chair leg on a wooden floor and then the door opens.

In the cafe after the meeting - the cafe afterwards is a ritual - Jane sips her coffee.

'So', she says and his senses, blunted as they are, still respond to the old predictable. The cliché of stocking on stocking, a glimpse of cleavage. She is lovely though, hair longish, reddish, that standard strand brushed aside continually from the eyes with that standard impatient gesture. They all do it and every time he could shout out loud - cut it off, cut the bugger off, and yet… she even has green eyes.

'Are you Irish?' he says.

'I was saying', and she is totally cool, focused, put together in her long swishy skirt and her beads.

'Yes, I will sponsor you since you ask. Are you asking?'

He begins the long trek back to sanity. At first it is impossible. So many aspects. What do you do with your time? What about the shakes? The awful longing for oblivion?

'Keep coming back'. They tell him and he does, somehow he does. In schoolrooms and in private homes, in church halls and on the wards of mental hospitals. He tells them his story and listens to theirs. It is the same story in every detail and he laughs with them when he is not crying. And it gets better. At first in hours. Then in days. Then a whole month goes by and his confidence grows. He is eating well, walks a lot. Tries to write, does write and a few snatches; a phrase, a sentence here and there becomes less awful than the rest.

Jane encourages him when he gets a few kids in.

'Write Young', his project, is an idea he has had for years. He has a talent. He should pass it on. And now the idea is reborn, out of his own need and to meet the advice his mentors give him to stop moaning and do something.

'Do something', they say, 'take your mind off. Stop feeling sorry for yourself'.

The kids are young, noisy, bouncing with eagerness and they are good for him. Jane brews the coffee, passes the cup cakes. Listens and watches him as he grows, as his enthusiasm for his own theories returns.

'They have no idea', he tells her, 'how difficult it is to write. To write well and they have to find that out for themselves. It's like swimming. Chuck a newly born baby in at the deep end and it will swim. It's only later, when we have told them how dangerous it is, when they have learned to fear, that they find they cannot do it'.

The days pass, and the weeks. It gets better, just as they promised. He does what he is told. He keeps coming back and, a day at a time, yes - it gets better.

Chapter Twenty One

'Phone rang'. Jane is in the kitchen. 'Something about some solicitors. This bloody tap, when...?'

'OK, love, I will, I'll fix it. I got the thing, the rubber thing, only... solicitors?'

'It'll be one of them fortune hunters; five hundred thousand quid and you're the only one to share it with. Perhaps then we can get a bloody plumber and Robert!' she removes his hand from her bum. He picks up the phone.

'It's one of them fortune hunters', Rob grins at her, covers the phone with one hand, reaches out for her with the other. 'Hello?' he says, reasonable, polite though it goes against the grain. He has a maxim... double-glazing, cash offers, lottery wins... bang the phone down. The voice is cool but with just a hint of urgency. Efficient. Practiced like on the telly. He'll be the fattish one, the guy on the phone, the boss of the team, striped, two-tone shirt and no coat on. Silver cuff links. Rows of microfilm in neat little boxes behind him. The typist banging away.

'The property is in storage at Lambeth', the voice continues, 'the exact details are a bit vague but basically it appears to consist of various items of household stuff, furniture. A full house by the sounds of it. All a bit spoiled, some of it by fire, some by water. We get a lot of that, water damage, from the fire brigade you see? Nothing serious. We've done a couple of these before, council clearances. Personal effects warehoused ever since the blitz and you may or may not want to see the stuff? We can of course get you a valuation done if it seems appropriate? The council has said a month to clear so no immediate panic eh?'

'Sixty years!' Jane snuggles up in the back of the taxi. 'I wonder if there's any clothes?'

'Not so likely', Rob says. He's done his homework. 'It was the first air raid of the war, 1940, and it gutted Lambeth.

119

They go round The Elephant, up Saint George's road, past the War Museum.

Jane half humming half singing; 'If you go down Lambeth Way, any evening any day... so they stored folk's things? Bombed out folk? And this particular lot has been traced to you?'

'That's about it', replies Rob, 'I suppose we can let Baldry, Newcombe and Baldry deal with it. Hardly be worth much'.

Jane turns to him, takes his hand and places it on her thigh.

'I wonder if there's any clothes', says Rob.

They are surprised to find just how small the collection is. A few pieces of furniture.

'Early Utility they called it,' Rob tells her, 'despised in its time, back in fashion now, might be worth a bob or two'. There's a wireless set, a Marconi Rob notes, Bakelite casing. He twiddles the knobs: Light Programme. Hilversum. Even has the trawler band. Three tea chests stuffed with stuff - crockery wrapped in newspapers. Rob unfolds one of the papers, smoothes the crinkling, yellowing sheet. It is the front page of the Daily Dispatch with the headline: 'Compiegne Forest Déjà vu. French Surrender in Historic Railway Carriage'. There is an old fashioned portmanteau made of stiffened canvas with leather strapping, brass fittings, a high, domed lid, and lastly, a few smaller packages tied up with string. That is it. The lot except for the clothes.

'Dresses!' exclaims Jane with delight. She has lifted the lid of the sea-chest and, dipping her arms and hands in she comes up with swathes of shimmering silk, colourful cottons, golden tassels. Stripes. Polka dots. 'Oh! My', she breathes. 'Look at these frocks'. But Rob is poking amongst the various pieces they have laid out. He selects a bulky envelope, lifts the flap, and peers inside.

'It's a manuscript', he exclaims. 'Now, if she wrote her life story, all will be revealed'. He flips through the pages. 'No, not a story, and yet, hang on, maybe it is a story'. He shows the front page of the document to Jane, she reads out the title: 'The Reel of the Hanged One. By Lizzie Reardon'.

'It's a choreograph', she tells Rob, 'sort of a direction... of a dance. A ballet perhaps? Who do we know at Sadler's Wells?'

They find the house. It is in a kind of alley just of the Brixton Road only it's not there any more.

'Bajun Rest and Coffee', the sign says.

A man is chalking a menu on a black board propped against the wall.

He's a dead ringer for Bob Marley, beard, tea cosy hat, and all that 'Hi! Man' laughter and the lingo. He tells them he came across in 1999, opened up and 'ain't doin so baad'.

'All the street was blasted', he goes on, 'so they tells me. John Lewis up The High Street? Gone. Flattened. Blasted all to hell. There are photos up the library'.

At the library they find Rob's grandmother. Rob shows Jane how to wind the film on, wind forward, scroll and there she is. Elizabeth Reardon. They follow the census references the solicitor gave them: 1871, 1881, 1891, 1901, every tenth year. They watch her grow. A scholar at five, the youngest in a family of eight. Ten years on and she's a shop girl, then in 1891, in digs at Derby. Rob traces a finger over the columns till he comes to "Occupation".

'Wowee!' he shouts. 'Actress!'

'Explains a lot', says Jane quietly. 'The dresses I mean'.

They work together, on the net, local archives, parish records.

'You'll get bitten', a friend tells them. 'It's like fishing. You'll sit for hours, days, sometimes years and then Bingo! A connection'.

The death certificate shows October 28th, 1940. Elizabeth Fortune, née Reardon. Cause of Death: Suffocation by bomb blast at 22 Dalton Place, Lambeth. Present at Death: M. Hancock, Niece.

A couple of days later, at the Theatre Museum, in back copies of 'The Performer', they find an obituary: 'Grand old Trouper passes on. Lizzie Reardon, Artiste Protean. Star of Europe and the United States'.

'Protean?' Jane queries. 'You're the wordsmith'.

'Well, yes, umm. Proteus? Greek God? Of the sea I think, son of Poseidon, able to change shape, so... a Protean Artiste must be, ah yes! Quick change Artist!'

'Clever Dick'. Jane tells him and then, not to be beaten, 'Stage Magazine'... their online archive. I took out a subscription, for a month, and look at this', she clicks the mouse, opens her 'shoebox' where she has saved relevant entries and up pops the first of dozens of Lizzie's engagements, starting with her debut at the Bolton Grand Theatre in 1888, to the last entry at The Palace Theatre in London in 1910. Page after page of announcements, titles like: *Billy Bung in a Fix*, at the Empire Glasgow. *Puss in Boots* at the Hammersmith Theatre of Varieties.

'Just look at her job descriptions', Jane jokes; 'Danseuses Extraordinaire', 'Terpsichorean Wonder'. And just look at the company she keeps: Mister Charles Chaplin, Marie Lloyd, Dan Leno. Even I've heard of them! And notice too, as I have', she nudges him playfully in the ribs, 'the dates. How close each venue is to the other. It's amazing how she got about. See here,' and she scrolls rapidly, skilfully to: 'The Alhambra, Belfast on September 18th. 1892 and the next day she's at Her Majesty's, Blackpool, having presumably crossed over on the ferry from Ireland, had a cup of tea, rehearsed and on with the show. What a life! Now then, where's that thing you found? Passenger Lists?'

Rob rifles through the small mountain of documents, papers, files.

'It'll be the last one', she says, 'It always is… Ah! That's it'. She stabs with a finger: 'RMS Campania, sailed Liverpool August 3rd, 1896 arrived New York August 11th. Mister James Fortune and Mrs Elizabeth Fortune!' She leans back triumphantly and smiles at him smugly.

'So?' Rob says. 'Who he?' Jane shakes her head slowly and then, impulsively plants a kiss on his cheek. 'Poor thing', she says, 'getting old'.

She rummages again in the pile of records and pulls out Lizzie's death certificate dated 1940. She points to the entry and mouths the words: 'Widow of James Fortune'.

'But still', It is Rob's turn to play devil's advocate, 'we do not really know, not for certain, that it is the same couple'. He looks at the top of the page of the ship's manifest and scans the columns, 'and look, there's a mechanic, a doctor, a servant; no occupation for him, or her and you'd have thought an actress..?'

'You are right of course, but wait a goddamn minute!'

She quickly removes the reel marked Ship's Manifests and feeds in Stage Magazine. She adjusts the page for centre and focus until, under the heading 'Entertainments in America' and the date August 12th. 1896 the following lines appear:

'Oscar Hammerstein's latest acquisition made her debut at The Olympia Roof Garden on Forty Second street last night. Miss Lizzie Reardon, a true English Rose, danced charmingly and to much acclaim. She was presented by her agent Mister James Fortune who is also her husband'.

Rob throws up his arms in surrender.

'I give up!' he says and she joins him as he laughs ruefully. Again she is moved to comfort him with a kiss.

'My little boy lost', she coos, 'come to your mammy who loves you'. She slaps his hand just as he begins to get interested, 'No giving up. There's plenty to look at here'. She shifts the screen from Theatre Engagements to News Items.

'Right', she tells him, 'I'm off to Mark's for a bit of retail therapy. Get stuck in. Surprise me'. She blows him a kiss as she goes out.

He is asleep on the sofa in front of the telly when she returns carrying the familiar carrier bag, which she holds aloft triumphantly.

'A new top?' Rob enquires.

'Two', she says. 'Marked down, though I'm not sure I like them, what have you found?' she nods at the laptop open on the table.

'Well', he says and she can tell it's something big.

'Well? What?'

'I'll show you', and he crosses to the PC, maximizes the page and there, 'what about that!' he stabs a finger at the screen.

It is an article in *The Stage* dated March 10th. 1910, entitled: 'Lewd Act Banned'. It goes on to say that The Office of the Lord Chamberlain has intervened to place a ban on further performances of *The Reel of the Hanged One*, which has enjoyed good reviews after a successful run in the West End and in the provinces. Miss Lizzie Reardon, the popular danseuses, was arrested and taken to Bow Street Police Station. She was later released pending any further action, which may be taken against her.

'The bastards eh?' Rob exclaims. 'Lewd? Where's that script thing... the score, whatever?'

He turns the pages, getting more and more angry.

'OK! OK! Channel it. I know, channel it'. He takes deep breaths. Counts up to ten. Does the serenity bit.

'Who do we know at Sadler's Wells?'

Tony Valance looks like the dancer that he is. Black stretch leotard, pumps, leg warmers.

'Full dress rehearsal', he tells Rob breathlessly. 'And I am knackered. Let's sit... coffee?' He goes to the machine in a mincing glide, small, tight; he reminds Rob of a musical note, a quaver; one arm extended, fingers dangling as he stirs his coffee.

He puts the spoon down and wafts a hand, fanning his face.

'Hilarion! Phew! What a part! And you are Robert? Rob! I saw your film, your latest... er... oops! What was it?' He cups a hand over his mouth. They both laugh.

'Anyway, I do the archive here, part time. He reaches beneath the coffee table and produces a folder. After your phone call, I got quite interested, and - well, here's what we've got so far.

'Lizzie Reardon worked for Sadler's Wells in 1886 not long after the reopening. Music Hall took over here from what had been a skating rink would you believe? It was a small troupe she ran called 'The Dainty Dots' in which she not only danced but also did the choreography. But then...' he delves once more into the folder, '1905 and she is big time. Her own production, in which she does the lot; half a dozen characters. Quick Change Artists they called them and there were quite a few about. Houdini himself took it up for a while. It was popular. Very popular'.

He shows Rob a poster, which he holds carefully. A slip of paper, old, parchment thin and fragile, the once vivid colours faded.

'It's a Handbill', Tony explains. 'Means what it says. You still get them today, shoved into your hand at the bus stop, advertising Pizzas and you let it drop as soon as you think nobody's looking. He points out the logo for "Pears Soap", another showing a little round box with the legend "Beechams Pills. Worth a Guinea an Ounce". Then there are the names of the management, Lighting By, Costumes, Courtesy of, Printed by. There then remains just enough room, in the middle, for the actual attraction.

MISS LIZZIE REARDON IN HER OWN PRODUCTION OF
THE REEL OF THE HANGED ONE
A Terpsichorean Representation of a True and Tragic Event.
Characters in order of appearance:
Tom. Sergeant. Chetina. Ship's Captain. Royal Gardener. Priest.
The Hangman.

'She's trying to tell us something', Rob mutters.

'Beg your pardon?' Tony replies.

'Oh. Just something Jane, my wife said, er... terpsichorean?'

Tony laughs. 'They didn't half come out with it didn't they? The big words? And the audience loved it. "Oooh!" They would go at each weird pronouncement. It means dance - pertaining too anyway, that's all'. He glances at his watch. 'Look, I'm interested. I think Jane is right. It's a story. There would be nothing new about that. All dance tells a story, or should do. The main aim of this place, Sadler's, has always been that. We're not just a pretty face and a trim little bottom you know. We do anarchy here as well as sugar plum fairies!' He retrieves the poster. 'Call me', he says as he flits through the door. 'Give it a couple of days'.

Jane keeps an eye on Rob. Always wary. As his sponsor she takes her responsibility seriously. Have trust, but tie up your camel is one of the slogans. He is the weakest link. If one of them falls, picks up that first drink, it'll be him, and she knows how hurt he is deep down. The talent that has produced three best sellers in a row. Financial success, film and stage adaptations - all this has left him unimpressed, disappointed. He dreams of dying in a garret. Penniless, starving. A fragment of immortal verse his only legacy.

'Christ's sake!' she tells him. 'Write as the bloody crow flies why can't you? Lord thingy gets away with it'.

They wait at the lights. He taps the steering wheel impatiently. Twitchy. She puts a hand on his.

'Your leg', she says, 'bouncing again'.

He grins. 'Good story that; *As the Crow Flies*'.

Rob and Jane sit by the river on a bench in the park. She feeds the ducks. Perfect, everything perfect. What more can she want? She asks herself the question knowing well the answer. What she wants is peace of mind. She sighs, leans back on the bench, and feels the warm sun on her face. Beside her, her husband is deep in thought, lost in some far off world of his own. He is writing, in his mind, and she has learned to know her place. If she spoke to him now he would simply ignore her.

'I never heard her name mentioned - at home, you know? You'd think they would have said something'. Rob rambles and she lets him ramble on. Another minute and she'll be asleep.

'Our Liz the actress, they might have said. Bragging. Showing off. And she appeared with Marie Lloyd you know. But no. Nothing. Not a peep. It's as if she never existed'.

Jane crumbles the bread. Tosses it to the ducks darting and squabbling.

'Grey hair she has. Silver really'. Rob mutters on, eyes fixed on the distance. Is he remembering? Or is he making it up?

'I'm a boy of five in a bob cap and there is this old, old woman. Long strands of thin, shining, silver hair. She combs it in sweeping strokes, sitting in the sun on the front step of a little house in a terrace in a suburb of a town. There is a brown streak in her hair, above the left eyebrow. A thin brown smudge and the fingers of her right hand are stained the same brown. When she kisses me I can smell stale tobacco smoke. An old smell mixing with her perfume. French perfume. Her lined face is powdered white. Her cheeks are brightly rouged. Her lips taste of anisette and she is smiling as she rises, enters her home, closes the door. Overhead, the slow throb of an aeroplane, labouring under the weight of its bombs, gets louder and nearer. Throb, throb, throb and the siren's wail'.

His voice is getting lower as he describes what he sees in his mind. The words flow. She catches fragments, the sound becomes a story as the pictures he is painting rise and fall in cadences. It comes naturally to him. He is a storyteller and she can imagine him in the courtyard of some ancient inn on the Old Silk Road telling tales as old as Apuleius. All he wants to do, and what he cannot do, is to write as his heroes wrote: Chekhov. Hemingway. She loses track and knows he has also, as the words spill out of him uncontrollably. A tap has been turned, and if she could just get him to his desk, lock him in, bind him. If she could just hold him long enough, he may or he may not write, and he may or he may not write well, and if he does not write well, he will drink, and she will leave him.

And yet he performs. Bounces back. Depths of dark depression one day, the next a ball of fire, energetically taking on a dozen things at once.

'That's handy', he says one morning at breakfast. '*Write Early*. It says here. This years conference is guess where?' She looks at him over her cup. Not one for quizzes first thing in the morning.

'New York! Should we go do you think?'

She nibbles her toast.

'Well dear, you are a founder member. *The* founder member. *President*, last I heard. Yes we should go, must go - and while we are at it we could look up some archives, see what there is, if anything, on Lizzie's New York appearances. There's that library - Performing Arts I think it is. Yes. And yes. Let's go'. She busies herself with the dishwasher.

'And why not', she adds later, 'while we are at it, why not a cruise? Fly to New York, do the convention, a bit of archiving, a quick look in Macy's perhaps and then a sea cruise. Do you good. I'll see what's going'.

Chapter Twenty Two

'Happy 10th anniversary!' she raises her glass of tonic. 'Two anniversaries, me and you, and little old you on your own. I never thought we'd make it - you'd make it'. She smiles.

'Not even a wine gum, as they say, except for, well, anyway - here we are'. He casts a sweeping arm to embrace the room as he swivels on the barstool. 'The Chelsea Hotel, New York City. Mecca of literary giants. Artists and their models. Model artists. Dylan himself, up those very stairs, dying of booze, and look at us, we got away with it. Not fair is it?'

They are awake early next morning. Things to do and a boat to catch. Jane piles her grits onto Rob's plate.

'Bubble and squeak for breakfast. No thank you', she tells him as he shovels it in.

'Yum yum', he mumbles through bacon, beans, two eggs easy over and scalding coffee.

Jane sips her decaf. Nibbles her toast.

The sun is out, drying last night's rain as they head out along Twenty Third Street to connect with Broadway.

'All the way up', Rob informs Jane. 'Can't go wrong in Manhattan, all straight lines and what's more you can walk most of it'.

At Sixty third they make a left and there it is: Lincoln Centre Plaza, where, at reception, they are directed to the Museum of the Performing Arts.

'You are Jane and Robert?' The woman is about thirty and she looks, Rob observes, like a librarian should look.

'Rob', he tells her 'and you are Cissie'. They shake hands formally and then the older woman gives each of them a hug.

'This *is* New York', she tells them apologetically. 'It's what we do'. She glances at her watch. 'We are booked in to number eleven suite at noon, you want coffee?'

Cissie has the apparatus already set up; all she has to do as the couple sit, is to wind on the film.

'Thirty five mil', she instructs them. 'A kind of compromise between Edison's Vitascope and the brothers Lumiere with their Cinematograph'.

She shows them the reel in its battered tin box.

'Kinda precious to an old buff like me'.

Rob squints at the writing on the box.

"Reel of the Hanged One" he reads. "Kineptikon Theatre, 1896. Prop: T. Pastor."

Cissie finishes winding on, she throws a switch and a bright light is projected onto the screen. The machine squeals and groans. There appears a rapid jumble of flashing lines. Weird squiggles shaped like fantastic monsters dance and squirm in the fierce glare and then, suddenly, a form appears out of the confusion. It is a woman, smiling directly and intently into the camera.

Outside, in the bustling avenues and through the thick curtained windows, Rob and Jane can just about hear the pulsating heart of Manhattan; a muted, erratic hum, background to the soft, electric whirring of the projector and the tick, tick, ticking of celluloid film as it weaves its way back in time from the twenty first to the nineteenth century. From the modern magnificence of one of the world's most prestigious institutions, to a flea pit vaudeville theatre in the red light district of Forty Second Street.

The images on the screen jerk and judder; each movement made at the exaggerated, comical speed normally associated with re-runs of old silent films. Even so, the thread of the dance is easily discerned. Cissie rewinds and runs the film again and again as Rob and Jane pick up the story. Jane takes notes and after the fourth or fifth showing they call a halt for coffee and conference.

'Eight characters I get', says Jane, 'eight changes, not only of costume but of facial expression, posture and I mean she actually *becomes* each person for the second or two that she plays it.

Rob begins a count on a raised thumb, ticking off as he goes with his forefinger.

'A sea Captain, Royal Navy I'd say. Two soldiers, one a Private, one a Sergeant. A young girl. Somebody in a white gown and hood. The executioner? Six I make it.

'The baby, says Jane, you forgot the baby, the doll at its mother's breast and what about the gardener or whatever? The man sowing seeds? That's eight'.

'What about the name?' Cissie asks. While Rob and Jane look puzzled.

'When the Captain is reading', she says, 'what looks like a scroll. Look, wait a minute while I... ah! There we go', and the machine starts up again, the sharp white light filling the little screen.

'I can stop it when I get to...there!' she freezes the picture. 'There is the naval officer in his dress uniform, gold braid at his shoulders, stern, forbidding, he appears to be shouting, proclaiming perhaps and behind him - look behind him', Cissie points with a finger. 'There', she says excitedly, 'just there, see it? Part of the backdrop, the set behind him, one of those lifebuoy things and a name on it'.

'HMS Rambler!' Rob jerks forward in his seat to peer more closely at the screen. 'Rambler! Tom! Thomas McSweeney! How?' He closes his eyes and begins to recite as the two women look on at him in surprise. At first Jane thinks it is a poem, or an extract from some play or other. Shakespeare perhaps. He is fond of declaiming out loud, often to her embarrassment in a crowded restaurant.

'Sacred to the Memory', he begins and she can see he is literally shaking as his voice cracks with emotion. She goes to his side and he pulls her into him, demanding and he can feel her next to him, her warmth, her strength flowing into him and he hears again her voice from long ago when she first told him, 'I can help you'.

They stand on deck as the cruise ship, side thrusters roaring, pushes herself off from the dockside and out into the brown whirling waters of the East River.

'These piers', Rob murmurs. 'What life they have seen! Hordes of hopeful humanity. Running, fleeing, seeking their fortune. Starving children, holy men, brigands, card sharpers, con-men and there...' He points to a pile, a jumble of building materials, where a giant bright orange crane casts its outstretched arm. Two massive girders, tons on tons of steel, dip and gently sway at the touch of a lever in the fingers of the miniature man up there in his sky cabin above Manhattan's East Side.

'That's where she landed, Pier Fifty-Eight, our Lizzie. RMS Campania, September 1896. Liverpool to New York. What a lady! Can't you just see her? There! See, her with her bonnet and bustle, telling them off for dropping her portmanteau'.

Their ship does a complete screw turn in the river. Rob and Jane stand at the rail.

'You', she tells him, 'are vibrating. Are you in love? With your Granny?'

The cruise takes them across the Atlantic to Europe. They laze in the sun, eat too much, play the one-arm bandits for cents. At Gibraltar they climb the steep paths up The Rock, sit on the wall in the shade by the

Castle. Keeping an eye on the apes keeping an eye on them.

Their last port of call is Malta, and as the ship, with two tugs attending, squeezes herself in through the dog - leg of the breakwater walls, Rob sniffs the air, listens for the bells.

'There are always bells' he tells Jane as they step carefully into the rowing boat that takes them across the busy waterway to Senglea.

'Not many tourists know this place'. He nods at an old woman, all in black, arthritic on the steps. 'Bongu', he greets her. They are in a little garden out on a pointing finger of land that hangs like an admonishment over the peaceful blue of Grand Harbour. The garden was once an olive grove; a dozen or so of the ancient gnarled trees still lean crazily against the fierce seasonal winds - the Grigale, cold from the north. The Sirocco, hot, humid, bringing sand from the Sahara. Before the olives came there were windmills, and before that La Vallette, with his handful of knights and a few peasants, beat off the Janissaries, using their severed heads as cannon balls.

'Arabs lived here, according to those that don't and wouldn't live here'. Rob tells Jane. 'Very parochial, the Maltese'.

They sit by the water sipping coke. The sun beats fiercely on the honey-coloured rocks. Children play in the dust at the feet of their mothers. Everything is muted, every sound gathered up by the porous lime stone of the ancient walls, hushed by the sheer weight of history and of time.

'Senglea' Rob tells Jane expansively. 'L'isla, to give it the Maltese. Barbary Coast to generations of sailors'.

Across the water a merchantman, a large tanker, is backing into her billet, nursed by the gentle urging of her attendant tugs. Lines of washing loll listlessly on wires hanging from every balcony of the crowded tenements opposite. A cat yawns, leaning for shade against a honey-coloured wall. And then the bells begin. At Saint Phillip's and at Saint Lawrence's, the pigeons, though you would think they'd be used to it by now, scatter in alarm from their belfry roosts, circling and soaring on the still warm air.

'I told you', grins Rob. 'And that's only Matins'.

'The other thing'. He has taken her by the arm and leads her into the shade of an old stone sentry box standing at the outermost tip of the little peninsular. 'This is the other thing. The Guardiola', he tells her. 'Look. See the ear? The eye? The nose?'

She looks up, squinting into the sun's rays, shading her eyes with her hand.

The three organs of the human senses, delicately worked in the soft stone, stand out proud, defiant through centuries of storms and high winds.

'They have been here for ever, watching for a sail, listening for battles cries, sniffing the wind for trouble but that's one story', Rob goes on. 'I prefer the other one where, when Suleiman threatened these walls, at the height of the siege, La Vallette asked for volunteers among the civilian population. Among these came women and children, many of whom, to show their contempt, cut off their own noses, cut of their ears and gouged out their own eyeballs, hurling them in defiance at the storming troops below'.

The couple lean with their backs against the warm wall. In front of them, beyond the park gates, a narrow street winds slightly up hill and away from them. Balconied houses crowd in on each other on either side, so close together you could hand a cup of tea from one bedroom to its neighbour opposite. A woman, belting the daylights out of a carpet, waves at them a welcome.

'And that', he tells her, pointing along the narrow, stepped street. 'That's where I was born'.

He glances at his watch. They sail at 1700. It is two-thirty. They walk past the church at the top of the hill; St. Phillip's with its red dome. Then down the hill towards the other church, the bigger one, affectionately called Il Bambini after the child's face on the statue of Mary its patron.

'Rumour has it', Rob tells Jane, 'that she used to be a ship's figure head and got washed ashore here after her vessel went on the rocks'.

They stroll down the hill and are just in time to catch a number four bus, which takes them to the next village, Cospicua, a short walk from the cemetery.

'This place was shut up when I was a kid', Rob steers Jane among the many new graves, some with photographs of the departed dead. 'That's Lawrence', Rob says pointing to a white marble statue of a monk holding a child in his arms. 'The place got blown up in the blitz so they locked the gates for safety'. They reach a grave in a remote corner. A metal railing has been erected around it. A fig tree lends its shade. 'Just look at the flowers, and look', as they lean over the railing.

'Candles', Jane gasps. 'And lit... who?'

Rob gets out his camera.

'That's a secret... a local family? Maybe more than one. After the bombs and the lock on the door they couldn't get near, so they fitted a pipe, see? An iron pipe and it's still there look, a stub of it. They poured holy water and oil down it, dripping it onto the grave hoping for miracles. He'd be canonised a saint, our Tom, if the folk around here had their way'.

Jane reads the inscription on a marble plaque embedded in the crumbling wall behind and over the plot.

Sacred to the memory of Thomas McSweeney, executed on HMS Rambler 8th.September 1845, Aged 23 years.

Rob is sitting on the little step that leads up to the plot. She can see he is moved and she comes to him, puts her arm around his shoulder.

'Rambler', she says. 'HMS Rambler - I see'.

'It was a put-up job' Rob begins. 'I've researched it for years and the people here are convinced of it. An accident, that's all that happened, but the British had an axe to grind. In any case, sentence of death was invariably commuted to flogging and imprisonment. I looked at six cases that occurred in the fleet about this same time, one of them a multiple murder. Not one of the convicted was hung. There was something not right, something hidden. I've come here as a lad, and I've sat on his grave and I've told him -Thomas McSweeney, son of the Swiney, Gallowglass soldier to the O'Donnell's of Tyrconell -I will find out'.

They walk slowly back to the bus, getting off at The Floriana Mall where they sip a cup of coffee before strolling back down Crucifix Hill to Customs House Jetty and their ship.

The Gharry Horse men are in full cry.

'Karrozin. Gharry. Ride to Saint Elmo. Valletta. Strait Street'. They have to dodge and weave to avoid them. Rob sniffs the air appreciatively.

'Horse piss', he says. 'Happy days' and they stroll hand in hand to the quayside gates at the bottom of the hill where she stops him, takes him by the hand and looks him straight in the eye.

'Why don't you?' She says. 'Find out?'

Chapter Twenty Three

Back home they begin trying to make sense of what they have found. The film. Lizzie's dance. The ship's name. Was it coincidence?

'Rubbish! Coincidence my eye'. Jane tells him. 'That was Lizzie in that film. Your grandmother. I'm convinced of it. She is doing her level best to tell us something. I can feel her, urging us on. So what's next?'

'Sadler's Wells', Rob says. 'Tony'.

'And Kew', she tells him, 'that's what we want. Public Records Office, see what they have on HMS Rambler, if anything'.

He's up early next morning, coffee already brewing. He kisses her good morning. She smells peppermints on his breath and she wonders. Toothpaste? Yes, probably but...she eyes him carefully over her cup, blowing softly to cool it.

'Cool it', she tells herself and watches. Rob bounces onto the bed and balances an A5 sketchpad on his knees. He draws a line under the name he has written.

'That's me' he says, born Malta, Feb 16th, 1946, to Robert Reardon born 1888, and Josa Vella'. He draws an arrow pointing upwards, crosses it with a horizontal line.

'Now', he says, my father must have had a father and a mother right? His mother, according to our solicitor friends, is Lizzie. Elizabeth Reardon, born 1866 at Bolton in Lancashire, died at Lambeth on October 28th, 1940. Right?'

Jane is well ahead of him but she lets him go on.

'So', he blinks, concentrates; 'My name is Reardon, my father's name was Reardon, we know my grandmother's name was Reardon, and we have seen census returns that show she comes from a family of that name also'.

Jane can stand it no longer. This man can imagine in his storytelling the most outrageous and convoluted scenarios, but place a fact on the end of his nose and he is as blind as a burrowing mole. Or is he confused?

'Well', she says, 'yes, you go all the way back to Lizzie, whose name we know was Reardon. So', she taps the sheet of paper with a finger nail, 'unless she married another Reardon, a bit rare in Malta I'd have thought - your father must be Lizzie's illegitimate son'.

Rob sighs. 'Yes, of course, just as I thought'. He is being playful. He sounds normal. Sounds OK. Christ! She's getting paranoid. But peppermints? She consults the family tree again.

'Pass me that calculator', and she dots in the numbers.

'So, for family tree purposes we are stymied!' Rob says resignedly. 'How do you find the father of an illegitimate child, especially if he doesn't want to be found?'

Jane has her eyes closed.

'Ssh!' She says, 'I'm thinking… first thing is, we know your birth date, 1946'.

'Right', Rob says again, knowing full well she has more up her sleeve.

'The Stage Magazine? we've still got credits remember? I've already looked and what do you know? from 1883, when she makes her debut at the Bolton Grand Theatre, until 1903 when the trail goes cold there are only two periods of nine months or more when she is not working somewhere, at some venue either here in Britain, or elsewhere'. She glances at her notes while Rob looks at her in total amazement. She smiles, just a little smugly.

'May 1887 to March 1888, and August 1896 to January 1897'.

Rob claps his hands.

'Bravo!' he cries. 'What a woman!'

She lowers her eyes and flashes her lashes demurely.

'Hang on', she tells him. 'I'm not finished yet. We already know about the latter dates, she was in America. Definitely. We've seen the film, we've seen her on the Atlantic Passenger Lists and there's an article also in The Stage. The only other time she could have had a baby is between 1887 and 1888'.

He just looks at her,

'A guinea a bloody ounce is what you are. Take that'.

He kisses her, at first in fun and then, with sudden urgency, his hand going automatically to her breast, he forces her mouth open with a probing tongue.

She pushes him away, far from angry but;

'Hang on. Whoa!' she pants. One thing at a time'. She takes deep breaths. 'At a guess, I'd say your father was born, in Malta, some time in 1888'.

She leans back on the pillows, her hair a halo about her bare shoulders. She wets her lips with the tip of her tongue.

'And incidentally', touching her hand to his cheek. 'He must have been a bit of a goer. He was nigh on sixty when he sired you.'

'Like father, like son'. Rob hoists himself on top of her.

'Mmm', she agrees and draws him down.

Hours later he cooks the spaghetti while she makes the salad. They eat, drink sparkling fruit juice and smile easily at each other. They are relaxed.

'By the way', she asks, 'have you changed your toothpaste?'

Two days later she finds the little stash of empty vodka miniatures in his sock drawer. Right at the back. Under the little packet of letters. Love letters. The ones she wrote to him when he was away that time and she missed him so much. She phones her sponsor for the first time in a long time.

'Elaine!' They hug each other warmly. Jane feels the old urgency in the other woman's touch, at once, it has never gone away. It has never been spoken but they both know. They see each other often, among friends. At meetings. They love each other. Jane knows she broke the other woman's heart when she made plain that what Elaine wanted could not be had. Jane can weep easily when she thinks how easy it ought to be to make this woman, whom she adores, so very happy.

The café is crowded. They huddle together; their heads close up against the din.

'Well, anyway, he's off again to Malta'. Jane is saying. 'Chasing this family tree business. There is something quite odd about it all I feel. You must come, see the dresses! And the stuff we are finding. Mysteries.'

Elaine orders two more cups.

'Nescaff', she reminds the girl. 'None of that bitter stuff'.

She grasps Jane's hands in hers.

'You know what to do if…well… you know, and if you need me you know where I am. If you need to get away… just for a bit say, you can always come to me. I'll not eat you. Not unless you ask politely'.

Jane smiles warmly.

'I know, love', she says.

The phone is ringing when she gets home. He has got as far as Hounslow. That's what she can make out. Missed his flight from Heathrow. Overslept. She can practically smell it on him over the phone. Whiskey it'll be, a good quality Scotch after the pretending with the little Vodkas. It's one of the traits and she recognizes it.

All alcoholics have traits. The same traits. Drinking, when you can afford it, the best there is somehow makes it more civilized, more acceptable and of course it is for most people but not for him, not for her.

His speech is slurry, he is rambling, furtive. She looks at the snowflakes forming on the windowpanes. White Christmas coming perhaps. Not for them though, not now.

'Go away', she tells him over the phone. 'Just go away. How dare you? How could you?' She knows she is wasting her time. She must get out of it. She knows the drill... withdraw with love.

'I'm withdrawing with love', she tells him and puts the phone down. The snow is sticking now and from their patio window the world outside looks obscenely clean.

Chapter Twenty Four

'Oh. Good Lord, the gifty gae us to see wa selves as others see us'.

Black Mac is on form.

Rob looks up from the bench. He could be at the Hilton of course if he wanted to be. He can afford it and there are plenty of drunks at the Hilton. This is his penance, his hair shirt, slumming with the rest of the bums, his very own flat stone under which he slinks and lies alone. He remembers the poem he once wrote. Fancied himself as a bard. A poet for Christ's sake....*and the owls in his bowels gasp and drown*...God! how fucking awful.

He sees the people scurrying. The real people. Back and forth over the bridge. Over the Thames. Hospital on one side. Seat of government on the other. How apt. Big Ben bonging out the hours and the people scurrying past. Going and coming. Nine till five and home in Surbiton by seven. Gravy and mint sauce on prime lamb chops. The wife in her patterned pinafore, just like the advert on telly. Walk the dog. Do the crossword. Get your leg over and don't forget to withdraw in time and oh. yes! Set the clock for morning so you can do it all over again. He would like to feel sorry, to be ashamed, but he cannot, it's not in the script.

'I've shit it Mac', he says. 'Big time'.

Mac swigs from a bottle held in a brown paper bag.

'Tek a wet', he commands. 'We've all shit it. See there, over there, Saint Thomas's?'

They have heard it all before.

Jock, another Scot, butts in sarcastically.

'The best fucking gall stones man in the fucking universe'.

'Laparoscopic cholecystectomy'. Mac corrects him heavily, 'Sixty minutes in an out and *Mister* McDonald to you if you please'.

The blossoms are out on the Plane trees along The Embankment, red buds, green buds, male and female. Sycamores, some call them but Rob has always preferred Plane. The Canadian backpackers think they are at home with their Maple Tree. The bright red leaf on their rucksacks. They often get down here in the spring and summer and the cops don't bother them.

Young folk. Travelling the world. Free.

'I never did that'.

'Did what?' says Mac as Rob hands him the bottle. Drinking mates they are. Everybody has one. A buddy in the gutter. There is a fear, a taboo about drinking alone, although they are all alone. Every one.

'Travel, I mean, see the world, not when I was young anyway and it's not the same when you have been young and you are young no more'.

During the night Mac hears a groan. Groans are common here in the dark and silence of the night. He goes back to sleep, turning this way and that on the hard, slatted bench. In the morning he gets up, staggers to the public toilet, which is just opening up. He pisses. Splashes his face at the grimy sink. He takes a squint into an open cubicle just in case. There is an empty cider bottle lying on its side, forlorn in the dirt behind the pan. He picks it up. Holds it up to the light. Sucks on it to make sure. He counts two bone-dry cough mixture bottles. One shit streaked pair of discarded underpants. He goes back to his bench, sits wearily and smells the blood. He knows the smell of blood. The iron smell. And then he sees the blood. A pool of it, oozing and already blackening around the wrought iron legs of the park bench. Rob is sitting bolt upright. Arms outstretched in supplication. Eyes wide open. His left wrist is a gaping wound, opened wide like a protesting mouth. Blood pulses from it in a regular rhythm. A rhythm oh so slow now, so weak. Mac knows he has no time; the very next beat will be the last. The man is dead.

He grabs the edges of the wound in his bare hands, clamps and holds them together.

'That stone!' he orders, aloud yet calm.

'What?' mutters Jock, standing there, gaunt, shocked, shaking.

'Under the arm, the armpit, shove it in hard. Now the arm down, press down, hold down. Press down hard'.

The commotion has alerted a few passers by, fresh off the tube, away to their meetings, their deals and their fortunes. They pause, rubbernecking, a bit of excitement on the way to work.

'Hey you! Mister! Telephone!' Mac addresses one of them who attempts to hurry on past in full stride, eyes averted, passing by, none of his business. 'Get on your bloody mobile' Mac insists. The man stands there, shocked, clean, pin stripes, regulation briefcase with the regulation pink newspaper neatly folded. He holds the phone to his ear and trembles only slightly.

'Tell them', says Mac. 'Now listen! - Tell them: Doctor at scene, male patient, arterial bleeding at wrist, cardiac arrhythmia possible'.

The man with the phone is trembling violently now. He wants to be sick.

'Volemia!' Mac insists. 'Listen! Hy... po...vol...emia! Yes you got it. Now sit down mister, you done a good job and Jock my bonny lad hold that fucking arm down!'

Elaine drives Jane into Westminster. They park in the grounds behind the Florence Nightingale Museum. "Critical Care", the sign says. "East Wing: Follow The Colour Coded Arrows". Their heels echo on the gleaming linoleum, a trolley handled by two burly porters overtakes them.

'Por favor', one of them says. A woman lies flat on the trolley, there is a blanket up to her chin, her face is old, grey. Is she dead?' The two men continue talking all the way down the corridor.

'Does nobody speak English anymore?' Jane says. Elaine squeezes her hand.

They sit on the hard plastic chairs. Dick Whittington looks down at them from a mural on the wall. Someone sneezes; once, twice, three times. The sound echoes rudely in the cathedral silence.

'Jesus!' one of the porters says, crossing himself and kissing his knuckle.

'Rob always does three'. Jane looks straight ahead. 'Sneezes I mean. I do seven sometimes and he shouts shut up, but he only does three'. She begins to cry. Elaine holds her hand.

'No', the ward manager tells them. 'You cannot see him. Nothing to see. He is heavily sedated. His chances? Well, he is very poorly. We'll have to see. It'll be some weeks'.

Chapter Twenty Five

The view from the convalescent ward looks out across the river to the Palace of Westminster, Big Ben, and The Embankment. The spring sunshine, even through the glass panels of the conservatory is not yet warm enough and Jane has arranged Rob's blanket about his legs. She is efficient, distant, detached.

'You've changed'. He tells her. 'Something different.'

He looks saintly, propped on the snowy pillows. A sliver of tissue is stuck to his chin where he has nicked himself shaving. He holds one arm tightly, close to his stomach. The other arm, wrapped up in bandages, is held high on his chest by a sling. She looks at his hands, trembling like two frightened birds. She has known those hands. Loving hands.

'Only a few more days they say. Just keep going'.

'Yes, love', he says. 'Going'.

Before she leaves she hands him a small packet.

'Read that', she tells him. 'I found it tucked inside an evening bag in Lizzie's trunk, and the brooch…?' she points to a small badge pinned in her lapel. 'It fell out of a pocket in one of the dresses. See the little lizard? I think it was Lizzie's good luck charm. She wants me to wear it'. She smiles wanly and leaves.

Rob watches her go, walking tall on her clicking high heels, purposeful, free He is her only liability, her ball and chain.

'Upset you has she', a Caribbean accent, warm, caring. 'They do that sometimes but they don't mean to. Cheer up, I'll fetch you a cup of tea'. The nurse waddles off down the ward, her black nylon stockings making the same old swishing sound as she goes.

Rob unties the thin red ribbon that holds together a small sheaf of notepapers, yellowing, fragile with age. He perches his glasses on the end of his nose, and shakily but determined, begins to read.

Offices of the Women's Social and Political Movement
Northern Division
The Crescent
Salford
Lancashire.
November 10th. 1903
Dear Miss Reardon,

Our mutual friend Christobel has asked me to write to you. She is prevented from doing so herself as she is presently, and we hope briefly, detained at His Majesty's Pleasure in Strangeways Jail.

She has asked me to say that she has followed your career with a mixture of pleasure and envy as you continue to charm your audiences, while at the same time using your talents towards ends perhaps more political than recreational.

May I join her in expressing the hope that you will endeavour to be as circumspect as your undoubted zeal will permit. Your contribution to our common cause would be sorely missed would the interests of certain quarters become so exercised as to seek to curtail it.

Regarding the matter of the hanged sailor, Christobel most earnestly advises that you at once abandon all present and any further investigation into that sad incident, the continuance of which, we are assured, would place you in considerable danger.

Our friend further requests that I send to you her most affectionate good wishes to which may I add my own,

Yours Sincerely
Barbara Leyland (miss) Secretary.

A nurse throws back Robs blankets abruptly.

'Right,' she says. 'let's have you'. And she helps him into his slippers, his robe; seating him firmly in a wheel chair.

'Tests', she tells him as they weave their way off the ward and out along the corridor.

The psychiatrist is a woman. Matronly, plump, foreign – probably Polish, Rob decides. She stands behind him. Holds out an arm.

'Rest your arm on mine', she tells him. 'The good one. Not the one you cut'. She is curt, matter of fact. No messing.

'Rest it. Totally. Let me take the weight – yes, rest it – good, good.' Moments pass. He can smell her perfume, mixing with the chemical, hospital smells. Her breathing is a slight whistling sound. He can feel the caress of it on the back of his neck. Tickling. She turns away from him abruptly and watches as his arm drops limply to his side.

'You have had your last drink'. She tells him. 'Your central nervous system is shot to pieces'. Hold out your hands: 'Yes – you see?' He watches his fingers as they jerk and jump.

'And your liver? Well – that will heal itself – given a chance. You have been lucky there and kidneys too. They have been working for the damaged liver you see.'

She sits at her desk and consults his records.

'A friend of Doctor Bob I note'.

It is the old greeting, the not - so - secret password between recovering alcoholics. Recalling a founder member, who, with one single fellow sufferer, began the movement that saved millions of lives.

The psychiatrist smiles at him.

'Keep coming back'. She says and then: 'You can go home now'.

Chapter Twenty Six

Rob looks around at the work Jane has done while he has been ill. Everything is laid out in what they still call the kids room although no kid ever played there. Pots, pans, clothing, everything in order and the most interesting bits she has put at one side for further investigation.

'I'd a lovely time with the frocks'. She tells him.

'Most of them are props of course, part of Lizzie's act. A greater part in fact. Much of the artistry, the illusion, was in the design of the clothes. Basically, one dress or outfit contained up to half a dozen more, hidden within its folds. Press-studs, buttons, loops, tags and the different rigs-outs were switched as the dance progressed. That's not all there was to it of course. Speed, practice and a real talent for the dance were just as important. And illusion. Magic. Our Lizzie was quite the magician apart from everything else'.

Rob doesn't know what to say. Why doesn't she get mad? Why did he have to spoil it all? Make amends, they tell him at the meetings, for the harm you have done, but how does he make amends to her now? What he needs is a kick up the arse.

'Look', she faces him over the kitchen table. 'I tried the recommended way – withdrawing - and it didn't work. Sometimes it doesn't. The Programme might be gospel but I am not that holy. You needed me, so I'm here. Sorting this thing, this mystery whatever it is, can only be good for you, perhaps for us. Let's do it and maybe... I don't know lets just do it'.

He nods.

'Yes, love'.

She walks away to let him cry.

They go together to Kew. It is agreed between them that he is not fit to go alone. It's going to take a few days, quite a few, before his screaming nerve ends calm down and he can drink a cup of tea without spilling it. They'll stay at the Coach and Horses on The Green, a bit old fashioned but the grub is good and hearty and that's what he needs. That and an interest to occupy him.

'They say those swans are famous folk, forgotten by history, trying for a place in the miles and miles of records'. Rob is puffed after the stiff stroll from the station. They sit on the wall that skirts the pond. Jane has brought most of her breakfast wrapped in a napkin. They look up at the massive concrete bulk of The Public Records Office as Jane feeds the birds. 'And they're all here': Rob is in instructive mode; 'King John, Lord Nelson, The dead of the Somme. You can find out the pay of any particular seaman in any particular year on any particular ship and…. come on, they're open'.

They go straight to the ADM catalogue- the series that deals with Admiralty affairs – ships, sailors and everything about them. Thousands on thousands of books, pamphlets, maps, logs. A seaman's life is recorded here, in detail, from his Attestation on joining, to his final Discharge when, depending on his circumstances and conduct, the appellation "Honourable" or "Dishonourable" will be applied. In many cases of course, especially in time of war, the record will be stamped "DC" which means Dead.

A small crowd is milling about, some of them full of purpose; they know what they are looking for and where to find it. Old hands. A few others look lost and head for the banks of leaflets that will tell them all there is to know about where to look. Rob nods to a couple of the regulars.

'Medals', he tells Jane, indicating a squat, scruffy looking man with a Fair Isle jumper on, who peers back at them myopically over wire-rimmed glasses.

Jane watches Rob as he chats easily with the man. He is animated, hands and arms articulating. She can tell every word he is saying by the language of his body. Later and throughout the day he goes from index to folio, from computer to record until he finds the piece he seeks. So sure. She always said he was the queerest alcoholic she ever met. His ability to bounce back. Dead one minute, alive and vibrant the next. Perhaps that was his downfall: he could not sink down far enough, hit the rock bottom most of them had to reach before crawling back over many years. She watches him now, Doctor Jekyll, as he waves a bit of paper about, the broad, boyish smile on him that could always warm her heart.

'Tea time', he says and they go down the stairs, through the turnstiles where, as usual, they fail to swipe the card correctly in the electronic slot.

'Other way up sir', the uniformed ex Sergeant Major says with a world-weary yet scrupulously polite inflection. They upturn the card and the trap doors open to let them out.

'Bitter', Rob says, pulling a face and grimacing into his cup. 'They used to do instant, still…'

He consults his notes.

'Get this!' he begins, waving a sheet of paper like a flag.

'From: ADM/300/4c/; Robert. B. Reardon - that's my dad - his Attestation Certificate, the document they sign to prove who they are and see here; all signed at St. Angelo, the fort I pointed out to you in Malta, remember? Just one thing though. Robert. B? I never knew he had a middle name but then...'

Jane watches his face, how excited he is.

'Then I looked up his original application - it's amazing, simply mind blowing the stuff you can find. Look!'

He produces a photocopy he has made of a letter his father sent to the naval authorities. His application. It is signed Robert, Baldacino-Reardon.

'Now', he goes on, 'I've asked a few experts and they tell me that signing on in the British navy as a Maltese, he'd have been classed as Locally Entered'. Rob pauses, getting it straight in his head.

'And', he continues, 'if he'd have done that he would have got local wages, lower than the UK rate. He had a dual passport and so he did the sensible thing and dropped his middle name. Became English'. He pauses again. 'Which is why I am English don't you know?'

Jane gives him an exaggerated round of applause.

'Sh!' Rob says. 'We'll get skinned! This is a library!'

'But what about his father?'

'Way ahead', Rob grins. 'All in hand', He opens his folder and comes up with yet another document copy.

'Thomas Baldacino. Captain, appointed Captain of the Dockyard, June 8th, 1884. Temporary Rank of Commodore.' He shuffles the bits of paper. 'And here... somewhere... Ah! Here we are—*his* Attestation Certificate'. He carefully lifts the frail, yellowed slip of paper from its box, lays it flat under the desk lamp. 'He enlisted at Malta... HMS Saint Angelo, same as my dad. As an ordinary seaman in 1860, and twenty years later he raises his pennant - did you know that a Commodore only has one ball? On his flag? A red ball - over the same barracks as he signed on at twenty years earlier. But look at this bit, where it says Date and Whereabouts of Birth. Jane examines the copy.

'Try this', Rob says, producing a magnifying glass. 'Courtesy of the house. They think of everything here you know'. Jane, squinting through the glass reads out the spidery, faded scrawl: 'Foundling. Certified by FR. Dom Alfred Spiteri on 9th Day of August 1845 in the Parish of St. Publius. Floriana. Malta.'

'Foundling!' Rob exclaims. 'Poor little bugger!'

They walk along the tree-lined avenues to Kew station and then past the famous Botanical Gardens to The Green and their hotel. They eat a substantial roast dinner and both are asleep by ten.

'Tomorrow', says Jane, just before she drops off. 'We tackle the Rambler and all her secrets'.

'Amen', says Rob.

It rains steadily all night. Jane awakes once or twice to nudge Rob to stop his snoring. In the morning the pavements are still wet as they again make their way the short distance to the Records Office. They check in and sit together in the foyer surrounded by the various leaflets. How to find. Where to find. Was your ancestor a Fireman, a Doctor, a Priest?

'ADM. again', Rob is confident, 'and we will go for our man.'

By lunchtime they have Thomas's name in front of them. They are using the map tables, as the record books are so huge. Rob caresses the pages with his gloved hands. Pages so delicate, so fine and yet what? Over one hundred and fifty years old, and the neat painstaking entries, in beautiful copper plate script, could have been written yesterday.

The title: "Ships Muster and Pay Book" is printed on the front of the ledger and below that: "HMS Rambler. July 1st to Sept. 30th. Eighteen forty six."

Rob props the open book on the soft supports provided and goes to the index.

He runs a finger down the list until he comes to "Royal Marines".

'Here we are', he continues turning the pages: Macdonald, Macnair, McReady and - Bingo!' He grips Jane's arm in his excitement, 'McSweeney!'

'McSweeney, Thomas'. Jane breathes and softly reads out the entries, left to right as they are written. Date of enlistment. Previous ships. A column denotes his rate of pay, mulcts for tobacco, soap and a pencilled in date notes his execution, the amount of wages owing to him at death; £2. 11. 6d. which included a sum raised by the auctioning of his kit. This sum being sent, the entry reads, via the parish priest of Mallow co. Cork, to Thomas's mother Bridget. The pencilled note adds. "A poor sum to pay for a life".

They take a copy of the entry and Rob goes to return the ledger.

'Hang on!' Jane stops him. 'Haven't we forgotten something? What about the sergeant, shouldn't he be listed?'

'Sergeant?' Rob looks blankly at her. 'What....'.

'The sergeant! Him in the ballet - Lizzie's dance!' She grabs the heavy tome and carts it back to the table.

'But we need a name', Rob protests. 'We have no name'.

Jane is already running through the listings: 'Royal Marines, Officers, NCOs -Sergeants!' she shouts finally and then, looking up at Rob with a devilish grin, 'and there is only the one -Sergeant J. Alun'.

Rob is at her side in an instant. She points, 'Look'. She turns to the other pages. 'Let's have a squint at the officers. Yes, the Captain of course, his First Lieutenant, the Boatswain, a couple of more naval ranks, midshipmen, and' - she grins and claps her hands like a child, turns and hugs a bewildered Rob. 'The gardener!' she almost shouts and then, more softly when she remembers where she is. 'The gardener in Lizzie's film, sowing his bloody seeds!'

Rob reads it out, at the bottom of the list of officers borne, the name: "Mister Alfred Coombes. PhD. FRS. Botanist. Age fifty-three".

Chapter Twenty Seven

'Email from Tony, our Sadlers Wells friend', Jane shouts through to the kitchen. 'We are invited to the ballet, bring your hanky he says and we can take him to dinner after'.

'Ballet!' Rob exclaims, wrinkling his nose. 'Well I might like the music and anyway, why not? Will I have to dress up?'

After the show they go backstage to Tony's dressing room, which is not quite the romantic scenario Rob has always imagined. Shared for a start with what looks like the whole of the cast. Albrecht is shedding his Ducal robes while Tony, as Hilarion, sits, completely naked, perched on a stool, dabbing at his cheeks with a tissue.

'What did you think of it?' he asks, swivelling on his chair to face them.

'Colourful', Rob asserts. 'All of it I mean. The theatre itself, the crowd, music, the whole atmosphere. Fascinating'.

'And the dance?'

Jane waits for Rob to put his foot in it.

'Ah! The dance. If only I understood it. But, well, it moved me, yes, I could see what you meant about bringing a hanky and the bit where Giselle and Albrecht do it together - the dance I mean'.

'The pas de deux', Tony interrupts.

'Yes, dance for two? And she's a ghost? Hell, yes, beautiful. But did I understand it? All of it? No'.

'Well you are not doing so badly, Tony assures him. 'It's been going since 1840 and the balletomanes are still at each other's throats'.

Jane thanks him. 'I cried', she says, 'so I must have enjoyed it and I do know a bit about it'. She looks directly at Rob as she speaks. 'An innocent girl, betrayed by her lover, who is then beset by demons. Her forgiveness of course. Her protecting hand. Redemption. Love conquers all'.

'Ouch!' Rob exclaims while Tony, looking on is pleased.

'That's it! That's what it's for. It's like your writing, or a painting in a gallery, it's about us and it touches us when we see ourselves in it'.

Their coffee is brought to them in a little booth in the lounge.

'A bit quieter here', Tony suggests. He lays Lizzie's manuscript on the table before them.

'And it's the same with this. I had some difficulty with the solo performance, but it's like you say Rob, the music, the dance, the scenery, backdrop, even the auditorium and not forgetting the audience, without whom it would be nothing. They all matter. We can each find the story, or *a* story anyway. So I'll tell you my take on it'.

Jane jots down the various interpretations as Tony describes them. The couple find themselves nodding and exclaiming in agreement as his rendition gels with the ideas that they themselves have already formed.

'Listen up!' Jane tells them and, holding her notes up to catch the light, she begins to summarise.

'The girl and the young soldier go walking. The other soldier, the sergeant, taunts the younger man, who clobbers him. The captain tries the offender. The sergeant is murdered in his bed. The young soldier is hung, comforted only by a hooded priest. The girl gives birth, and we see her first offering her breast and then abandoning the child, leaving it, tied to the rocks at the doorstep of a cottage.

Tony nods enthusiastically in agreement.

'And if we put that together with the film and all the other bits we have I'd say we are getting there'.

'But what about the Gardener?' Where's he when he's at home?'

'My turn', Tony laughs as he produces a couple of A4 sheets stapled together.

'Description of scenery', Tony tells them, 'backdrops, stage sets and so on: He reads the scene list.

Scene 1. A field of green crops, waving in the wind, as first the girl alone and then together with the boy, dances joyfully in a sylvan setting.

Scene 2. A dark figure scatters seeds over crops.

Scene 3. A fight between two uniformed men.

Scene 4. The courtroom scene with the naval Captain prosecuting.

Scene 5. The crops have withered as first the boy is hung and then the girl casts herself onto the rocks.

'Fields of green crops? A scattering of seeds? Crops withering? Come on!' Tony urges. 'What more do you want? Who or what is the gardener? What was he there for and what part does he play in the drama?'

'Mister Coombes next stop', says Jane. 'Who is he? What has he to do with whatever it is Lizzie is saying, what they stopped her from saying when they put a ban on the reel. Comfort to the enemy my bum, Lizzie was no traitor. That was a ruse. Whatever it is, this Coombes is in there somewhere - find him and it's my bet we will find out what has really been going on.'

They go to "Free BMD" - Births. Marriages and Deaths on the web.

'That he was fifty-three in 1846 is what we know from the ship's register. So he died after that.' Jane punches in what they know, searching the first five years till 1850 and bingo! A five star rated name comes up; Alfred Coombes, died third quarter, 1846. Surrey.

'Jot that page and folio number down', Jane says, 'we'll order the certificate'.

Both of them are on edge for the next few days. People did say they'd get hooked.

'It's like fishing', Rob reminds her. 'And we keep getting nibbles'.

'It's here', Jane yells out one morning a few days later just as Rob, in the bathroom, is negotiating those awkward bristly bits under his nose.

'Shit!' He yelps as the blood springs out. He flies down the stairs, dabbing at the tiny nick with a tissue.

Jane already has the envelope open.

'Ta... Ra!' she exclaims gleefully. 'August 6th. 1846. Alfred Coombes. PhD. F.R.S. 26. Orion Crescent. Narrowdown, Oxfordshire. Cause of death: Exsanguination (by self inflicted wound). Present at death: O. Coombes, daughter'.

'Suicide!' Rob exclaims and he blushes awkwardly - bled to death - ....' and Jane grips his hand, squeezes hard.

'Sshh!' she tells him, 'Sshh!' and the moment passes. 'So now what?' She closes her eyes, drums her fingers, deep in thought and then:

'Suicide... I wonder? Wasn't it illegal to kill yourself? In those days I mean, surely there'd be some sort of investigation?'

He grabs her by the waist.

'Once more the oracle! Coroner's Report; why didn't I think of that?'

'Do we know where is Narrowdown?' Jane asks.

Rob replies at once. 'I know it well, lived there once. Nearby anyway. It's on the Thames, or Isis as they call it up there. That narrow boat I told you about in my hippy days, nothing to eat but nasturtium leaves and wacky baccy for afters. No point in going there though. What we want surely is a local newspaper'.

'Colindale', Jane tells him. 'Newspaper Library near Hendon'. They've got the lot, even foreign papers'.

The Northern Line takes them straight there. Colindale, one of the many small villages that make up outer London, consisting mainly of a single busy main road lined by rows of semis, a park, some pubs, a scattering of Asian shops, a Greek deli, and a couple of caffs. The archive is across the road from the station.

'Ten o clock they open, I checked on the net', says Jane. 'Let's have a coffee, it's only twenty too'.

Polska Caffe, it says over the door, pensioner's getting their Full English, discount price, to last them all day, The Mirror and The Sun propped up against the brown sauce bottles. Lovely smell of frying bacon.

'Two coffees', Rob tells the man, 'please... you got decaf?'

At the Archive, Rob flashes his British Library card and they are in.

'Last time I was here it was all card index', he nods at the computer stations scattered around the room.

Jane picks up a leaflet.

'How to find a newspaper for a particular town', she reads out. 'That sounds like us'.

They soon get into it, daunting phrases such as "Integrated Catalogue" and "Subset" quickly becoming familiar.

Jane stabs a finger at the screen: "Jackson's Oxford Reporter" sounds a good bet'.

Jane brings up a list of dates. Types in the date of Coombes's death, and in half an hour, the item they order is delivered to their numbered seat.

'The real thing', says Rob in surprise. As, with difficulty, he lifts the file of newspapers. 'I was expecting a fiche or microfilm'. He hoists the heavy, stiff backed volume onto the rack provided on the desk in front of them and begins turning the brittle, yellowed pages.

'August sixth 1846 it said on the Death Certificate. So here we go', and they are both silent, eyes focused on the fading sheets of newsprint, as, page by page, the search goes on.

'Trouble is', Rob tells Jane, 'it's hard to resist sometimes stopping to read... look! See what I mean? Who could resist that?'

"Man Auctions Wife at Bicester Market: Alec Simpson of..." Jane slaps him on the wrist. 'Get on with it for God's sake, we've not got all day'.

Suddenly, towards the end of the quarter, there is an article, the one they are looking for. Jane, looking over Rob's shoulder, reads the highlights.

'Mr Alfred Coombes, lately released from Admiralty Commission. Verdict suicide, controversy concerning evidence, daughter to appeal verdict'.

'Jesus! Rob exclaims. 'Now we are getting somewhere, what does it say in your leaflet about making copies?'

They fill in the little slip, hand it to the attendant and go off to find the restaurant.

The coffee machine baffles them both.

'Press button, press button. Where the hell?' Rob steps back, hands on hips, defeated. A young girl, about ten, here with her Mammy, taps the screen with a delicate finger. The coffee gushes into the waiting cup.

'Button', she tells them.

'So, where are we?' Rob has the bit between his teeth, and Jane is happy for it.

'Appeal? Isn't it likely that the same paper would cover any appeal?'

'Yes', Rob's tone is tentative. 'But when? Could be months later, even years. What we need is an index. Let's ask'.

'No', the girl behind the desk is apologetic, 'not for provincial papers but "The Times" - it has an index going back years. Palmer's Index 1741 to 1905. If your event was in that bracket and important enough, depends'.

It takes them minutes to find the entry, which gives them a volume and a date. Half an hour later they have their item.

'Appeal Denied in Coombes Case'. They take it in turns to read.

Miss. Olive Coombes of Narrowdown was today refused Right of Appeal in the Crown Court Oxford. Her prayer was made in respect of the Coroner's Verdict of June 10th. 1846 when the Recorder investigating her father's death pronounced a verdict of Suicide. The Appeal Judge Mr Justice Knaresborough observed that subsequent to the Inquest the Recorder had placed a seventy-year restriction on his findings and this being so, an Appeal could not be heard at this present stage. Interviewed, Miss Coombes told The Times that she was convinced her father did not take his own life. It was she who found his body not half a mile from their home, and whereas the Coroner found massive loss of blood the principle cause of death, she herself noticed no blood at all when she found her father dead. Our correspondent reports that, according to a police source, the only weapon found near the body was the man's penknife, which his daughter said was the one he used to scrape the bowl of his pipe'.

'What about Maltese papers?' Jane asks. She sniffs her bacon butty and rolls her eyes in delighted anticipation. 'Whilst we are here. I don't know about you, but I think we've too many open questions, too many loose ends; we could do with resolving at least one of them. What are we looking at?'

She raises a thumb, joins her finger to it.

'One, your family tree: your father's father was born in 1845 and that's as far back as we go with that. Two: we know Thomas McSweeney was executed in 1845. Lizzie's dance or ballet tells the story of a boy who is hung and of a child being born. There just has to be a means by which I can convince you, er... and me too actually, that what I feel in my water is what really happened and before you shout women's intuition', she holds an admonishing hand up, 'pin your ears back and listen'. She does the thumb and finger trick again, pauses for breath.

'Thomas Baldacino is Thomas McSweeney's son. The girl who bore that son is the girl who, in the ballet, dies jumping off a cliff. I've said it before and I'll say it again---Lizzie is trying to tell us something in that ballet and to me at least, it could not be plainer'.

She sits back, looks at him. 'Well?'

'Malta Gazette', Rob says and they go back to the computer station. 'Integrated Catalogue, Subset, Newspapers, International. He rhymes off the various steps: 'Getting to be a dab hand at this', he says as the long list of available dates opens up.

'It's a good job they open late tonight', Jane looks at the clock on the wall as Rob patiently scrolls down on the microfilm. 'Gone five now and stop! Hold it! wind back, wind back slowly, and stop! What is that then?' Rob squares the article in the centre of the screen, adjusts the focus ring and there it is.

ABOUT WITH THE GLEANER

MAY 10th. 1886

Your Gazette last week gave us the spectacle of certain strident women parading with no apparent shame in the grounds of our beloved il Foso in pursuit of advantages, which your scribe for one finds quite objectionable. The Rights of Women, while always at the forefront of our political intentions, are surely best assured by the continued, careful considerations of our elected administrators than by a bunch of shrill and ill-informed women, no matter how sincere their motivation.

Today I can record a happier event not unconnected with the above audacity which will perhaps serve as a timely reminder of God's Intentions for women and of His never failing Compassion in the matter of their rights.

Miss Elizabeth Reardon, rising star in the entertainment world and travelling companion to the so called Suffragettes, gave birth last Saturday to a charming if noisy boy while under the patronage of Lord and Lady Brackley at San Anton Palace. Your gleaner can reveal that a suitable arrangement regarding the child has been formulated between the unfortunate girl and that well-known and respected Gentleman, Thomas Baldacino, RN. Captain of Her Majesty's Dockyard and his wife Hannah. Miss Reardon will sail for England, unaccompanied, in SS. Alaunia on the 30th inst. When she will continue in what promises to be a glittering career'.

'Yippee!' Jane shouts, covering her mouth and looking around apologetically.

'Well, bloody well! What time have we left?' says Rob with a grin, looking at his watch. 'Two whole hours and at the rate we are going we will crack it'.

They return the film and go back to the catalogue.

'Anything about 1846 is what we want', Jane says and the machine screams in protest as Rob scrolls hard over on the fast forward key.

'June, July, August, September, 1846', Rob yawns, stretches as Jane takes over. The machine's whirr slows and softens to a gentler pace as she delicately nudges and coaxes the film along.

'Getting near time', Rob says impatiently.

'I've got that certain feeling', Jane sings softly to the tune of an old pop song. Then, with a start, 'what's that? - Baldacino! - Mrs Baldacino!' She positions the article in the frame, zooms in and the article springs to life.

'*A Gift from God*', '*Is what Mrs Baldacino is reported to have said when a new born baby appeared on the doorstep of the cottage she shares with her husband Alfredo at Pinto Heights Valletta. Mr Baldacino had gone to milk his goat when he heard the unmistakable cry of an infant. He found the baby, warmly attired and secured to the trunk of a carob tree. The child's origins are unknown, but it is reported that the body of a young woman was also found later that same day, lying on the rocks at the foot of Pinto Heights. An autopsy has revealed that she had recently given birth. The two incidents are the subject of an ongoing investigation by the constabulary. Mrs Baldacino asserts the baby will be Christened Thomas, as that was the name found written on the child's forehead. She would neither confirm nor deny a neighbour's affirmation that the name had been written in blood.*'

Back at home in the comfort of their own surroundings, feet up, his arm about her shoulder, Rob and Jane go over the findings of the day.

'No wonder you have felt so much for Thomas over the years;' Jane sips her tonic water. It's almost as if you were truly related and I suppose their will be a legal term for it; your relationship, let's do a chart, get it all straight'. She gets out the sketchpad and begins to draw.

'We only need the male line, so - your father was Robert'. She begins the backward descent in time. 'One hundred and fifty years we are looking at, give or take. Let's see', she raises a thumb again and begins ticking them off. 'That's six monarchs worth. Two Queens and four Kings'.

'Fascinating', says Rob. 'But isn't it all conjecture? I mean, I can see your points and I'm as sure as you are that that's the way it was, and if it was then I am the great, great, step-grandson of Thomas McSweeney, if there is such a relationship. Perhaps that does explain my fascination, even fondness for him but what about Lizzie? Where did she learn the tale? Why is she involved? Why was she so concerned as to write it down in a dance?'

Jane interrupts his flow. 'Why was she leaned on? Why was her ballet banned?' They pause, gaze helplessly at each other.

'All we have is why's', Jane says. 'But somehow they are all connected. There must be a key'. Not for the first time they find themselves thinking and then saying the same thing.

'Coombes! Mr Alfred Coombes!' and Jane finishes it for them both. 'PhD. F.R.S. and suicide my arse!

Chapter Twenty Eight

If you had met Arnold Pilling in another age, the 1920s say, you'd have called him a card. The sort of fellow, who belts you on the back down the pub and who, although you hardly know him, calls everybody squire. A short, ruddy man, who wears - and this is long after Harold Wilson -one of those silly macs that made a Yorkshire valley famous. Add to this a hat, an actual pork pie hat, and you will know at who we are looking.

He comes up the subway steps at ten to nine every morning, waits with that scattering of early arrivals, for the lights to change. The Prime Minister rolls up on his bike of course... and here comes the old muck raker - the one they call The Beast, with his out of date haircut, demob suit, his lunch time butties dangling in a Tesco's shopping bag - on his way to work like anybody else. Arnold falls in step behind him as they pass by the striding bronze bulk of Winston Churchill. There is Emily Pankhurst with her finger raised and Nelson Mandela, the latest addition, the legend, still living.

'Morning squire'. We may suppose Arnold nods, familiarly to each one as he passes.

At The Green, the MP's veer left as a smiling bobby opens the Member's Gate. Arnold carries on to enter, along with the common herd, via The Old Yard, and thus to the Jubilee Café where he sneaks a miniature whisky into his latte and settles himself to observe the Member's Lobby where, already, as Big Ben bongs the hour, small groups are dotted here and there like kids at some school yard game. Satellites about a central moon. Shifting, murmuring over this or that motion, amendment paper or pending Division.

Arnold Pilling is not a prizewinner. He will not be seen on the box, hosting *Have I Got News?* or airing his views on *Question Time*. Suburban syndicates are his meat and drink. He is good at that and after thirty years of phone calls, assignations, pub crawls, he is on speaking terms with just about every provincial editor this side of Cape Wrath, as well as a few 'over the pond' to employ his own vernacular.

The couple opposite are familiar to him - the bloke is anyway. Arnold watches as they sip their coffee, good coffee here. He is pleased when they are pleased.

'Mmm!' Jane says grinning at Rob over her cup. 'More like it!'

Arnold eyes them again. He definitely knows the bloke. Yes. Seen him…Yes! Got him! He gets up from his perch and goes across. Never backward at coming forward, Mister Pilling.

Rob is embarrassed. He always is. They'll say, 'Oh! I've read them all. Your books. And the film, " Perpendicular?" Wow!'

And Rob is left wondering which book, what incident, which film and then, always, they'll say, 'What's your latest about?' As if he knew and 'God knows' he'll say to himself, signing the bit of paper 'for the missus'.

'Robert Reardon I presume?' Arnold sticks out a hand.

'You look lost... Pilling...Arnold Pilling, Press'.

They shake hands.

'My wife Jane', Rob offers and, 'yes, we are in awe. Waiting for our MP…' he trails off.

'Doing the tour are you?' the newsman asks as Rob begins to get fidgety.

Jane puts a hand on Rob's thigh. He glances at her, catches the raised eyebrow.

'Prime Minister's Questions', he volunteers. 'We hope, today being Wednesday, and then, well, a bit of research. Not!' he forestalls the question, 'for a book'. He finishes lamely.

Another man appears suddenly at their table, pin striped suit, Guard's tie over Turnbull Asher shirt, even the bloody carnation Jane observes and Christ! The greying sideburns! Do they open a box or what?

Arnold gives Jane his card.

'Anything I can do', and he is off across the stone flagged floor towards the Press Gallery.

'Bloody man!' The Right Hon. Percy Arnstable - Swift, MP, twitches with two fingers the spotless white handkerchief poking its nose from a top pocket.

'Vultures. All of them. Banging on. Practically invented the expense account'. He leads them into the great Westminster Hall, pointing out the hammer roof, the brass commemorative plaques: Warren Hastings tried and acquitted. Sir Thomas More getting his head chopped off.

'We English have a long tradition of pillory when it comes to our public servants'. The Honourable Member leads them up the great stairway and into the care of a Sergeant at Arms who directs them to their seats just in time to hear The Speaker set Mr Cameron onto Mr Brown for the weekly ding dong.

'Childish!' Is Jane's opinion as they make their way to The Terrace. 'Bloody school boys. 'Oh. Yes you did. Oh. No I didn't!'

157

Arnstable - Swift serves them himself. Weaving in and out of the crowded tables, a tray held aloft. They sit in the sun and watch a barge glide by. Across the water is the hospital balcony of recent memory; to their left The Embankment where Rob's blood still stains the pavements.

She reaches out and takes his hand in hers.

'Now', says their MP. 'The other matter. I have discussed this with Her Majesty's Keeper of Records at Kew PRO and it would appear that the reason you are being denied access to the documents you seek is that they are still subject to Public Interest Immunity'.

Jane interrupts. 'We looked at that', she says, 'and it does not make sense. The original gag... then called Crown Privilege, was set at seventy years, which meant we could have seen the thing in 1915'.

Their advisor is beginning to look uncomfortable. Something is up here. Rob glances at Jane who presses her point.

'OK! Let's say nobody is interested. All those years. No call for it, as it were. But we are interested now, and what about Freedom of Information?'

The Honourable Gentleman shifts in his seat, cornered.

'Oh dear! I do fear something is up as you say Robert'. He spreads his hands, hesitates. 'Appeals dear boy. The Crown has appealed on three separate occasions over the years and has been successful in extending the period of immunity by the maximum of seventy years on each occasion'.

Rob jumps in.

'Latest appeal?'

'Nineteen eighty-five'.

They walk down the Embankment towards Millbank, cut into Horseferry road and sit at a small round table soaked in sun under a coloured waterfall of banked spring flowers that hang from baskets set into the windowed arches of a typical London pub.

'Pages Bar', Rob notes the inn sign over the door. 'Who he I wonder?'

'The street', Jane points to the street sign in its distinctive red white and black enamel. 'Page Street'. She shakes her head, smiles at him and cocks her wrist to scan her watch. 'Five thirty he said'.

With that the pub door swings open and there he is: Pork pie hat, daft mac and, in one hand, a half drained pint.

Rob winks at Jane.

'What's your poison?' the reporter says and they just about manage a straight face between them as he skips back into the pub.

'Is he real or what?' Jane says.

They sit in the sun; the waiter brings their drinks, the bustle of Westminster all around them as the couple fill the other man in. Arnold listens carefully, jotting a note here and there in florid shorthand and a good two hours go by before they all walk together towards the tube at Pimlico.

'So!' Arnold exclaims. Pausing to stroke his considerable nose. 'Interesting' Jane always swore afterwards that she actually saw the nose twitch, seeking the faintest whiff of a story.

'Basically', he has his fingers steepled like a preacher, 'all you are doing is your family tree?'

Rob nods.

'And you are stuck at what? Great Grandfather? Great-great? Something like that, but then your Granny, Lizzie - and I do like the sound of her - she has, or so you believe, some sort of a connection'. He pauses again, wags his supplicant fingers up and down, forcing the thought. 'A connection, possibly, with a guy who appears to top himself, and about whose death, for some reason', he pauses, 'we are being kept in the dark'.

They come to a halt at the Drummond street entrance to Pimlico Tube Station.

Arnold Pilling is still sniffing.

'One never knows', He says and Jane and Rob again exchange glances. 'Topicality!' He turns to Rob. 'You're a writer, you know the score. If you can get your tale, no matter how old, wrapped around a current event... similar event?' The couple nod politely.

'Think Iraq', he suggests. 'Think Weapons of Mass Destruction', he waves them goodbye with it, head on one side, quizzical. 'A suicide? A Coroner? A Gagging Notice? Send me what you've got and I'll write it'. He pats his pockets as the dialling tone of his mobile starts to do its nut. Finding it at last, he speaks into it.

'Ah! Norman! Just the man!' he places a hand over the mouthpiece, raises an arm in a farewell salute to Rob and Jane, points apologetically at the telephone, and waddles off up the road, deep in earnest conversation with a man across the water in Ireland.

Chapter Twenty Nine

'Good morning sir', Norman Daly offers a fresh, clean napkin to the minister. A slim man, good looking, tanned, nervously dashing about on the balls of his feet A worried man too by the look of him and no wonder, Norman thinks to himself, with half his cabinet set to knife him. As he was telling Mary, his missus, that very morning at breakfast.

'They're all there, all the top dogs, all night sittings and getting no nearer and that's Ireland for you. Talk and talk and Sinn Fein won't trust the DUP and vice bloody versa. Still fighting over the Boyne they are, battling with pikes. Nothing changes'.

'It'd be different', Mrs Daly smoothes her pinafore, 'If only that lovely Mo Mowlan was still at the castle. She'd jolly them up'.

'And Good Morning to you Norman, and how is Mrs. Daly today'? the man, zipping his fly with a flourish, takes the towel and drops a pound coin in the little saucer.

'She's fine sir - and good luck with the voting'. Norman watches as his first customer of the day strides purposefully away, ever the statesman, on show, even here where all men really are truly equal.

The copper pipes gleam like old gold. Ceramic surfaces spotless. Pure white hand towels arranged attractively on marbled basin tops. Mirrors gleam, reflecting and deflecting the soft glow of concealed lighting. Norman takes off his protective pinafore, dons a smart white jacket, adjusts his bow tie and stands, hands neatly folded, as he listens for approaching footsteps, ready, at the exact instant, to fling open the door to his distinguished clients: Prime Ministers, Presidents, Secretaries of State, Aides de Camp. He has seen them all and each one, eventually, after all the in fighting, negotiation, compromise, will stand here, in Norman's emporium, legs splayed, prick in hand, pissing contentedly in the common pot.

Norman discreetly turns a bright brass tap to allow a small tinkling dribble into a pristine bowl. The man with the beard, blinking like an owl behind thick framed glasses, head bowed over the urinal, relaxes and allows his own tinkling dribble to follow suit.

'It's nerves'. Norman tells his wife. 'All pent up they are and some of them do have that little difficulty. I do my best. Part of the job'.

Norman proffers a napkin, smiling sympathetically as the other man removes his spectacles, polishes each lens carefully. His eyes, the attendant notes, close up and without the glasses are softer, kinder than you see on the telly. You just cannot imagine him squinting down the barrel of a rifle or priming a bomb with those lily-white hands.

'Thanks Norman', the man says, his heavy Ulster accent echoing among the marble walls as he lets the door swing shut behind him.

Norman has been in the job most of his working life, but got quite worried when the AIDS scare came along and they began boarding up the old establishments. Cleanliness; that was his hallmark, soap, hot water, disinfectant, and lashings of Brasso. Like a palace, his last place was. Everybody said so. A shining, underground palace and he knew most of the regulars: Lawyers from the Courts nearby; teachers from the college; a banker. The usual rough trade of course, as well as the odd rent boy. Scrubbing off the graffiti from the backs of cubicle doors was one of his more interesting - if often disgusting - tasks. Lurid drawings, requests for assignations, lists of predilections, some to make Norman laugh, a few to turn his stomach.

'Takes all sorts', he would tell his wife and, the very soul of discretion, he'd put a finger to his lips and wink.

Then the big job came along and he jumped at it. Suited him and of course Mrs. Daly welcomed the promotion.

Every couple of days Norman will get on the blower, letting on discreetly to one or another of his many friends and media contacts: Who's come, who's gone, who's not speaking to whom, whose threatening to resign. The little brown envelopes that pop through their letterbox are much appreciated and the contents, under Mary's supervision, go straight into their savings account at the post office.

Meanwhile in London, at his desk, Arnold Pilling is writing up his copy. He has already sounded out the most likely buyer, and he is confident The Telegram will take it on. Even so, that twitching nose of his, sensing danger, does appear to be trying to tell him something. Scrap it perhaps? Bollocks! Good story like that? The lawyers will sort it. He presses on.

Jane opens one eye. Rob is just creeping in through the bedroom door. He has not drawn the curtains thank God, one of the first things she taught him. He has brought her a cup of tea. A cup of tea? He never brings her tea. Something is up.

'What's up', she cries as he drops the paper on the bed.

"IRISH FAMINE—ENGLAND CULPABLE?" she reads the headline.

They scan the report together, Jane reading out loud the main points.

'Evidence emerging... a poisonous weed... genocide...young sailor hung... mysterious suicide... Christ! He's got the whole lot in! Talk about a can of worms!'

The phone rings. Jane picks it up, recognising the estuary English straight away.

'There may well be... er... repercussions I fear',

'It's him', Jane puts a hand over the mouthpiece, nodding at the newspaper lying open on the bed.

'I will resist all and any attempts, be assured of that, to name you as my source. That's what they'll be after, my source. They can't, dare not touch me though they will make things hot. Basically of course you – we - have done nothing wrong but it's the times you see, current events, political manoeuvring going on. Peace talks at a delicate stage. Anything, any item reflecting on Ireland, on England's attitudes. Past, present, future, true or false. Anything likely to upset any tentative balance. Anything they may be forced to acknowledge for the sake of peace. If one of those political factions can find a way to gain a political advantage over the other, if they can be given a lever they can use to destabilise the opposition, they will not hesitate to use it. Just think what the Irish Catholic majority would make of it!'

'But it's all so long ago', Jane interrupts. 'Past. Forgotten'.

'The Irish', Arnold tells her solemnly, 'never forget'.

Chapter Thirty

Tracy Kennet concentrates on trying not to blink too much as the flash and glare of a moving wall of cameras attacks her from every angle. Careful study of her face in the bathroom mirror has convinced her that blinking, combined with the exaggerating thickness of her bifocal specs, gives her the appearance of a startled owl. Facial spots don't help her image either and the awful frock her mother has insisted on, is, she has decided, the ultimate insult, the keenest betrayal in all the fourteen long years of her insufferable life. Winning first prize ought to be thrilling and she has willed herself to be thrilled but how can she be? How can anything be thrilling when life is so cruel?

She looks up at the stage and there he is, her love, the only love of her life. Forever. She glances to her left, to the poised grown woman at his side, his bitch wife, as she stands and applauds her man. The knife twists and turns in the very core of Tracy's being. She blinks and blinks again as the tears start.

'It's the cameras', she assures her mother. 'I'm fine'.

On the podium, Rob raises a hand and the noise subsides. He is wearing the corduroy jacket, jeans, and a spotted bow tie. Jane's marketing.

'More writerish', she tells him.

'More twatish', his reply.

"Write Early," he begins, 'goes from strength to strength'. He pauses to let the audience catch on. Acknowledges the groans with a grin. 'Exactly! Cliché! Awful easy cliché, so what do we do?' A hundred voices, young eager voices bellow it out.

'Show. Don't tell!' They yell out the mantra. 'And if you have to use a cliché make it your own'.

'Right, so that's my speech done for yet another year. Now for the prize winners and always remember, we can't all be winners...' He cocks an ear to the crowd.

'But we can try!' the children shout.

Tracy does what she has to do as she smiles, touches his hand, receives her prize, and as she turns away and descends the steps, Jane, seated in the front row, shudders suddenly and almost recoils as if from an icy blast as she finds herself looking straight into the hell of the young girl's eyes.

'That girl', she begins as Rob, concerned, puts his arm around her.

'You ok?' he asks, 'you look…'

'No, I am not ok', she shudders again and Rob holds her close.

'Was it something I said?'

'That girl! Is she, is she…alright..?' Jane repeats.

'Trace? My prodigy? Fourteen going on forty? Well no, she's not alright, a bit weird actually, but she can write'. He shakes his head in admiration. 'She will be good, I mean really good, and if the last ten years of Write Early has only produced a talent like hers then it will have been worth it'.

The press are waiting for them as they leave the building. Questions from all angles, the usual stuff, fodder for a few remote columns in even more remote tabloids. Rob recognises the man from *The Mail.* He is surprised to see a national turning up.

'Will you resign?' asks the reporter and before Rob can answer, 'Is it true you have refused to submit yourself for a C.R.B check in respect of your involvement with young persons'.

Rob grabs Jane's hand, pushes the man aside roughly; they both turn, startled as the camera flash blinds them. A hovering taxi pulls up and they stumble inside.

'Bloody newspapers', the cab driver turns to them. 'Where to mate?'

Back at their own home Jane brings Rob his coffee. They sit in the garden under the apple tree they planted when they first moved in. All those years, she muses. They have been so lucky. Why have they been so lucky?

'Did you?' she asks. 'Refuse?'

'What? The Criminal Records thing? Yes! I bloody well did refuse! Wouldn't you? Nosey bastards! I told them if you want to know whether I am a paedophile or not, ask me. I'll tell you no and that will be that. How dare they investigate me behind my back? I have done nothing wrong. Bloody fascists!'

'Still', Jane says. 'They will wonder won't they? I mean…'

'Let them wonder!' he bursts out and he is very angry. 'They can bloody well lock me up if they want. I will not bow down to their squalid diktat!'

The leaves on the apple tree ripple with a sudden gust of wind causing pink white clusters of blossom to become detached and fall like snow on the manicured green of the lawn. She shudders, pulls her cardigan up around her shoulders.

'Getting cold', she says. 'Bed time'.

Chapter Thirty One

Jane awakes first. The sound of tyres on the gravel of their driveway. A squealing of brakes. Voices, commands, car doors banging. A beam of light sweeps over the window, then bang! The front door is rammed in.

'Stay where you are!' a voice screams out. 'Do not move!'

The clump of feet on the stairway. Their bedroom door opening.

'Police'! a woman's voice, quiet now, polite, at odds with the rudeness of the entry.

She speaks without entering the room.

'Will you get dressed ma'am, and then come with me downstairs? And Mr Reardon, will you also get dressed? We will require you to come to the station'.

Rob has seen it before. On the telly, the Bill bring in the suspect, usually assumed to be guilty. He sits opposite the two officers, the old formula: one of them kind, understanding, a real Father Christmas, the other a bastard.

'We have it all stitched up', the bastard says. 'Christ! You are in the shit aren't you?'

He shoves a photograph across the little table and Rob can feel his own isolation. They are so sure. Whatever it is they are after. What are they after? Why so sure?

'I want my lawyer', he tells the man and 'of course you do', is the reply. 'She is coming. We have phoned her, she said she was on her way – traffic - what can you do?' He shrugs in a gesture of mock helplessness.

'Just look at the photo, do no harm, while we wait'.

Rob looks down. It is the girl. Tracy. His star pupil.

Outside, from the corridor, comes the tap, tap, tapping of approaching feet. There is a murmuring at the door and a smart young woman, soberly dressed, pops her head in enquiringly.

'Ah!' she says and takes a seat at the table.

'My client will not answer any of your questions until I have had a chance to talk to him in private and I will take the opportunity now to tell you that we will make a formal objection to all the police actions that have thus far taken place this morning'.

Rob's lawyer is brisk as she taps a small sheaf of documents on the tabletop.

'And when this matter is resolved to the benefit of my client, we will of course commence immediate proceedings on his behalf in the matter of reparation'.

'Oh dear', says the policeman with a stifled yawn.

Bailed in his own recognition, Rob walks unsteadily out into the car park. His lawyer, Janet, click clacks alongside him on surprisingly unprofessional high heels. He can hear the swish of her black stocking thighs under her modest black skirt. In the car park she fiddles with the remote, the car doors give out their usual satisfactory clunk, the lights flash.

'OK?' she queries.

'I could do with a drink', Rob says.

Jane meets them as the car draws up at their front gate. She runs out to greet them and flings her arms around Rob as he and the lawyer walk up the drive.

'What?' she asks, looking from him to the lawyer and back again.

'What the bloody hell...?'

'Let's see', Janet plonks her brief case down on the settee beside her while Jane stares blankly at Rob.

'The girl is alleging improper conduct', the other woman says as she rifles through her collection of A4 sheets. 'Fondling apparently, breasts and so on?'

Jane gasps. 'That girl? That girl... Tracy was it? I knew... something!'

Rob looks up at her sharply.

'Something!' he thunders. 'You believe this shit?'

Jane is embarrassed as she realises how her reaction, her immediate assumption has cut him. She is his wife for God's sake. She has to be on his side. Doesn't she?

The lawyer intervenes.

'Let's get it all out. Let's get it on the table. All that they have'.

'All? Jane replies incredulously. 'How much more is there?'

'You got any coffee?' Janet asks as she crosses her long legs making herself comfy.

Jane glowers at her and at Rob as she goes to the kitchen.

'What we have is…. on the girl's side, is….ah! here it is - the fondling. Over some considerable time... since she was ten?' His lawyer looks up at Rob. 'You paid her... she alleges you paid her, five pounds a time, on… several she says, several occasions.

Jane bangs the coffee pot down on the glass-topped table.

'For fucks sake!'

Rob has his hands over his face.

'I need a drink', he mutters and his voice is a desperate plea.

Jane turns on him in her anger, opens her mouth to speak. Thinks better of it.

'What's the use?' she mutters, utter disgust in her tone.

'And of course,' the lawyer presses on. 'There is the computer evidence... the alleged web sites. Have you downloaded? Are you in the habit...?

'No!' Rob bursts out. 'Never! Not once. I've had some spam... who hasn't? But, no I…'

Jane cannot contain herself.

'How do you know that?' she asks reasonably.

Janet looks at them both.

'Is there something I should know?' The silent pause is palpable, prolonged, until Jane, with a sigh, answers.

'He... we... are alcoholics. I don't drink. He doesn't, mostly anyway but...'

'I have slipped,' Rob owns up ruefully. 'A couple of times in twenty bloody years... two times in fact, but I would know – of course I would know!'

'Well,' his lawyer is calm, matter of fact. 'I take it you deny these charges? All of them?' Rob nods while Jane eyes him carefully. She continues to stare at him, at his face, shocked, ashen. At his hands shaking now as he places a flat palm to his forehead, an old familiar gesture, one of dozens she knows so well. Loves so well. This is the man she loves. She would know.

'I know', she tells him as he turns to her and she buries him in her arms, patting his back and shoulders. Soothing, murmuring. A mother with her child.

'I know'. She repeats softly. 'I know'.

Janet, the solicitor, in her smart suit, manly cravat, chiselled composure, clicks shut the combination locks on her smart leather brief case, crosses and then uncrosses her legs, coughs discreetly.

'Have you', she enquires of Rob, 'pissed on anybody's chips lately? Any enemies?' She delves in the depths of her handbag as her mobile goes off with a vengeance. Purse, compact, an embroidered handkerchief, note book, lipstick, all go flying until she finds the phone and puts it to her ear.

'Sorry', she mouths to the couple and then into the phone, 'Arnold who? Pilling?' she raises an eyebrow at Rob who nods. 'Well, I am representing him', she goes on. 'His solicitor. Yes he is here...' and as Rob shakes his head, puts both hands up, mouthing a silent but distinct 'No!' the lawyer, ignoring him, addresses the phone.

'Tell me', she says and resting a notepad on her knee, begins to take notes as the voice drones on at the other end. Her shorthand, both Rob and Jane note, is as swift and efficient as she herself as she nods, agrees, questions. Finally, folding the phone, she places it neatly in its little black pouch and leaning back in her chair, consults her notes.

'There appears to be, according to Mr Pilling, some considerable regret over the manner in which you have been treated. He is of the opinion that, were the police as confident in their evidence as their conduct towards you would suggest, they would have nailed you by now. You would not be out on bail and the story would at the very least be either leaking, or else a full press release would have been issued. Evidently forces beyond the police remit are taking an interest, and he himself has detected signs which indicate to him that his own best interests will not be served by his continued involvement'.

'Rat!' Jane explodes. 'Talk about a sinking ship!'

Rob, far from downhearted at the news, appears positively cheerful.

'I think', he says. 'That if I were writing this story, my knight in shining armour would be girding his lusty loins and mounting his trusty steed just about now. And if that is a cliché or two, then fuck it!'

Chapter Thirty Two

Joseph Boniface Scicluna is not a priest. He looks like a priest: sober suited, black cloth, black shoes highly polished. A seminarian perhaps? There are many about in the Enclave. Young men of all and every nation, fresh faced, eager. They criss-cross the great square, in and out of the hallowed halls, via certain doors and portals through some of which not even a Bishop's Crucifix could gain admission.

Joseph – Joe to his colleagues – admires his reflection in the mirror, straightens his tie, spits on his palms, and smoothes his black hair. The girl watches him silently from the bed. Her legs are spread, her hair, tousled about her pretty face is fiery red against the whiteness of the pillow. Her eyes, he notes, are deepest blue.

He strides over to the bed and takes out a billfold. He counts, 'One, two, three hundred?' She shrugs, reaching out a hand to brush the fly of his trousers. He grins. Bends suddenly to kiss the soft russet triangle between her legs and then, turning abruptly, he leaves, closing the door softly behind him.

The taxi edges carefully through the crowds that are already forming in the early sun. Along via Greggoria, under the great arches of Porta Coreleggio, it rattles over the cobbles of a dark back lane and stops beside an iron studded oak door to which, incongruous in these ancient surroundings, is affixed that modern day replacement for the original Swiss Guard—the swipe card receptor. Joseph pays the taxi driver and fishes under his shirt for the plastic card. As usual it takes three or more swipes and a deal of cursing before a soft click is heard and the door swings open.

The curator is a nun. A Carmelite. Not much older than himself and Joseph, remembering the excesses of the previous night is conscious of his own shame. Will she see? Can she smell the sex on him? Will she chastise him? He has a quick memory of Sister Agatha and he, a boy of ten, bent over the stool. The swish of the cane. The incantation stuttering from the depths of the old woman's hatred as: 'Dolor ea Buen!' she hissed. 'Pain is Good!'

'Morning Joe', the curator greets him cheerily, peering up at him. 'You look like shit. Had a busy night?'

They call her Miss Moneypenny and her boss, him in the inner sanctum, is of course known as 'M'.

Her given name is Margaret, Sister Margaret of the Little Sisters, and she has everything ready: flight tickets, briefing, target details, hotel reservations.

'You will be met at Heathrow - look for the badge' and automatically Joe touches his own lapel. 'Yes', she says, ' I see you have yours the right way up for a change'. She reaches out, straightens the little lizard anyway and for a moment he thinks she will kiss him. He closes his eyes. 'Read the brief on the plane, it's all you need'.

She pats him on top of his head. Good little boy. Dismissed.

'I'll get it'. Jane sings out from the kitchen as the doorbell goes through its maddening repertoire yet again. She yanks the door open. Forces a smile. At first she thinks Mormons? Jehovah's? But they always come in pairs. He *is* all in black though, and then she sees the badge.

'The little lizard is a Chameleon, adopted by the Carmelites, it is a symbol associated with the Virgin Mary, and it is also used by The Rujarjanti'. Joe has made himself comfortable by the fire.

'Good coffee this... not bitter'.

Jane smiles.

'Now who or what is Rujarjanti?'

Joe laughs out loud.

'Well, I'm one for a start - the modern version. A kind of policeman really - the Vatican KGB some say. We are not priests; we may not be particularly religious. The Vatican is a sovereign state, and like all states we have our secret services. Think CIA without the missiles'.

He helps himself to another scone, butters it carefully, liberally, bites into it with obvious delight.

'And where', Rob asks, 'do we come in?'

'Ah! Yes. Well, you are in trouble. The source of your trouble is of interest to us. You hurt and we hurt. I am here to stop the hurt'.

Jane has brought in the badge she found in Lizzie's trunk and she lays it on the table. Joe unpins his own badge and places it alongside hers.

'The lizard', he says. 'Our common ground, and you recognised it straight away. Mine is the simple model, just the little beast, no ornamentation, but yours - that is to say Lizzie's -well, I'll give you the heraldic words – *"a fess vert charged with a reptile argent between three boars passant sable."* That's a silver lizard on a green stripe surrounded by three boars. More or less. Now then...' He is teasing them. 'Who do you know who would have boars for an emblem?'

Jane is ahead of him.

'Pigs? Swine...? Sweeney! She shouts it out in celebration. 'Tom, our Thomas, son of the Sweeney!'

'And you know the story, most of it anyway and of course you must then know why you are up to your neck at this moment. You are not the first - Thomas himself, Lizzie, the botanist Coombes. All three silenced, the two men for what they knew and your friend Lizzie for trying to find out. Which is where you are - on the point of being silenced - and our interest? The church? It's complicated, but briefly, we - and I mean our intelligence services - we are a bit like Edgar Hoover, we know the dirt on many things: On people, on governments, on situations. We concentrate a good deal of our efforts on it. Remember, we have no army, no ships, no fighter planes. What we do have is a massive network of details, potentially embarrassing, compromising details, which we can and do use, via our diplomatic branches, to... let us say... lean on people. Blackmail them if you like. And we are successful'.

'And what about your own dirt?' Jane cannot help putting in. 'Bent priests, the collusion with dodgy regimes. Pius Twelfth and Hitler for God's sake'.

Joe puts his hands up. 'Mea culpa, mea culpa. Any more of that coffee about?'

Rob puts a hand on Jane's, gives it a squeeze.

'I think he's a friend, love, although I'm not sure why'.

Joseph ladles sugar into his cup. Sips.

'Yes but what does he want?' Jane will not let it go. 'What can he do?'

'Let's start with what *they* want', Joseph is calm, business like. 'They being the authorities, the British police, or whoever is controlling them. We are talking Ireland! The curse of Ireland! England's bed of nails for centuries. And here and now, as we speak, peace talks at Hillsborough Castle. Peace! In sight! After all those years and those very talks hanging on a thread. Concessions being given. Blind eyes being turned. Murderers let out of prison. They just cannot afford the embarrassment, none of them. The shocking impact of the headlines. Just think what the media would make of it if they got a sniff of the possibility that a British government, no matter how long ago, had sanctioned... nay, instigated, chemical warfare and genocide. The Maltese fungus Thomas told us about, the involvement of the Navy, the dodgy suicide of a man who knew too much. The story is as virulent, even if only symbolically, now as it was in reality then. It's potential to poison is not diminished by time. Of course, we, the Holy Church, would like to keep it that way. A very useful diplomatic tool that strange little weed has been!'

'So, I take it', says Rob, 'you can magic away my little troubles if I keep my mouth shut?'

'Exactly! We have already put a hold on the false charges. Oh, yes! We are quite powerful when we want to be. In fact, and not to put to fine a point on things, I really do urge you to go along while you can. Things change rapidly in my business'.

Rob closes his eyes, trying to reckon the angles.

'What if I do "go along" and then - at a later date say - spill the beans anyway?'

Joseph reaches out with both arms across the little coffee table. He puts a hand gently on the cheek of each of his two companions. He sighs softly. His voice is a whisper.

'Do you remember Pope John Paul the First? Was he or wasn't he? Did he or didn't he? The conspiracy theories?' He begins to squeeze each cheek. He is a big man naturally, but the relaxed demeanour, which made him palatable, even friendly, has gone. His eyes, flicking one to the other, first Jane and then Rob, are spheres of ice in a face of stone.

'We got away with that didn't we?' He smiles now, the friendly, boyish grin returning.

'Let's be friends, after all we go back a long way. Oh, yes'. He notes Rob's quizzical look. He picks up the McSweeney badge. 'Did I tell you how your grandmother Lizzie got this?'

He has their attention again.

'You will have recognised my Maltese origins from my name, Scicluna? Common, as you may know in those islands. We are in fact the relics of a once great Sicilian noble family. My great grandfather, Phillip, was a Rujarjanti, of the old school, in Malta, and his father attended Tom McSweeney at his incarceration and at his death. He was also Thomas's controller in collaboration with the fledgling Fenian Brotherhood of Ireland. Anyway, family letters suggest that Phillip met and fell in love with Lizzie who was living in his sister's house at San Anton. This would be in 1886. He could not declare his affection of course, since he was wedded to the church. It is doubtful she ever knew. Nor, it seems, would she know just who her benefactors were in later life.

Jane gets to the point first while Rob is still evaluating what they have just been told.

'So it was Phillip who gave Lizzie the badge? And...the story? He told her the story!' She turns to Rob. 'The ballet...'

'Ah! The ballet', Joe chimes in. 'That was her undoing. They closed her down you know?'

'We gathered', Jane agrees.

'She never worked the stage again. Cut off at the height of what should have been a brilliant career. All her hard work. Abused by her father, her child wrenched from her by unfortunate circumstance, abandoned by her husband. She became ill. When the Brotherhood found her she was in a Lunatic Asylum, sectioned on trumped up evidence, languishing indefinitely to await the Royal Pleasure.

He looks up sharply at Jane's cry.

'Oh. God!' She covers her face, weeping uncontrollably, her head buried in Rob's shoulder. He holds her to him, comforting her as she has so often comforted him. It is his turn. Years have passed by since they first made their pact. Their common enemy has been held at bay by their common need and together they have fought it. Yes, he has been the weaker, and when he has fallen she has lifted him. They have embraced their recovery together, absorbed the rules so that acting as one person has become the most natural thing to do. In all circumstances. Together they are strong, but one of the rules means that they can never both be weak at the same time. It was her turn for strength and now it is his and he holds her close.

'Sorry! Sorry', she says, recovering though still shaky. 'Thanks', taking the handkerchief Rob hands her.

'Don't know where all that came from'. She blows her nose, stares fixedly into space, remembering. 'Well, I do know, I mean, really. I do know. I have felt her you know, little things, over the past months, felt her near to us, to you actually'. She turns to Rob. 'Genes I suppose'.

'Which', says Joseph, 'is perhaps another way of saying reincarnation'.

'So, really', Rob sits on the edge of his chair. 'The Catholic Church has been just as anxious as the British government to keep this aspect of the Irish Famine secret. They want to keep quiet the fact that a chemical agent was possibly used by the British Government to starve a million Catholics to death'?

Joseph spreads his hands, shrugs.

'Not only that', Rob presses on, 'but the subsequent deaths? Two that we know about. What about the botanist? What happened there?'

Joe shrugs his shoulders once again. Rob can see the Maltese in him, the gesture, one of many employed in that country, the open palms, the innocent plea. "Alora! What can you do?'

'The Brits took care of Mister Coombes'. He says finally.

Rob is not satisfied.

'So', he says again, 'I get lucky because the church finds it expedient to keep the lid on one of its dark secrets'.

'It's our ace in the hole, surely you can see that', Joe counters. 'And yes, it is the only reason. Your nightmare is already over. We are assured by the police that the facts leading to your arrest are provisionally acknowledged to be mistaken, an enquiry will be held, compensation may be offered. Relax, take it easy'.

'And the girl?' Jane asks. 'Tracy?'

'Guilty!' Joseph says at once. 'Of a schoolgirl crush. Aggravated of course by some fancy scripting by your tormentors. She's all right. She'll get over it. A good Catholic girl'.

They say their goodbyes at the door, Jane and Rob follow Joe down the drive to where his car awaits.

'Compensation? You mentioned?' Jane begins.

'Oh, yes', Joseph grins. 'Get what you can, just ask, you will get it. All you have to do is keep your mouth shut.

Chapter Thirty Three

Jane's mobile begins its relentless racket the moment she shuts the door. She runs through to the sitting room, locates her handbag and grabs the phone by the scruff of its neck.

'Ugh!' she glares at it, presses the tit to shut it up and then, sweetly. 'Hello?'

Rob watches her as she takes the call.

'Mmm. Yes. I see. Great! Yes, yes, we'll certainly do that'.

She puts the phone back in her handbag while Rob waits impatiently.

'What?' he asks.

'The niece', she begins. 'At Lizzie's death, present at death it said, d'you remember? M. Hancock? Well, that was the fortune hunter fellow, Ted. She's turned up, and as she may have a claim on Lizzie's effects, he thought we would like to know'. She goes to the file, finds the death certificate, points out the entry to Rob.

'M. Hancock, and her name is Maureen'.

The District Line takes them to Richmond where they alight and head up the hill, past the Poppy works, to the magnificent bulk of The Royal Star and Garter Home with its superb views over the bridge and the Thames.

'What a place to end it all', Jane exclaims as they pause to take in the view.

'And what, may one ask', says Rob, 'did she do to deserve such splendour?'

'Whatever it was, she got the BEM. for it', Jane is a bit sharp, 'twenty odd years in the Queen Alexandra's Army Nursing Corps, lost a leg in Borneo. She's eighty bloody four. On her own. What do you want?'

They are met at the main door by a nursing sister who escorts them to the terrace.

'She's so excited over your visit', the nurse tells them. 'She's got photographs, letters, all sorts'. She points to a small table around which three chairs have been placed, one of which is occupied by the lady herself.

She is old, of that there is no doubt, but she is straight, neat, disciplined. A colourful handkerchief is tied about her hair. Carefully polished shoes, sensible shoes, poke out from under a long floral skirt giving no hint of a missing limb. Her chin rests lightly upon hands clasped about a stout walking stick and, as Rob and Jane approach, she cocks her head slightly to one side to welcome them as they make their way over the manicured lawn. A beaming smile lights up her face.

Rob hesitates and Jane tugs at his arm.

'What is it? She hisses, still quite annoyed with him.

'My next novel', he tells her. 'I've just seen the opening paragraph'.

'Call me Mo'. The old lady instructs, offering a rouged cheek. 'They all do', she fusses, making sure they are comfortable. 'I've ordered tea and scones and she'll bring them in a minute, but I thought scones would be nice - they were Betty's favourite'.

Rob is obviously lost while Jane, catching on, takes a frail hand in her own and kisses it.

'We are more used to calling her Lizzie', Jane says. 'Did they all call her Betty?'

'Turn your head young feller, no, the other way', Mo tells him, reaching out and positioning his face.

'Yes! Now look at that'. She holds a framed photograph to the side of Rob's head for Jane to appraise.

The photo is faded, sepia, full length. It shows a woman in what is obviously theatrical costume. She appears to be about twenty five and is leaning forward in a posed attitude, head tilted slightly to one side. A grin, which Jane instantly recognises, lights up her pretty face. The likeness is immediately obvious, and Jane, moved to tears again, dabs at her eyes as the old lady begins.

'Betty, yes, most of us did, I always did. I preferred *Aunt* Betty of course, but she wouldn't have it, very forward she was, for the times. She was my father's elder sister. Those with the name Elizabeth got called all sorts of things then; Betty, Liza, Beth, and of course we knew her stage name was Lizzie. My father was quite old - fifty something - when I was born.

Jane and Rob study the faded photograph.

'There's more, isn't there?' Jane suggests as the older woman nods and grins.

'Yes', she says, as she extracts a single sheet of notepaper from a tattered manila envelope. 'There is more'.

She perches her spectacles on the end of her nose, and then without once looking at the paper, she recites:

'Darling girl, it cannot go on. You are too good to be treated as I have treated you. You know I have tried and you know how I have failed. I am afraid that I am just too rotten to ever change. You will be better off by far without me. You will soon forget and know that what I now do is for the best. I have loved you and I do. Jimmy'.

She hands the letter to Rob who notes the embossed legend at the top: Hotel Belle Vue, 42nd Street. New York', and the scribbled date 'Aug. 10. 1896'.

'And all those years', the old lady continues. 'Poor Betty thinks the worst, indeed, by an even crueller turn of fate, she once told me that someone had sent her a cutting from the New York Times dated a couple of days after she had sailed for Liverpool alone. Someone had informed the police that the body of a man had been sighted in the East River. It had been thrown up among the swirling muddy waters by the propellers of the Campania, the very ship my aunt was sailing in. The body was never identified'.

'Tea up!' a young girl places a tray on the table beside the old woman's.

'And this is Annie', Maureen tells them with a warm smile as the girl fusses with the cups and a loaded cake stand.

'I'll pour', the old lady says. 'Thank you Annie, you are a love'. The girl tucks a blanket around Maureen's legs before tripping off.

'They are so nice here, talk about beck and call, only it is closing you know - this one at Richmond anyway. There is another one just opened up near Birmingham and yet another planned at Hampton Court'. She looks out across the winding Thames, the bridges at Richmond and Putney and sighs, 'Lovely, and I have been so lucky'. She is lost in her thoughts momentarily, then with a shake of her head brings herself back to the present

'The way things happen in a life. The changes, contrasts, bad, even wicked one day and then good, so good you think you'd burst. That's how it was with my Aunty Betty. Such a hard life, such tragedy and then, in the end, such happiness, for both of them, in their final years together'.

She is getting quite tired, a nurse is hovering discreetly, so Jane suggests they come again some other day but the old lady will have none of it.

'No', she tells them, and waving away their concern she collects her thoughts and continues.

'The programme was on the Home Service, *In Town Tonight*, it was called, and me and my mum listened in every Saturday night. I was sewing a frock at the time. I'll never forget it. I was only half taking notice. They must have mentioned her name three or four times before it dawned on me. I caught a reference to Protean Dancer, Music Hall and then her name

- her stage name -Lizzie Reardon and they were talking about her career and her interests. I wrote to the BBC who forwarded my letter. She invited me to visit her and James, which I did. She was reunited with my dad, her brother, and then, although I was only twelve, it was arranged that I should go to live with them as a sort of companion. Almshouses they were, or had been and they had the end one next to the church. Two up, two down and an outside privy. A little garden at the front. Nice. I loved it and we all squeezed in, me, Betty, and James of course. Oh! He was a smasher with his gypsy curls and the stories! All over America he'd been, hitching rides on the railroad - boxcars he called them - sleeping rough, and then Hollywood and the film stars. Chaplin! Mae West! Comfy and warm we were. James bought the house from the church people, did it up a bit, he was not short of money that I do know, kept it in a trunk under the bed and they used to joke about it, saying it would all be mine one day - only it didn't happen. The bomb took care of that'.

The sun is dipping low in the sky and a chill has settled. The nurse appears and this time she is adamant.

'Right', she says. 'Let's have you Mo, you'll catch your death and it's no good you pulling rank, I'm gaffer here'. Jane and Rob help to get the old lady into a wheel chair and they push her, up the slope to the conservatory where it is warmer and where, as if by magic, yet another pot of tea awaits them. The old lady has hardly paused for breath as she has relived what are quite obviously, memories of a time of much pleasure and sweetness.

'I never saw such love', she tells them. 'You could feel it all over the house and the laughter!' She is silent and then. 'Like a pair of kids they were and we were all so very happy. Her voice has become a whisper and they can see the tears in her eyes. 'I never saw such love as that', she says again. 'Never again. Not once in all those years'.

Rob pours the tea. He is silent and Jane can almost see the stories as they tumble about behind his half closed eyes. They sip their tea quietly.

'And the bomb?' he says at last, breaking the spell.

Maureen takes a handkerchief from her bag. Blows her nose determinedly.

'We were out of candles', she begins. 'James had made some toffee. Treacle toffee. He could do things like that. It'd only just set and they were eating it already, laughing as they licked the hot syrup from their fingers, him and her, sat by the fire, together. The corner shop had no candles so I cut across the park towards the ironmongers on the Brixton road. Then the siren went so I ran for the shelter at the Underground. It was the first real raid of the war and it was morning before the all clear came. Then I went home and the fires were still burning in the streets as I passed.

Incendiary bombs they dropped, the Germans. I ran and ran and I thought I could see them still sitting there just as I had left them, and I hoped there'd be some toffee left but they were gone. All gone. A warden in a tin hat stopped me and I could hear the hiss of steam as the firemen drenched the flames'.

The old woman is drained. Jane anxiously takes her hand. They can hear the sounds of the evening meal being made ready. The rattle of cutlery, clatter of plates. Rob and Jane stand awkwardly while the noises of normality echo around them. Rob puts his arm around Maureen's frail shoulders, kisses her cheek.

'Thank you Mo,' he says.

Chapter Thirty Four

Dawn is breaking as the plane goes into its tight banking turn. Looking out of the window Rob watches the tiny island tilt and yaw below them as the pilot steers his aircraft steadily around, gradually levelling the nose, until the horizon, swaying wildly, stills, steadies and then levels out into a firm, straight line. He puts his engines into coarse pitch as, suddenly, like a kite catching the wind, the aircraft settles back on an even keel and the long, jagged coast-line at Dingli Cliffs comes into view. White faced walls topped by honeyed rocks, a scattering of wild herbs: rosemary, thyme, fennel. Line upon line of tumbling dry stone walls, centuries old. Forming small square pockets of hard fought soil, safe from searing winds, lashing rains and the sun's incessant glare.

'Nice to see you back Mr Reardon', Passport Control gets better, Rob notes. It used to take ages in the old days when Luqa was still an air force base. They pick up the keys for the hire car, drive out past MacDonald's, and turning left towards the big roundabout, they set off on their pilgrimage. They are booked in for the weekend at The Phoenicia in Floriana, but Jane insisted and Rob was happy to agree, that they would do the grand tour before they did anything else.

Rob winds the window down to catch the warm breeze as they pass the temple ruins at Tarxien. Swaying and jolting over the pot-holed tarmac, he skilfully dodges the early morning traffic, the honking buses. The smell of hot cheesecakes cooking tempts them as they reach the big square at Paula. The sun catches the silver domes of the Church of Christ the King and all the bells clang out to welcome them.

'Malta!' says Rob. 'Land of Hells, Bells, Smells, and Pregnant Women'.

'You love it', Jane has given up trying to protect her hair against the blast through the window.

'I do', says Rob gravely. 'I do indeed'. Turning left, they head up the hill in the direction of Rabat. Cats and old men snooze under spreading carob trees. An ancient bus, belching black smoke, snarls and coughs around impossibly tight corners in villages unchanged in centuries. Rob is at home in this place, forever home. At San Anton they park the car under a wall violent with scarlet bougainvillea, and as they approach the gate, Rob puts a finger to his lips to avoid waking the sentry snoring gently in his box.

Princes, Presidents, Commanders-in-Chief and their Ladies have all lived here and, as the couple walk among the exotic plants, giant tropical trees, and shaded bowers; the warm weight of history, forever near, cries out to be remembered.

'Lizzie walked here', Jane tells Rob and her tone is matter of fact. 'Look! She sat on that wall by that fountain, heavy with your father inside her. I can hear her crying'.

They sit on the wall. Rob puts an arm about Jane's waist, and they are silent as they listen to the tinkling of water among the water lilies. Jane rests her head on her husband's shoulder. She sighs contentedly and just at that moment a sycamore leaf, rustling aimlessly along the stony path is driven by a sudden gust of warm wind. They watch it rise into the air, dipping and dancing, carried on the current, soaring and pivoting up and up until, with a final graceful bow, it disappears among the surrounding trees.

'Bravo!' cries Jane, clapping her hands and smiling.

The drive to Cottonera takes less than an hour, the landscape changing as they leave the rural, better-off suburbs of Attard and approach the dockyard area of The Three Cities. They follow for a while the line of an ancient aqueduct, its old stone arches appearing and then suddenly disappearing among a rash of show rooms, car parks, mini-markets - the rude intrusions of advancing modernity. In front of them now is Cottonera Lines, the huge bastion wall built on the hills of Bormla in the seventeenth century to protect the port and the Three Cities: Senglea, Vittoriosa, and Cospicua. The acoustics change as they enter the tunnel, a dull roaring in their ears that lifts suddenly as their car bursts out of the dark and into the sunshine.

Fortification is everywhere. Here the Knights of Aragon, Provence, Italy, England, Germany, France, combined to form a mighty military force - The Knights of Malta, Protectors of European Christendom. At their umbilicus were the mysteries and disciplines of the Holy Roman Church and its internal conspirator Opus Dei.

The Tuesday Market is in full cry as they park the car and walk up the slope towards the cemetery. Plastic buckets, flowerpots, bolts of bright cloth, fruit, six-inch nails, votive candles. Everything you need, and more that you don't need can be found in this colourful cacophony of commercial theatre.

The graveyard is hidden. Sandwiched between a cement works and an ancient fortified gate with its armorial arms still intact atop strong, limestone pillars.

They walk among the neatly ordered lines of gravestones, plastic geraniums, exhortations to the saints, platitudinous poems, and coloured photographs of the smiling dead.

Thomas is in his corner still, where Rob has always known him to be. The figs are ripening on the overhanging tree. Rob knows these figs. He picks one. Bites into it, the warm flood of liquor bitter sweet on his tongue, bringing with it the memory of the long ago boy, seated on a stone, looking down at the grave, and the promises that he made.

Jane leans over the iron railings. She wipes clean the face of the inscription with her handkerchief and together they read aloud:

SACRED TO THE MEMORY OF THOMAS McSWEENEY
Executed on HMS. Rambler, June 8th, 1846
Age 23 years.

They stand in silence. Jane nudges Rob gently. 'Go on'. She tells him and he continues. Reading from the words newly chiselled beneath the old.

PARDONED POSTHUMOUSLY
By the Criminal Cases Review Commission of Great Britain and Northern Ireland January 11th, 2011.